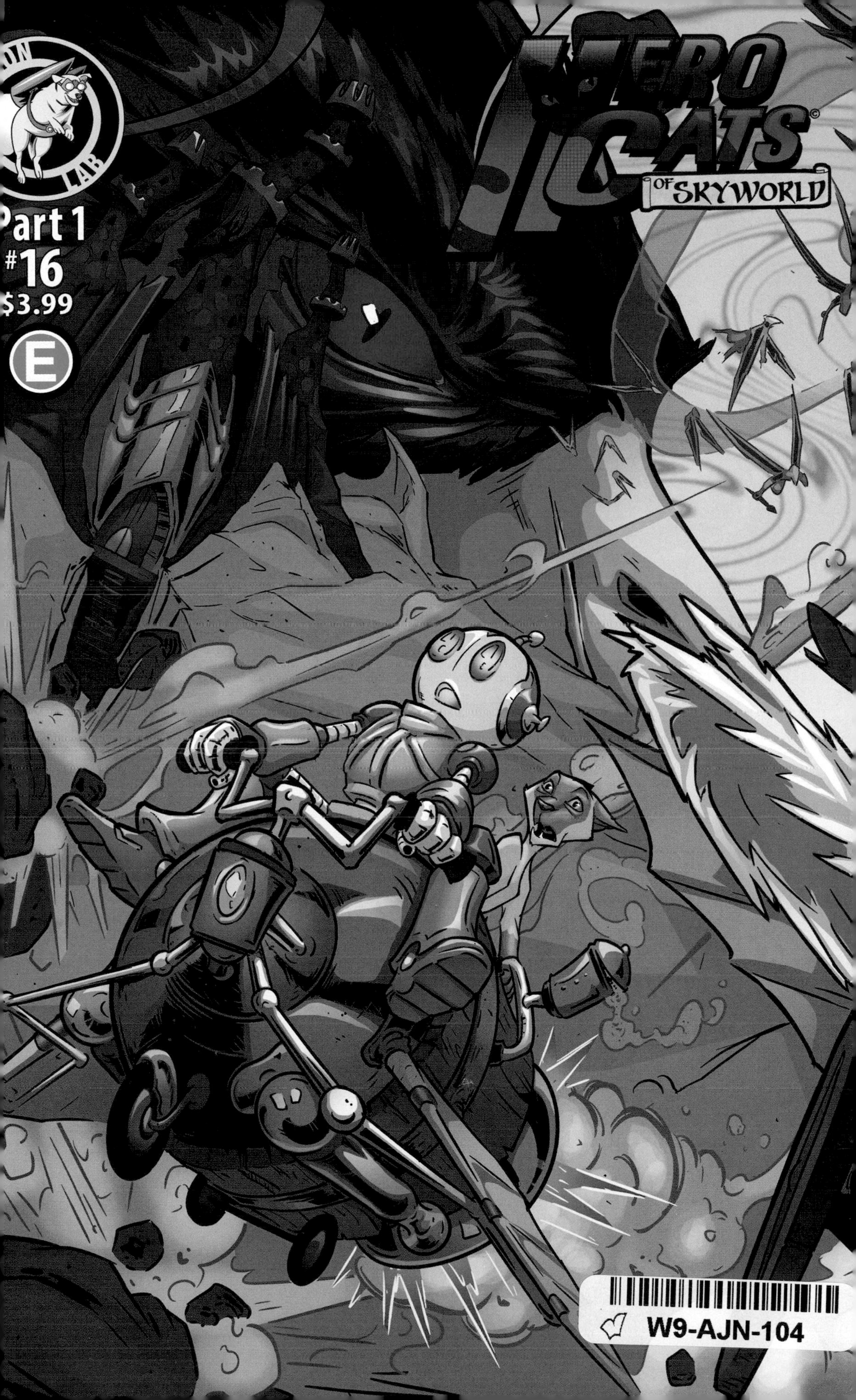
HERO CATS
OF SKYWORLD
Part 1
#16
$3.99
E
W9-AJN-104

FROM ALL-AGES TO MATURE READERS ACTION LAB HAS YOU COVERED.

 **Appropriate for everyone.**

 **Appropriate for age 9 and up. Absent of profanity or adult content.**

 **Suggested for 12 and Up. Comics with this rating are comparable to a PG-13 movie rating. Recommended for our teen and young adult readers.**

 **Appropriate for older teens. Similar to Teen, but featuring more mature themes and/or more graphic imagery.**

 **Contains extreme violence and some nudity. Basically the Rated-R of comics.**

 FIND YOUR NEW FAVORITE COMICS.

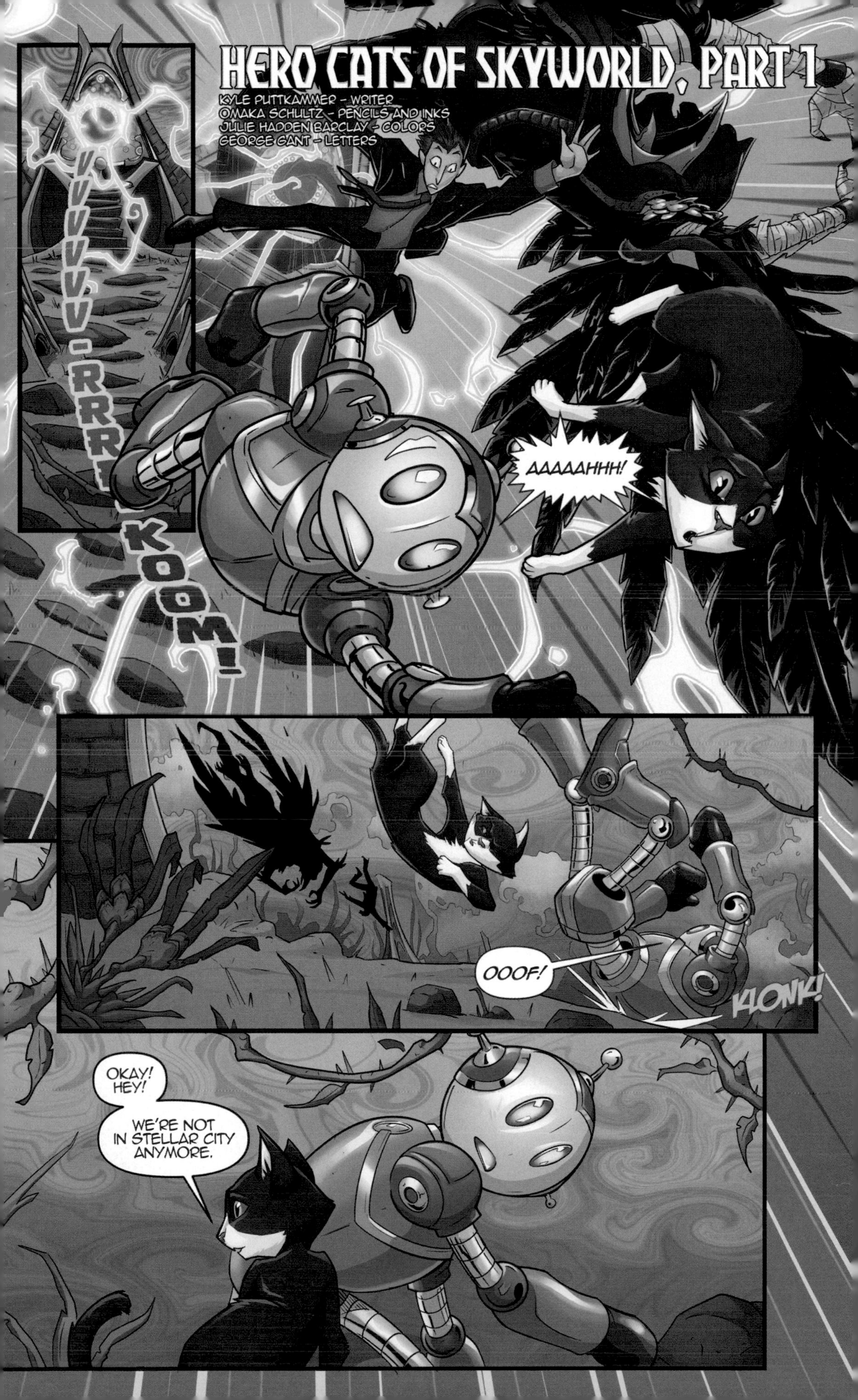
HERO CATS OF SKYWORLD, PART 1
KYLE PUTTKAMMER - WRITER
OMAKA SCHULTZ - PENCILS AND INKS
JULIE HADDEN BARCLAY - COLORS
GEORGE GANT - LETTERS
VVVVVVV-RRRR
KOOOM!
AAAAAHHH!
OOOF!
KLONK!
OKAY! HEY!
WE'RE NOT IN STELLAR CITY ANYMORE.

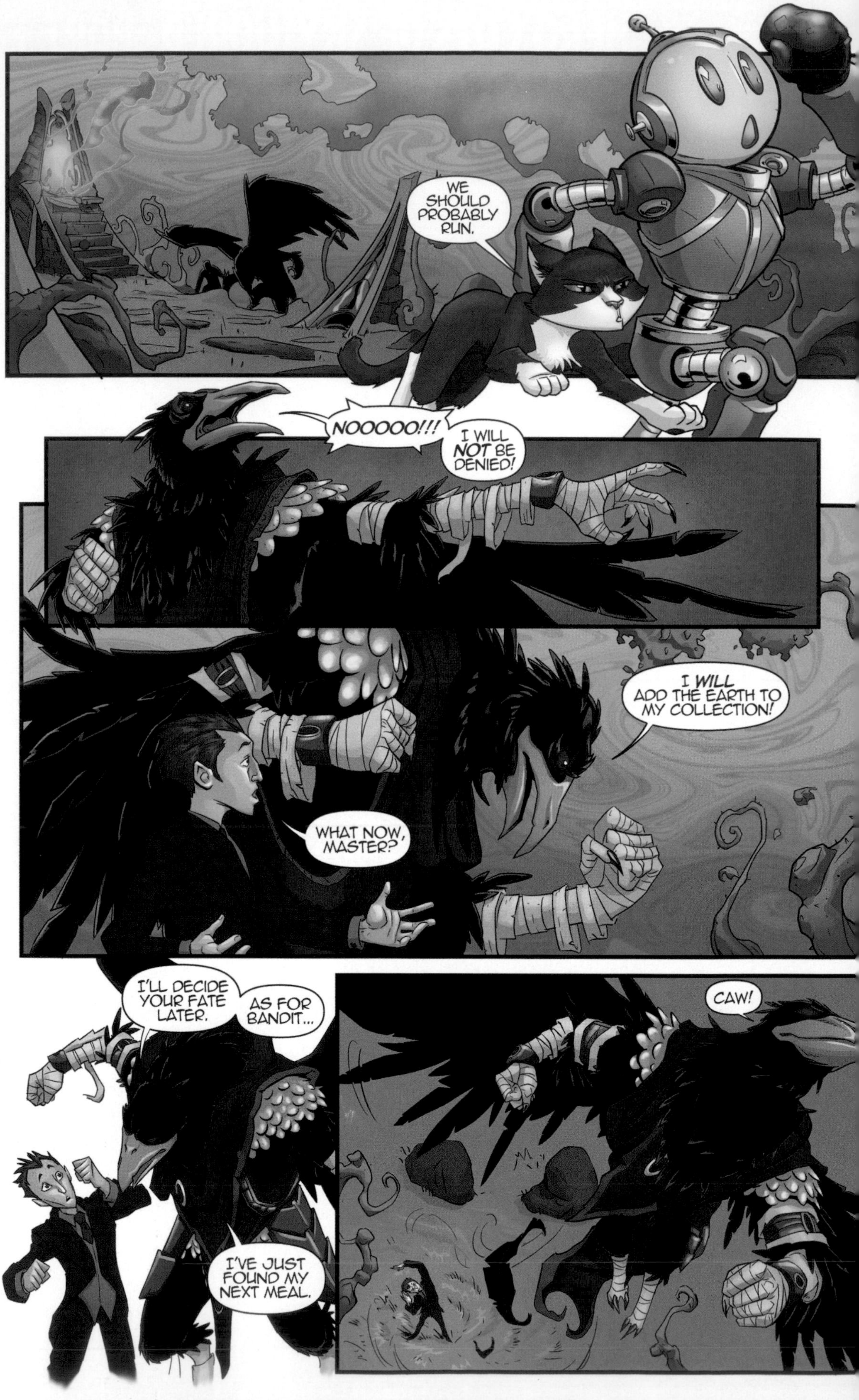
WE SHOULD PROBABLY RUN.
NOOOOO!!!
I WILL NOT BE DENIED!
I WILL ADD THE EARTH TO MY COLLECTION!
WHAT NOW, MASTER?
I'LL DECIDE YOUR FATE LATER.
AS FOR BANDIT...
I'VE JUST FOUND MY NEXT MEAL.
CAW!

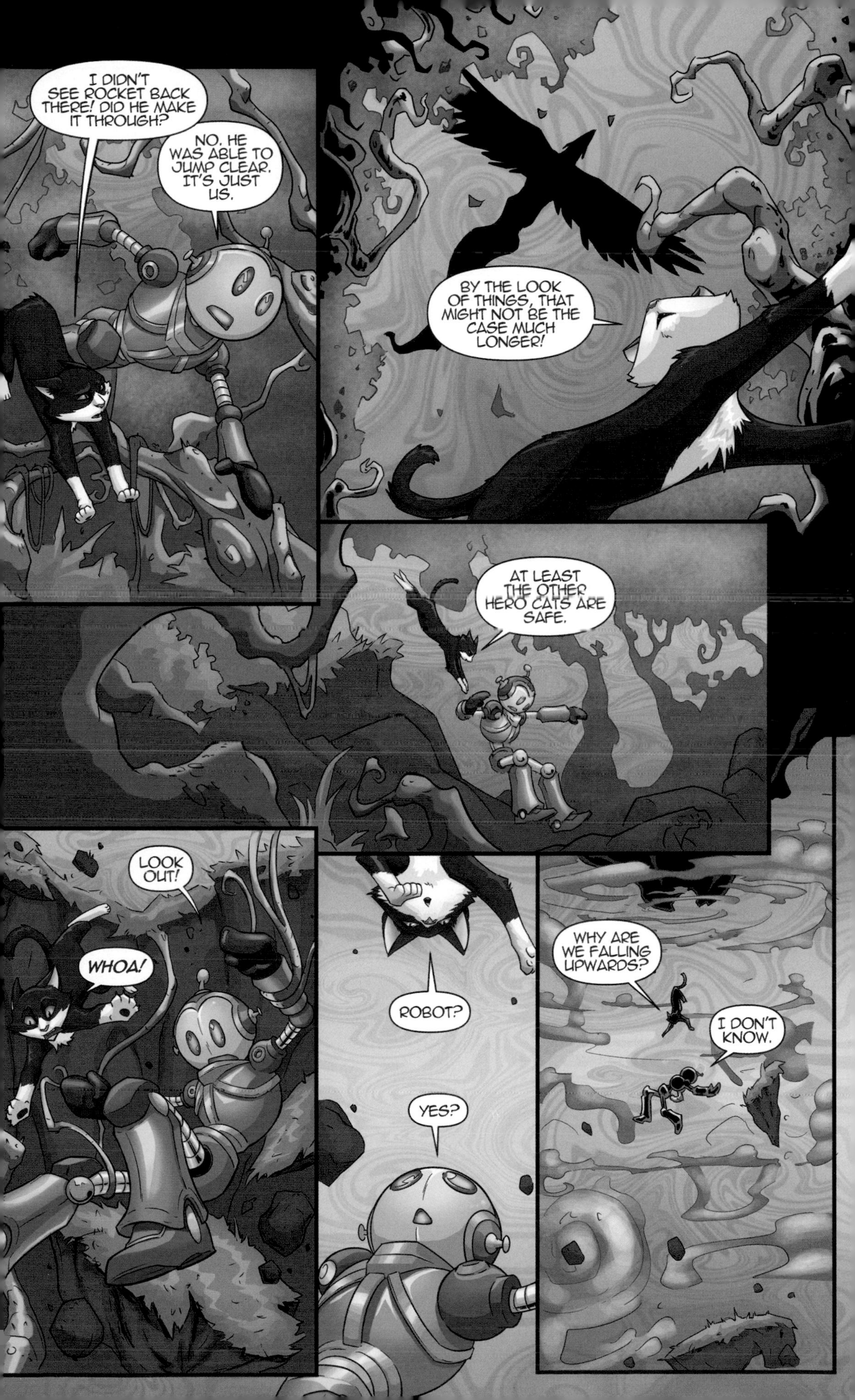
I DIDN'T SEE ROCKET BACK THERE! DID HE MAKE IT THROUGH?
NO. HE WAS ABLE TO JUMP CLEAR. IT'S JUST US.
BY THE LOOK OF THINGS, THAT MIGHT NOT BE THE CASE MUCH LONGER!
AT LEAST THE OTHER HERO CATS ARE SAFE.
LOOK OUT!
WHOA!
ROBOT?
YES?
WHY ARE WE FALLING UPWARDS?
I DON'T KNOW.

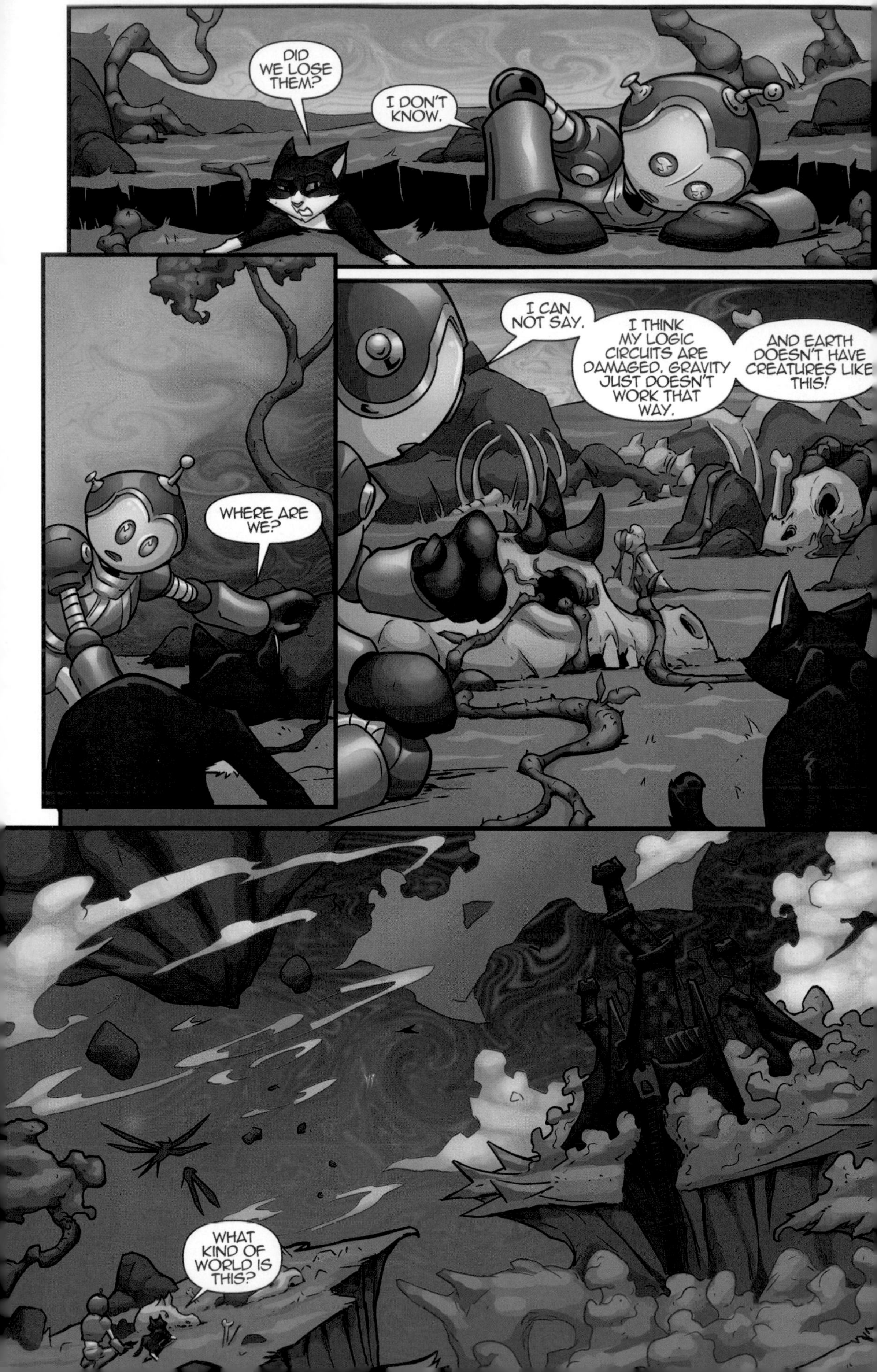

DID WE LOSE THEM?
I DON'T KNOW.
WHERE ARE WE?
I CAN NOT SAY.
I THINK MY LOGIC CIRCUITS ARE DAMAGED. GRAVITY JUST DOESN'T WORK THAT WAY.
AND EARTH DOESN'T HAVE CREATURES LIKE THIS!
WHAT KIND OF WORLD IS THIS?

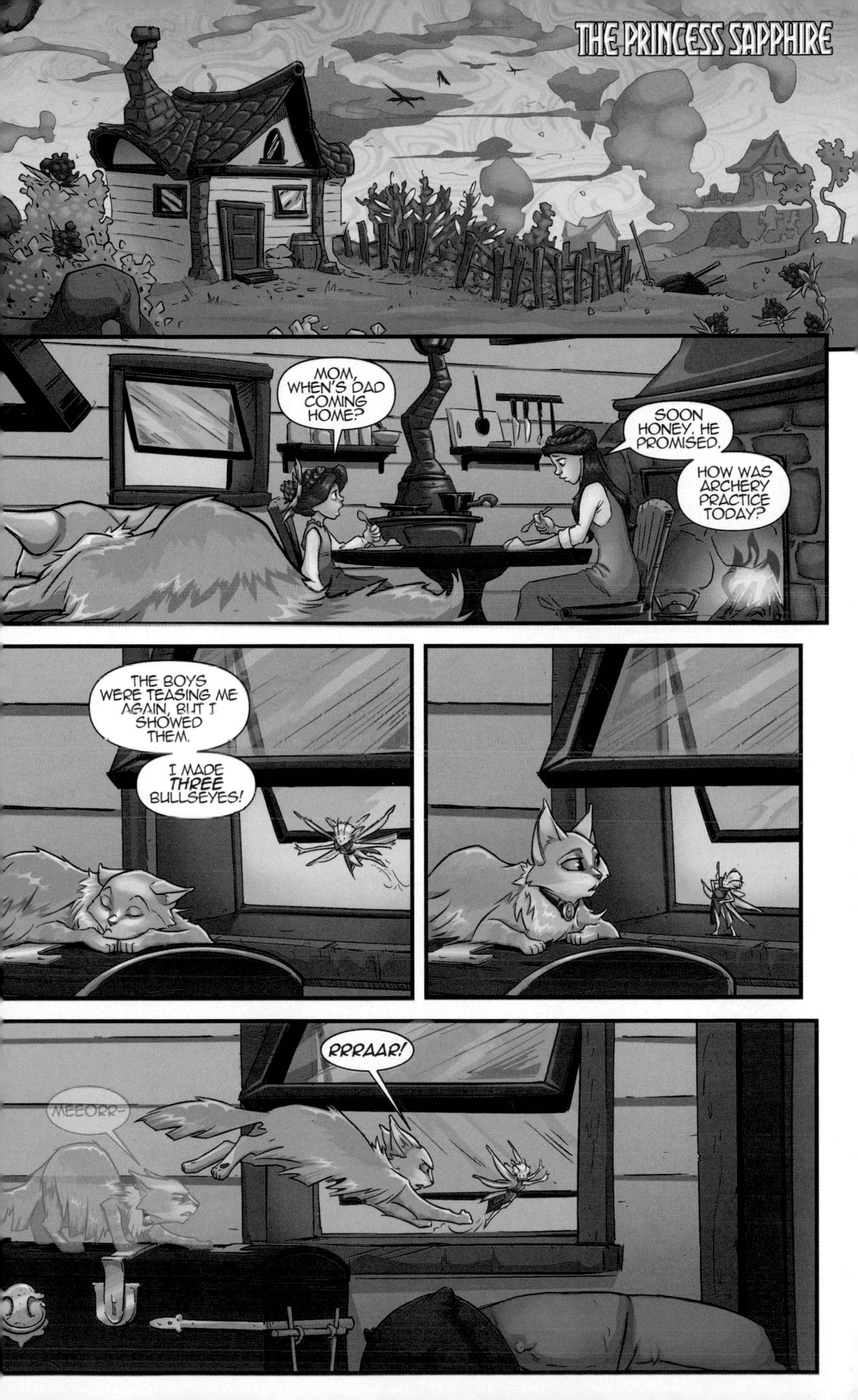
THE PRINCESS SAPPHIRE
MOM, WHEN'S DAD COMING HOME?
SOON HONEY. HE PROMISED.
HOW WAS ARCHERY PRACTICE TODAY?
THE BOYS WERE TEASING ME AGAIN, BUT I SHOWED THEM.
I MADE THREE BULLSEYES!
MEEORR-
RRRAAR!

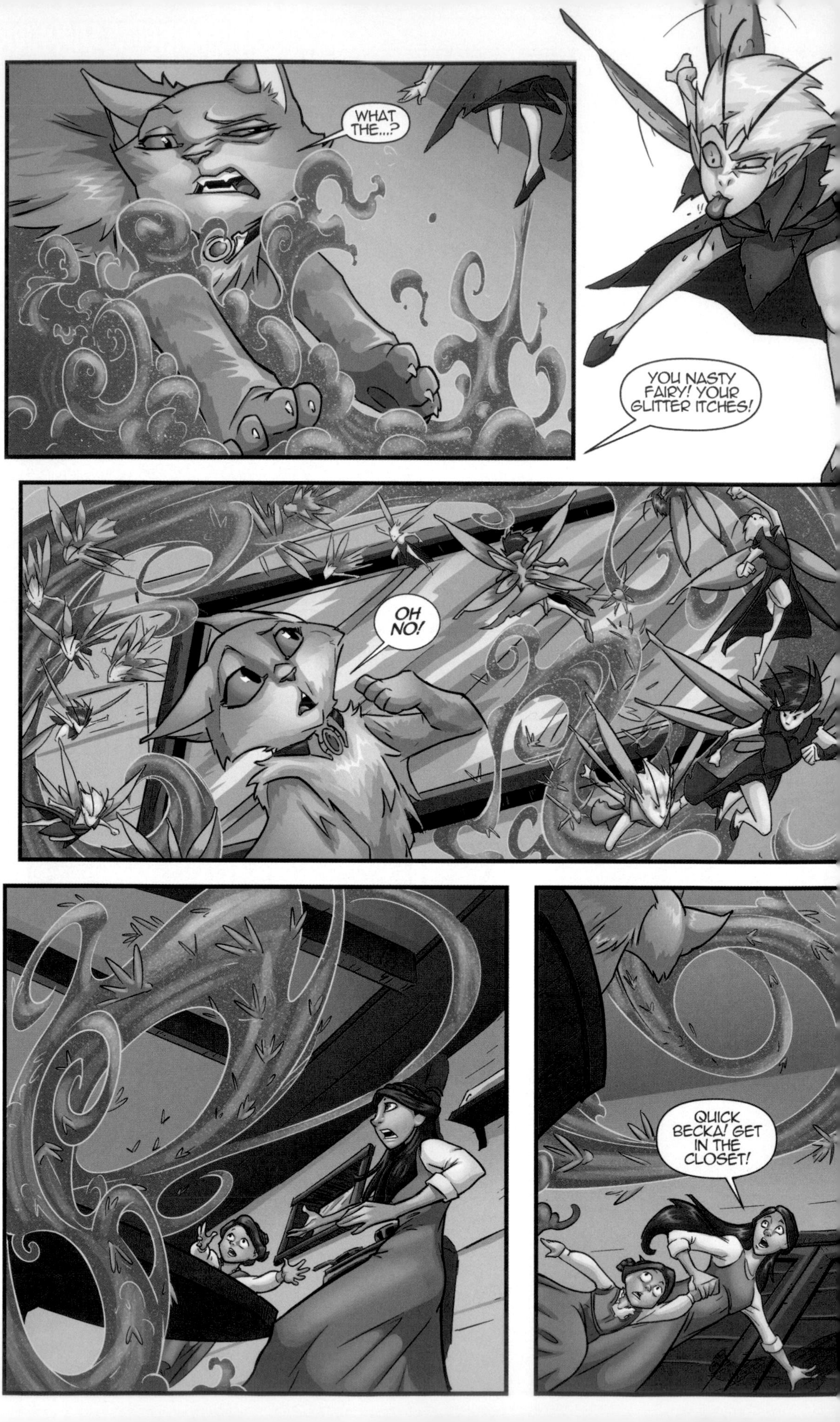
WHAT THE...?
YOU NASTY FAIRY! YOUR GLITTER ITCHES!
OH NO!
QUICK BECKA! GET IN THE CLOSET!

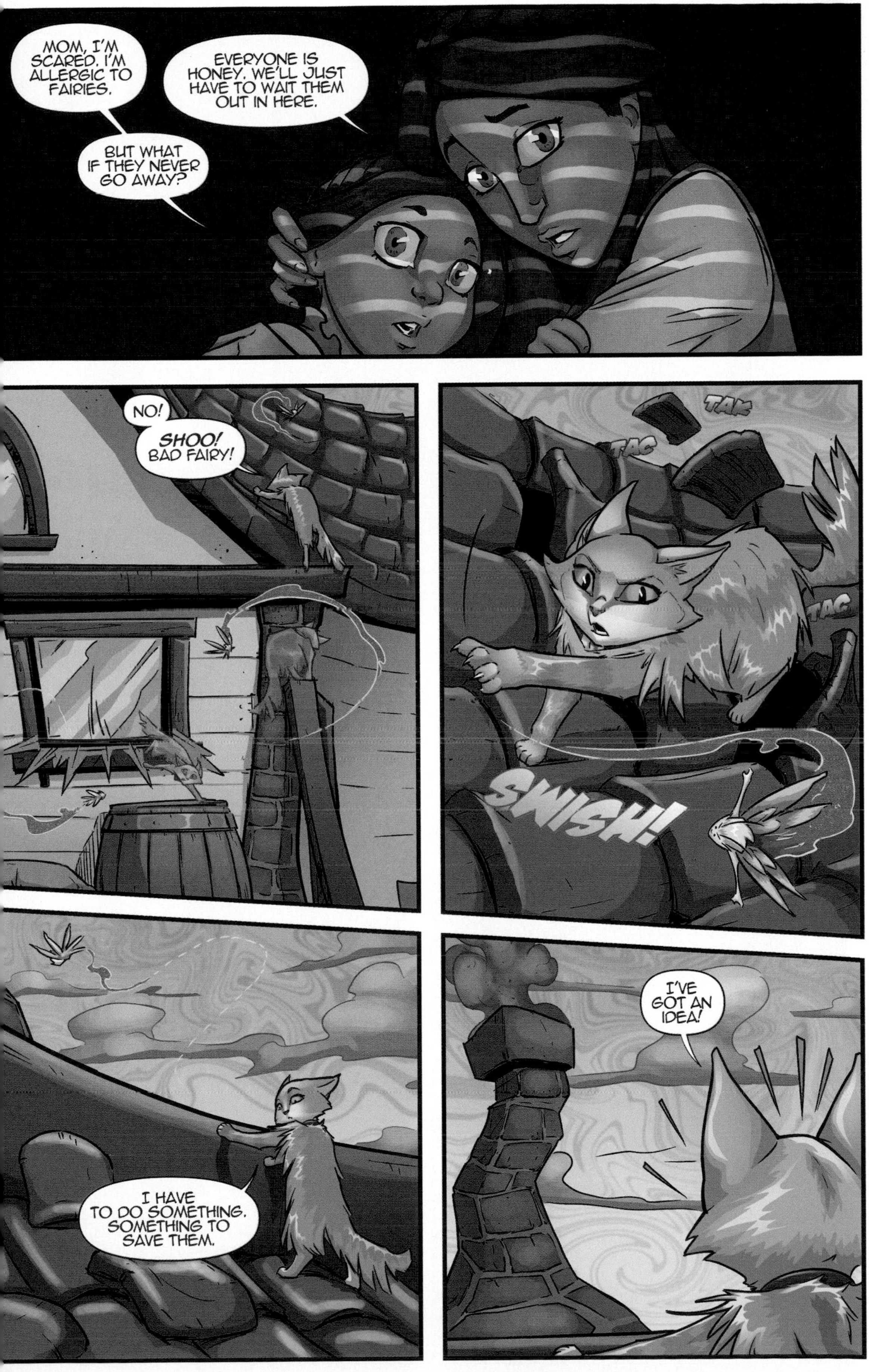
MOM, I'M SCARED. I'M ALLERGIC TO FAIRIES.
EVERYONE IS HONEY. WE'LL JUST HAVE TO WAIT THEM OUT IN HERE.
BUT WHAT IF THEY NEVER GO AWAY?
NO!
SHOO! BAD FAIRY!
TAK
TAC
TAC
SWISH!
I HAVE TO DO SOMETHING. SOMETHING TO SAVE THEM.
I'VE GOT AN IDEA!

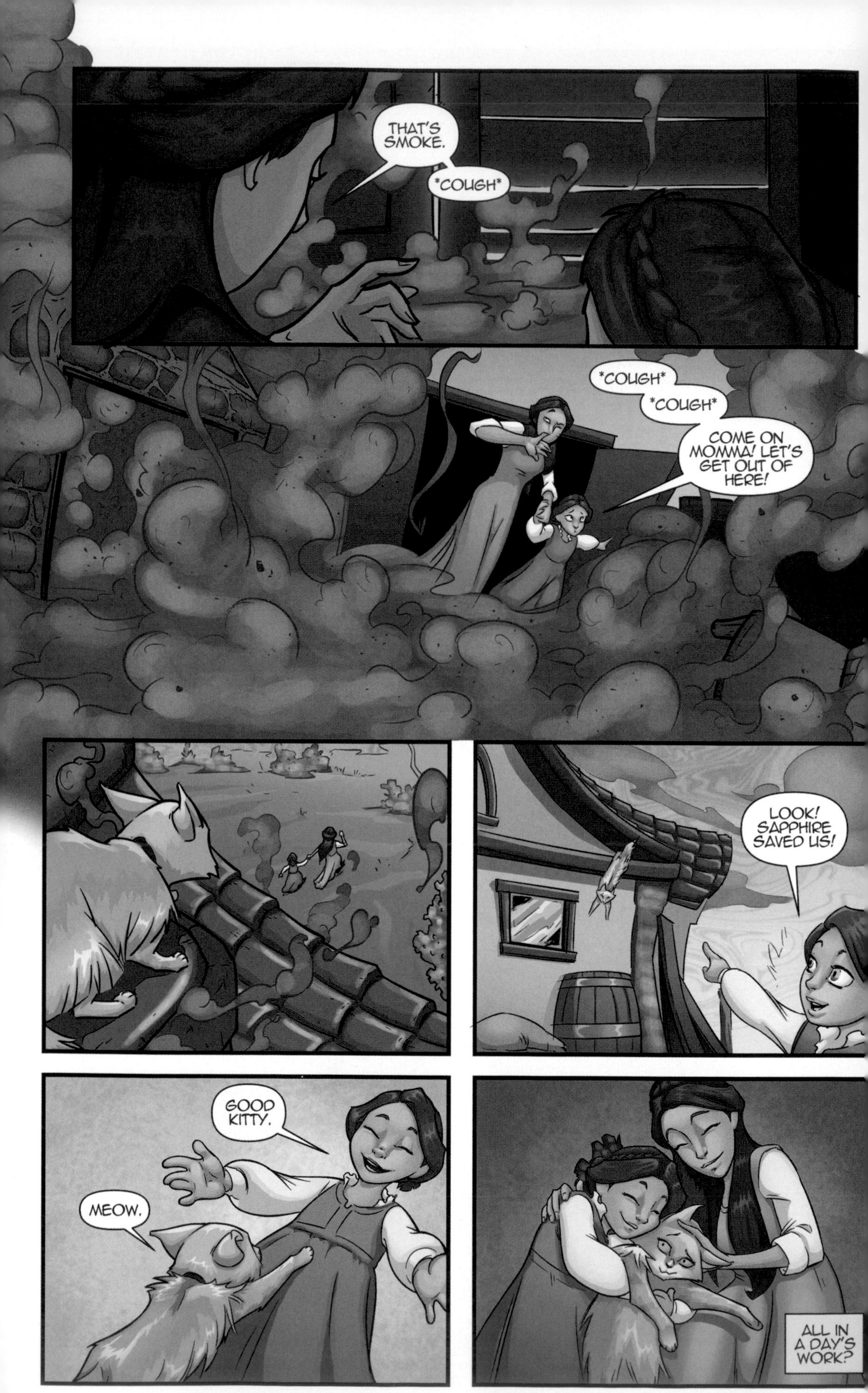
THAT'S SMOKE.
COUGH
COUGH
COUGH
COME ON MOMMA! LET'S GET OUT OF HERE!
LOOK! SAPPHIRE SAVED US!
GOOD KITTY.
MEOW.
ALL IN A DAY'S WORK?

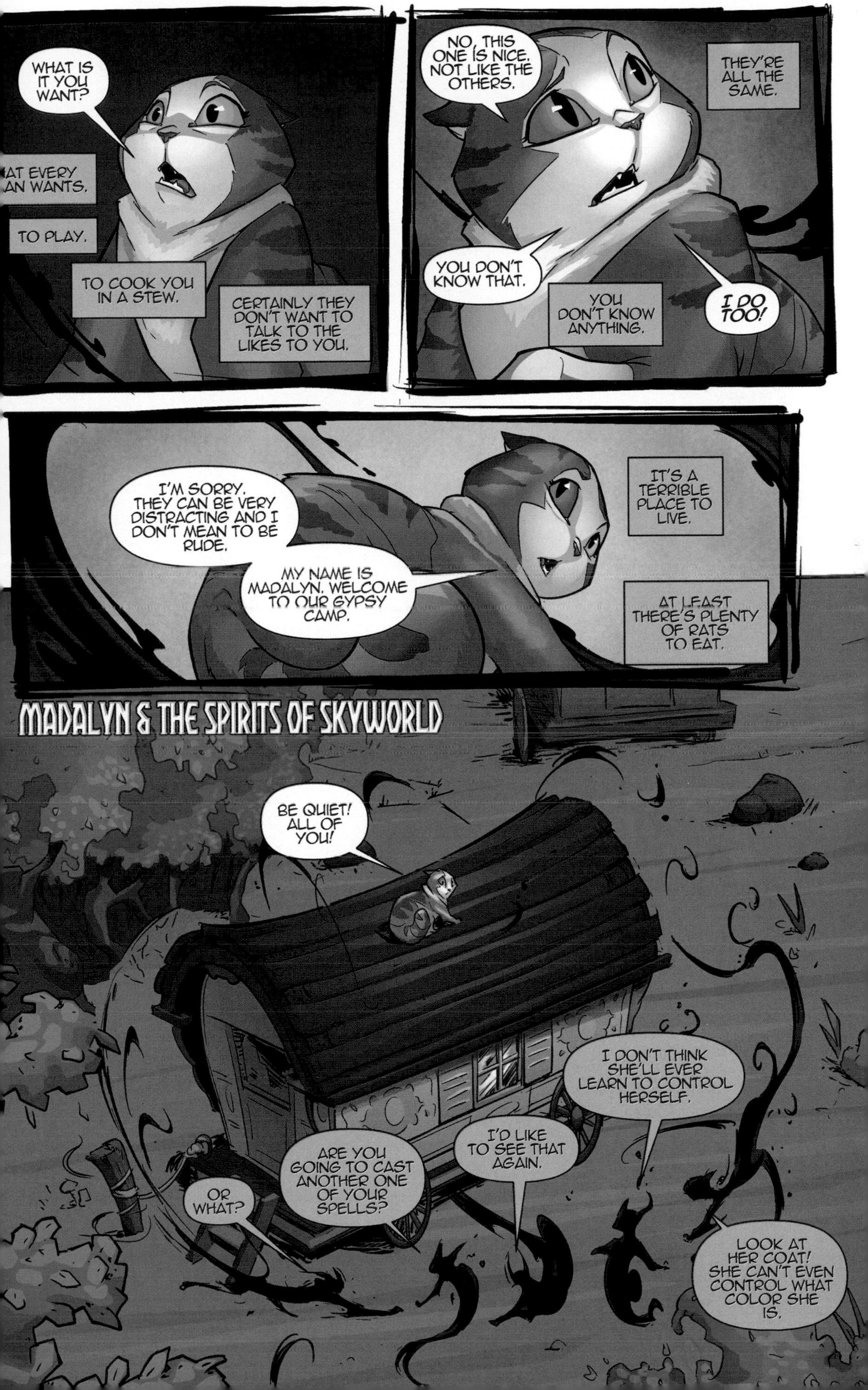
WHAT IS IT YOU WANT?
AT EVERY
AN WANTS.
TO PLAY.
TO COOK YOU IN A STEW.
CERTAINLY THEY DON'T WANT TO TALK TO THE LIKES TO YOU.
NO, THIS ONE IS NICE. NOT LIKE THE OTHERS.
THEY'RE ALL THE SAME.
YOU DON'T KNOW THAT.
YOU DON'T KNOW ANYTHING.
I DO TOO!
I'M SORRY. THEY CAN BE VERY DISTRACTING AND I DON'T MEAN TO BE RUDE.
IT'S A TERRIBLE PLACE TO LIVE.
MY NAME IS MADALYN. WELCOME TO OUR GYPSY CAMP.
AT LEAST THERE'S PLENTY OF RATS TO EAT.
MADALYN & THE SPIRITS OF SKYWORLD
BE QUIET! ALL OF YOU!
I DON'T THINK SHE'LL EVER LEARN TO CONTROL HERSELF.
I'D LIKE TO SEE THAT AGAIN.
ARE YOU GOING TO CAST ANOTHER ONE OF YOUR SPELLS?
OR WHAT?
LOOK AT HER COAT! SHE CAN'T EVEN CONTROL WHAT COLOR SHE IS.

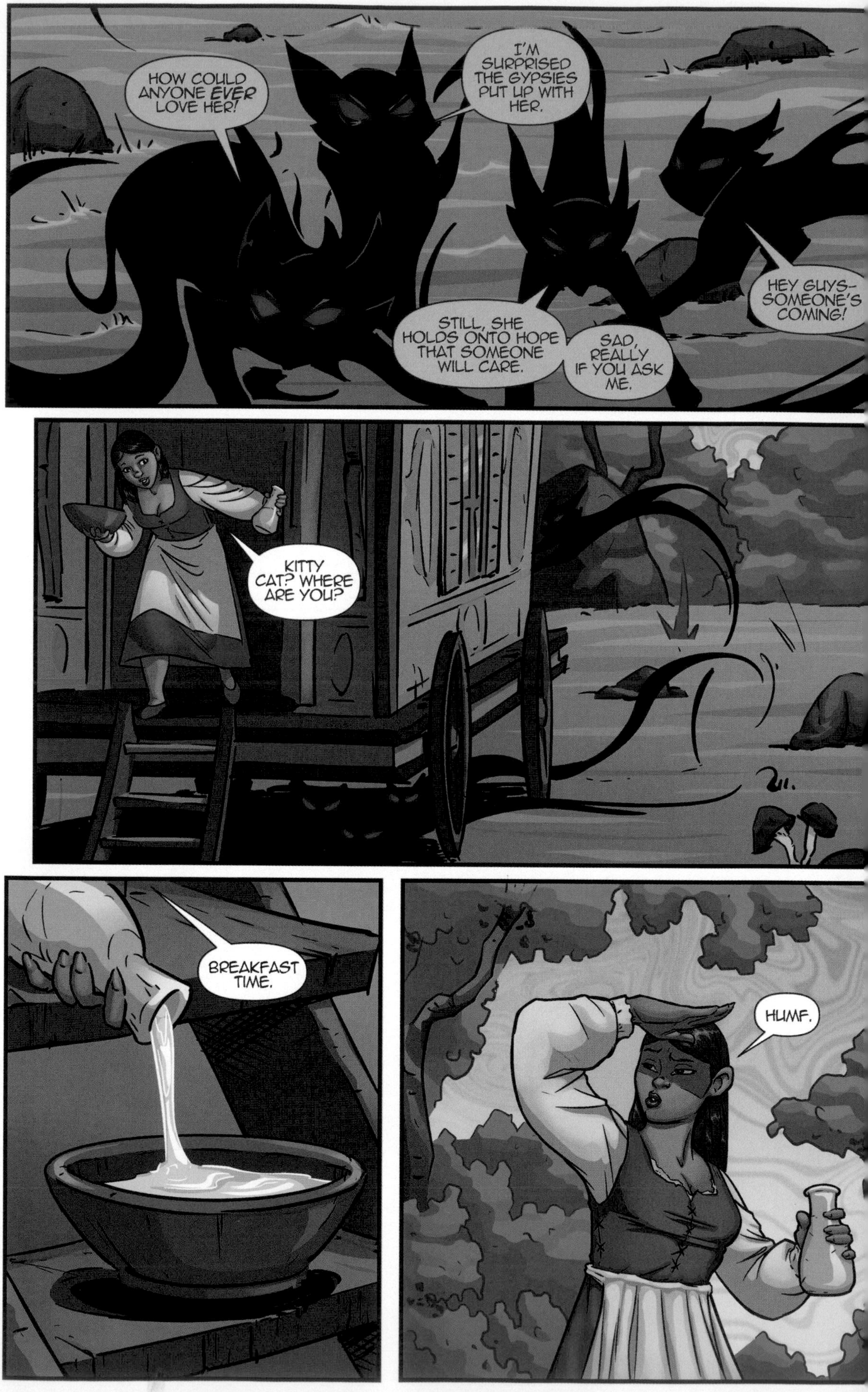
HOW COULD ANYONE EVER LOVE HER!
I'M SURPRISED THE GYPSIES PUT UP WITH HER.
STILL, SHE HOLDS ONTO HOPE THAT SOMEONE WILL CARE.
SAD, REALLY IF YOU ASK ME.
HEY GUYS- SOMEONE'S COMING!
KITTY CAT? WHERE ARE YOU?
BREAKFAST TIME.
HUMF.

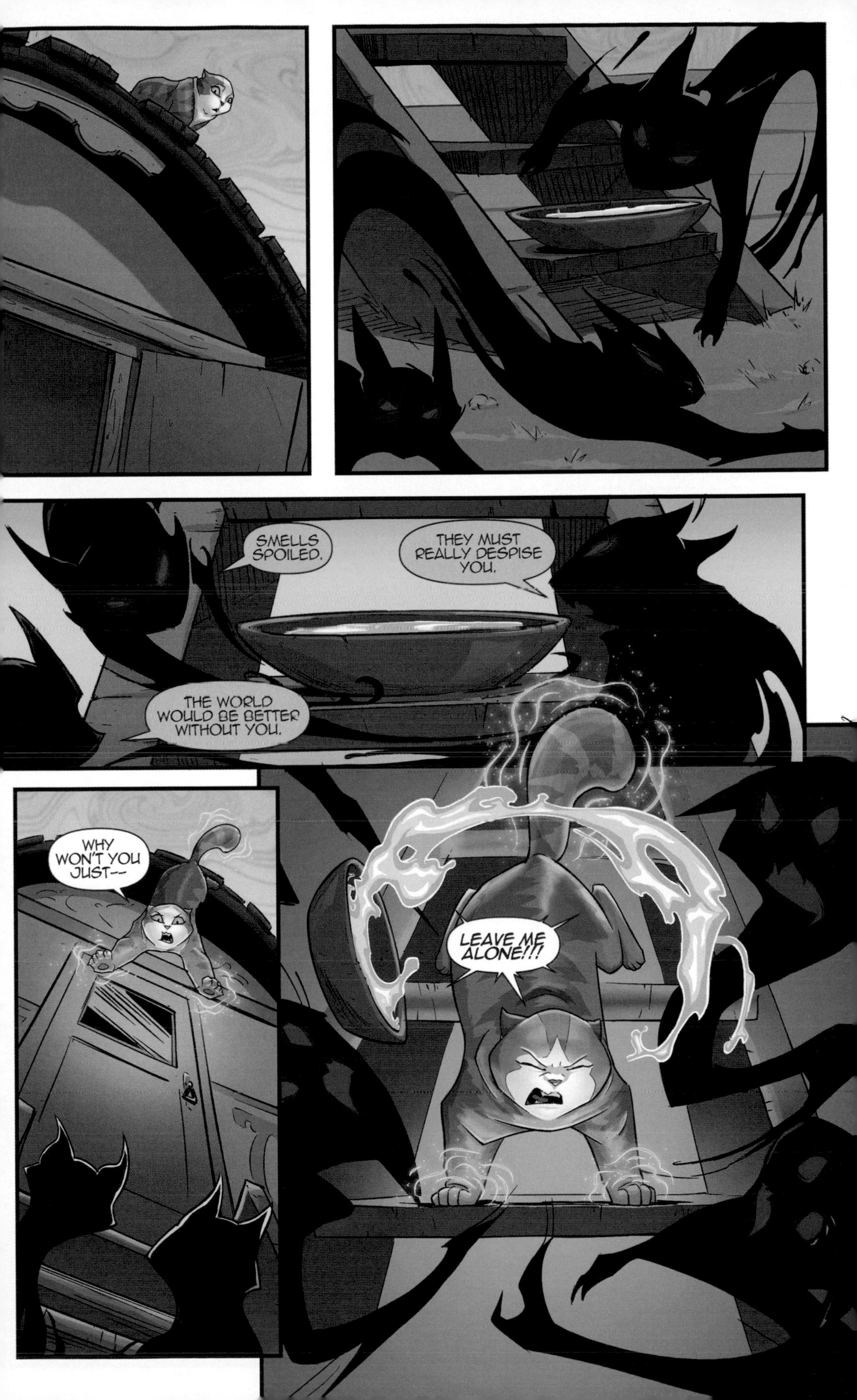
SMELLS SPOILED.
THEY MUST REALLY DESPISE YOU.
THE WORLD WOULD BE BETTER WITHOUT YOU.
WHY WON'T YOU JUST--
LEAVE ME ALONE!!!

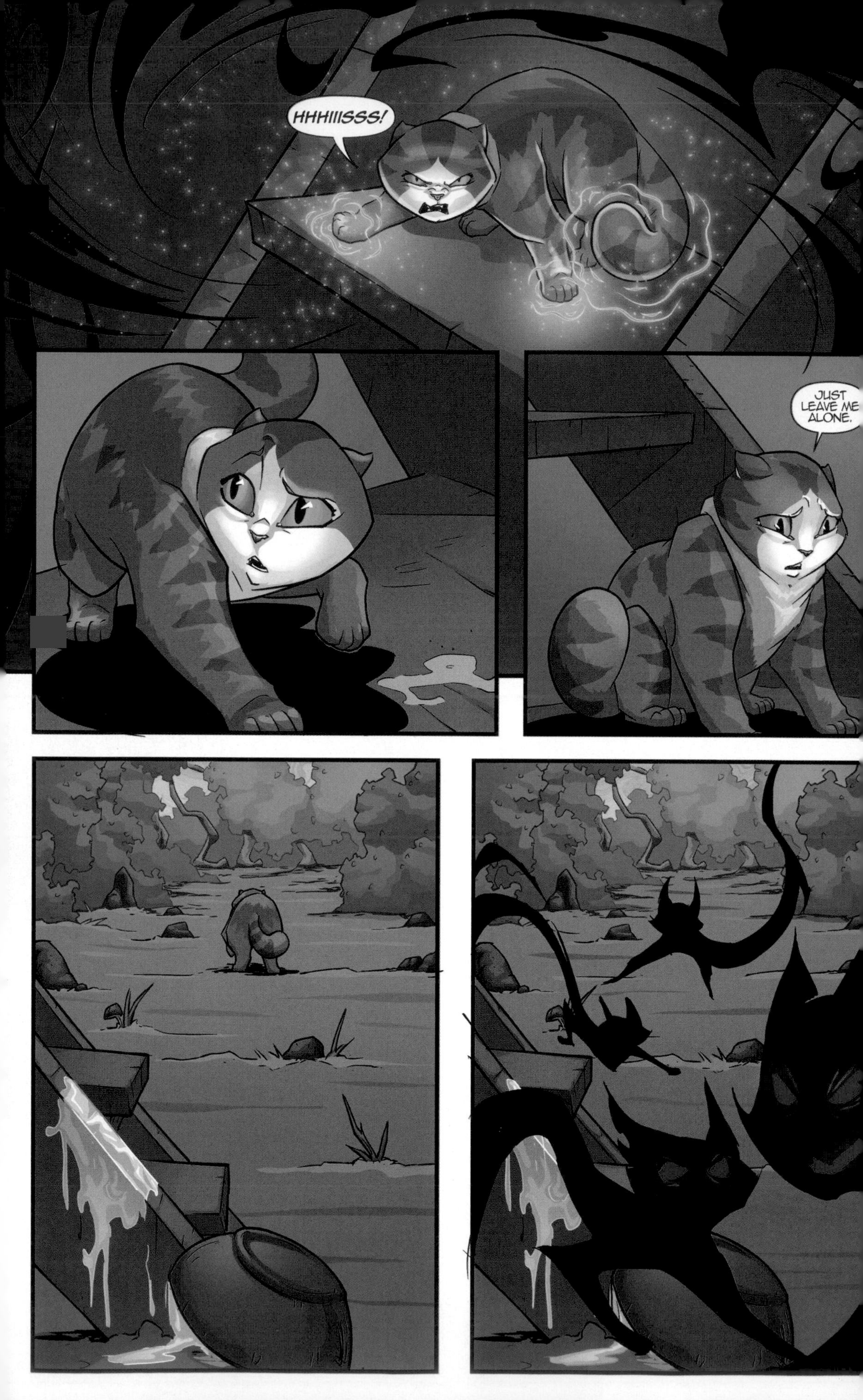
HHHIIISSS!
JUST LEAVE ME ALONE.

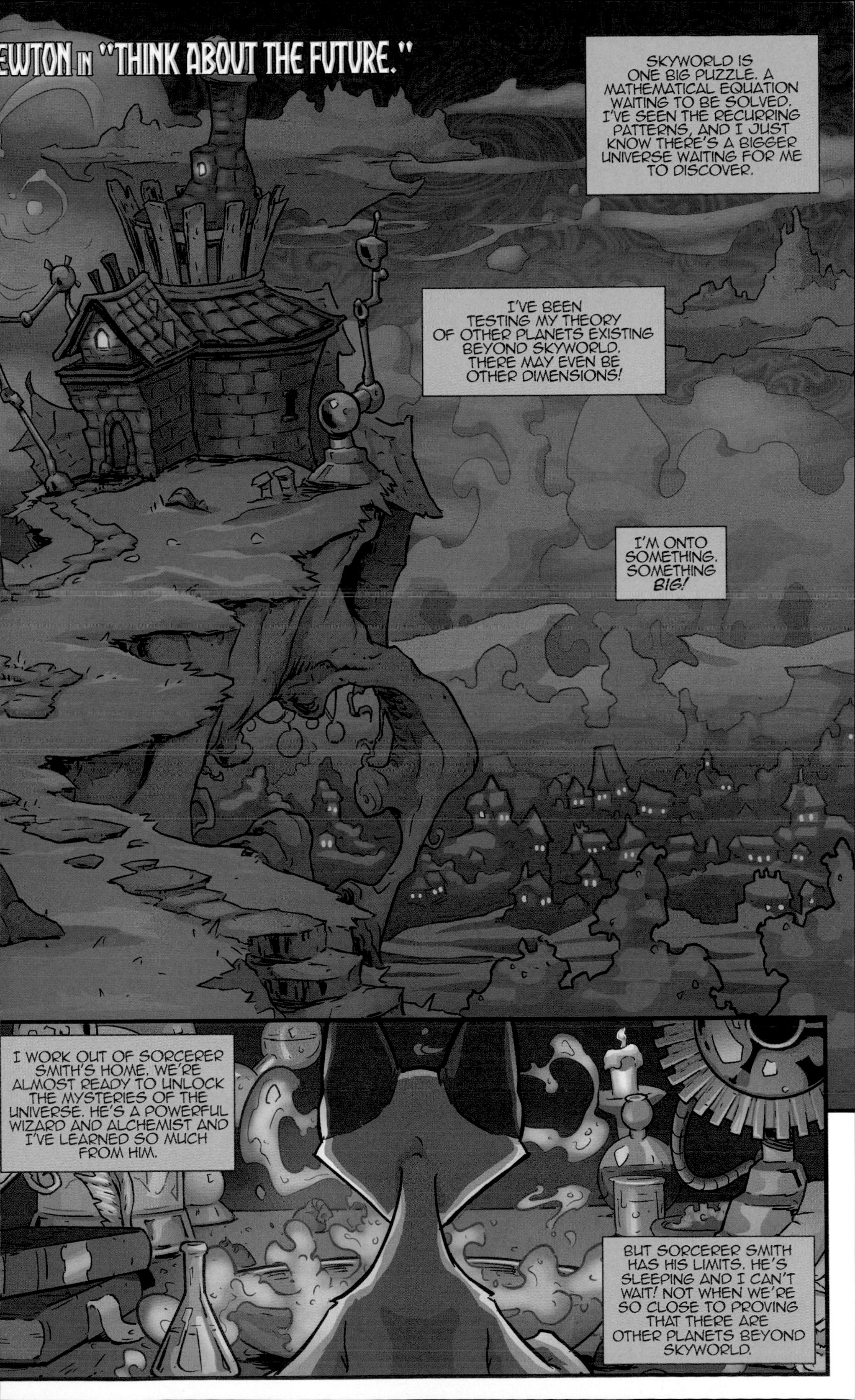
EWTON IN "THINK ABOUT THE FUTURE."
SKYWORLD IS ONE BIG PUZZLE. A MATHEMATICAL EQUATION WAITING TO BE SOLVED. I'VE SEEN THE RECURRING PATTERNS, AND I JUST KNOW THERE'S A BIGGER UNIVERSE WAITING FOR ME TO DISCOVER.
I'VE BEEN TESTING MY THEORY OF OTHER PLANETS EXISTING BEYOND SKYWORLD. THERE MAY EVEN BE OTHER DIMENSIONS!
I'M ONTO SOMETHING. SOMETHING BIG!
I WORK OUT OF SORCERER SMITH'S HOME. WE'RE ALMOST READY TO UNLOCK THE MYSTERIES OF THE UNIVERSE. HE'S A POWERFUL WIZARD AND ALCHEMIST AND I'VE LEARNED SO MUCH FROM HIM.
BUT SORCERER SMITH HAS HIS LIMITS. HE'S SLEEPING AND I CAN'T WAIT! NOT WHEN WE'RE SO CLOSE TO PROVING THAT THERE ARE OTHER PLANETS BEYOND SKYWORLD.

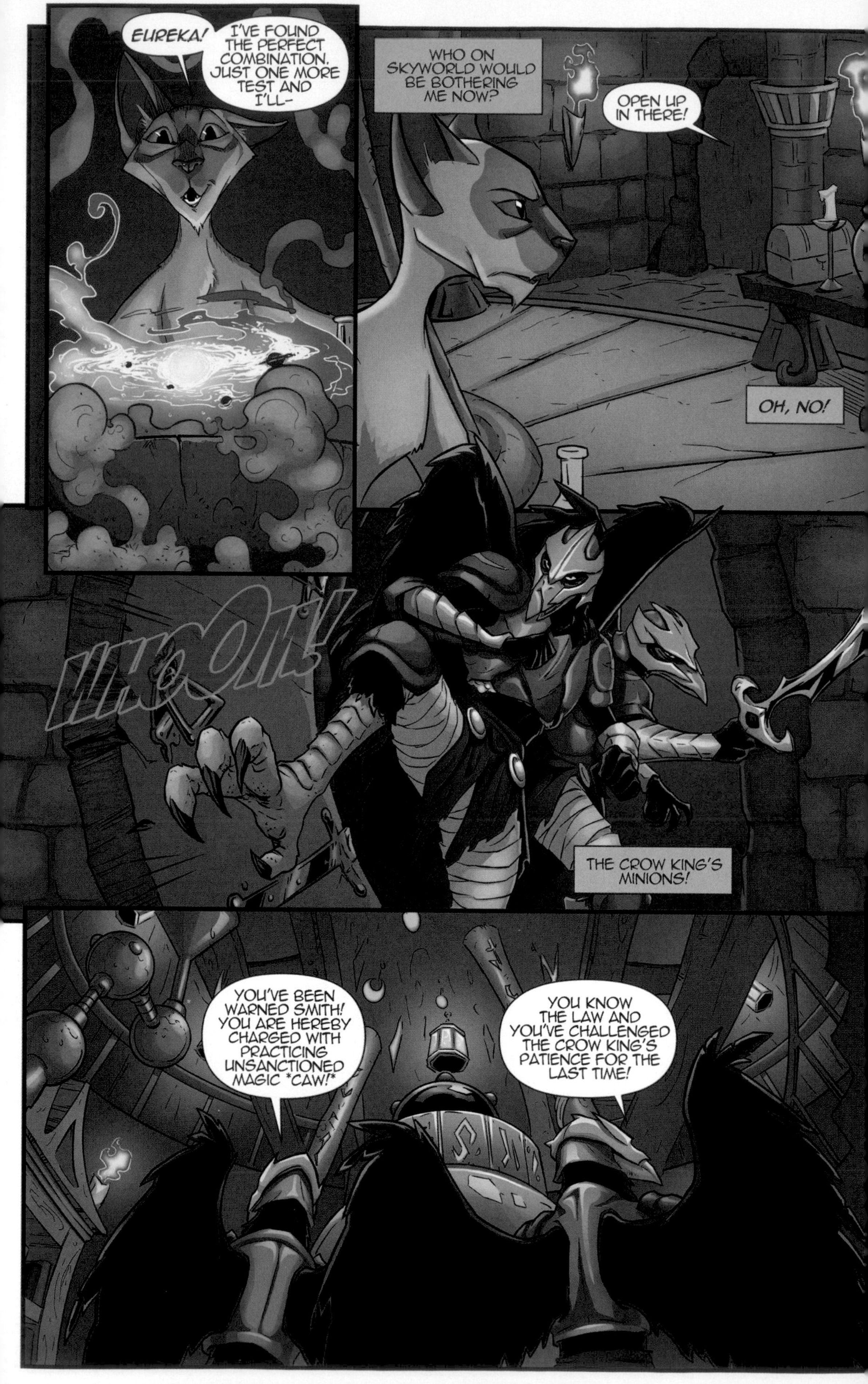
EUREKA!
I'VE FOUND THE PERFECT COMBINATION. JUST ONE MORE TEST AND I'LL-
WHO ON SKYWORLD WOULD BE BOTHERING ME NOW?
OPEN UP IN THERE!
OH, NO!
WHOOOM!
THE CROW KING'S MINIONS!
YOU'VE BEEN WARNED SMITH! YOU ARE HEREBY CHARGED WITH PRACTICING UNSANCTIONED MAGIC *CAW!*
YOU KNOW THE LAW AND YOU'VE CHALLENGED THE CROW KING'S PATIENCE FOR THE LAST TIME!

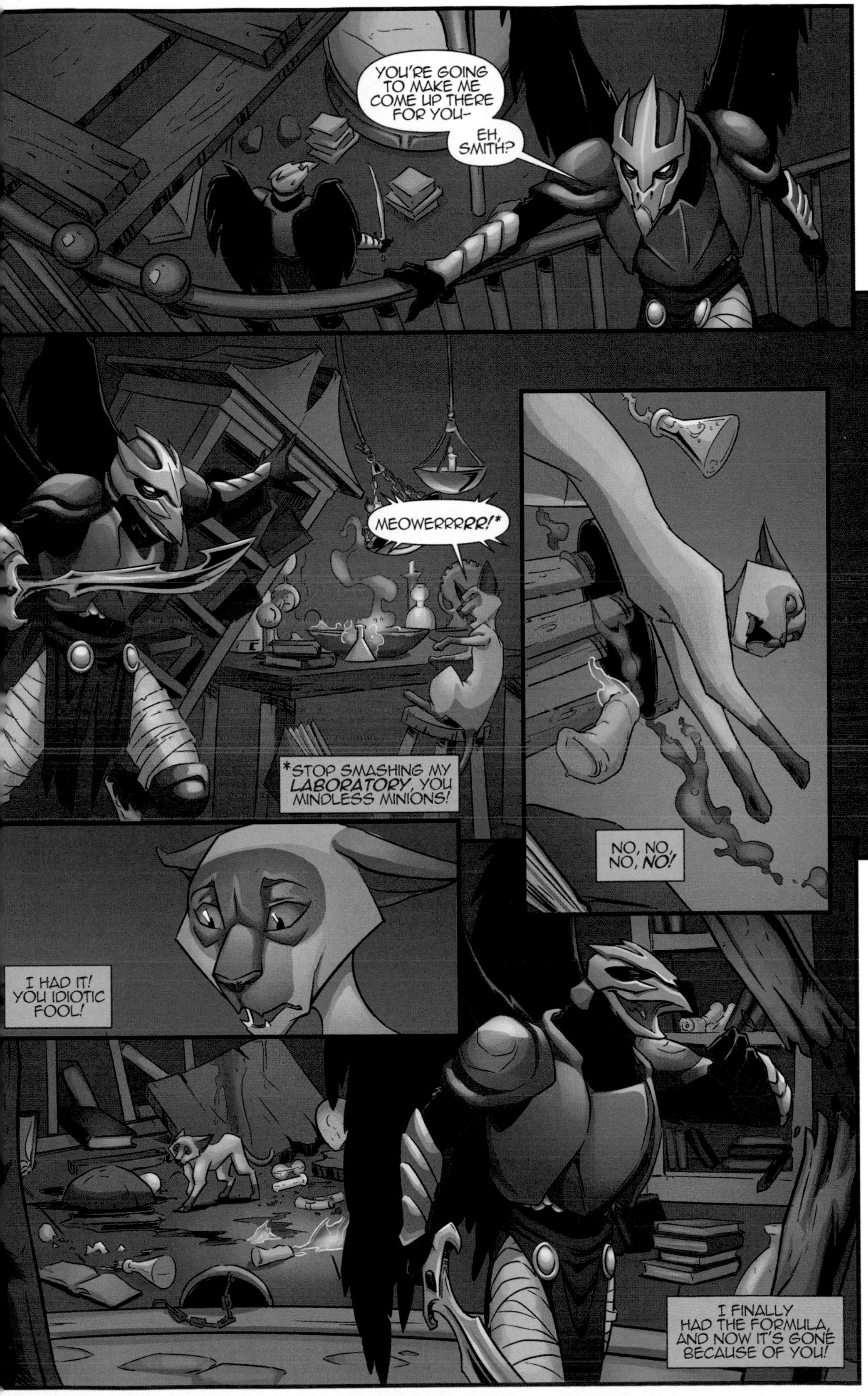
YOU'RE GOING TO MAKE ME COME UP THERE FOR YOU-
EH, SMITH?
MEOWERRRRR!*
*STOP SMASHING MY LABORATORY, YOU MINDLESS MINIONS!
NO, NO, NO, NO!
I HAD IT! YOU IDIOTIC FOOL!
I FINALLY HAD THE FORMULA, AND NOW IT'S GONE BECAUSE OF YOU!

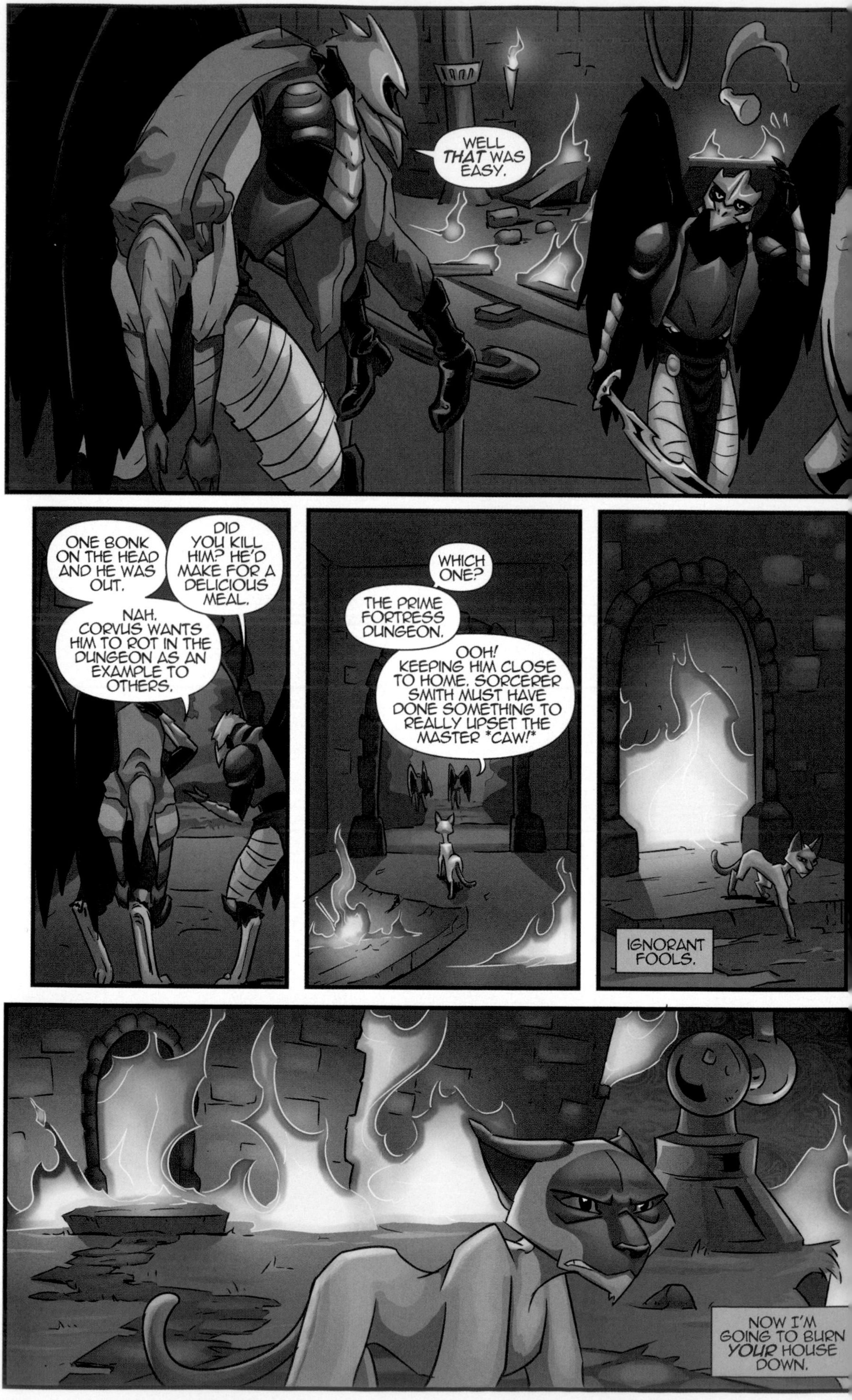
WELL THAT WAS EASY.
ONE BONK ON THE HEAD AND HE WAS OUT.
DID YOU KILL HIM? HE'D MAKE FOR A DELICIOUS MEAL.
NAH. CORVUS WANTS HIM TO ROT IN THE DUNGEON AS AN EXAMPLE TO OTHERS.
WHICH ONE?
THE PRIME FORTRESS DUNGEON.
OOH! KEEPING HIM CLOSE TO HOME. SORCERER SMITH MUST HAVE DONE SOMETHING TO REALLY UPSET THE MASTER *CAW!*
IGNORANT FOOLS.
NOW I'M GOING TO BURN YOUR HOUSE DOWN.

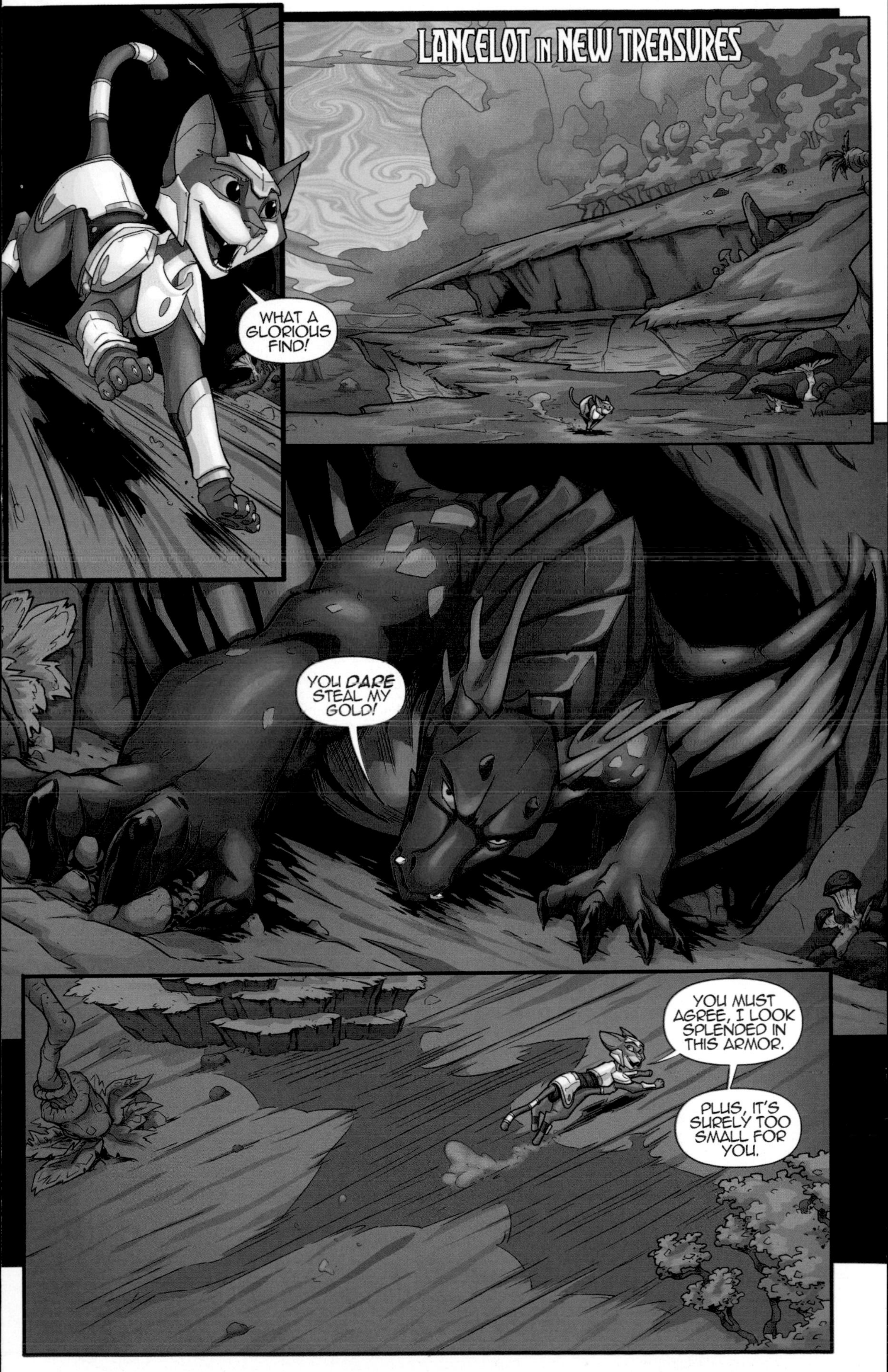
LANCELOT IN NEW TREASURES
WHAT A GLORIOUS FIND!
YOU DARE STEAL MY GOLD!
YOU MUST AGREE, I LOOK SPLENDED IN THIS ARMOR.
PLUS, IT'S SURELY TOO SMALL FOR YOU.

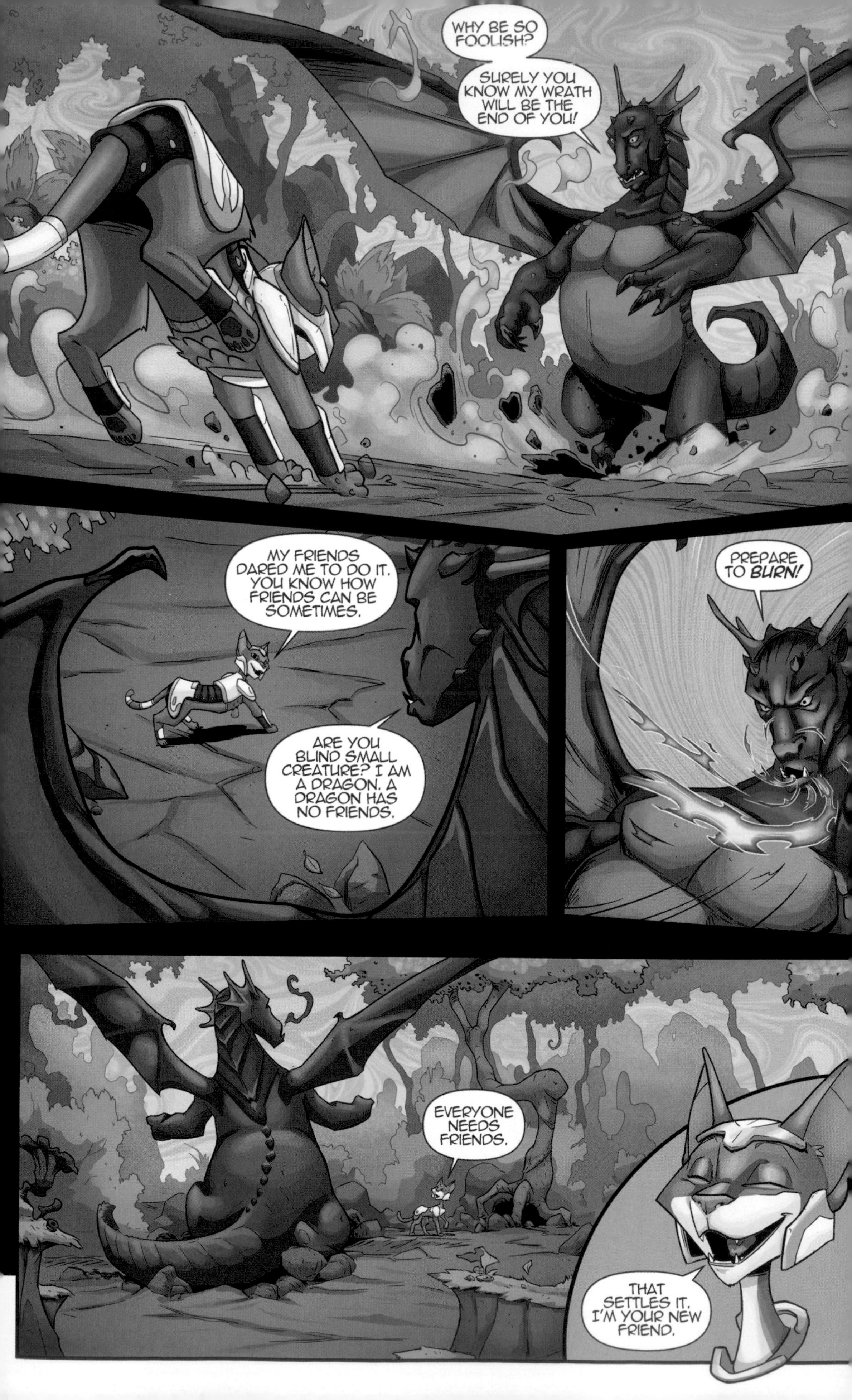
WHY BE SO FOOLISH?
SURELY YOU KNOW MY WRATH WILL BE THE END OF YOU!
MY FRIENDS DARED ME TO DO IT. YOU KNOW HOW FRIENDS CAN BE SOMETIMES.
ARE YOU BLIND SMALL CREATURE? I AM A DRAGON. A DRAGON HAS NO FRIENDS.
PREPARE TO BURN!
EVERYONE NEEDS FRIENDS.
THAT SETTLES IT. I'M YOUR NEW FRIEND.

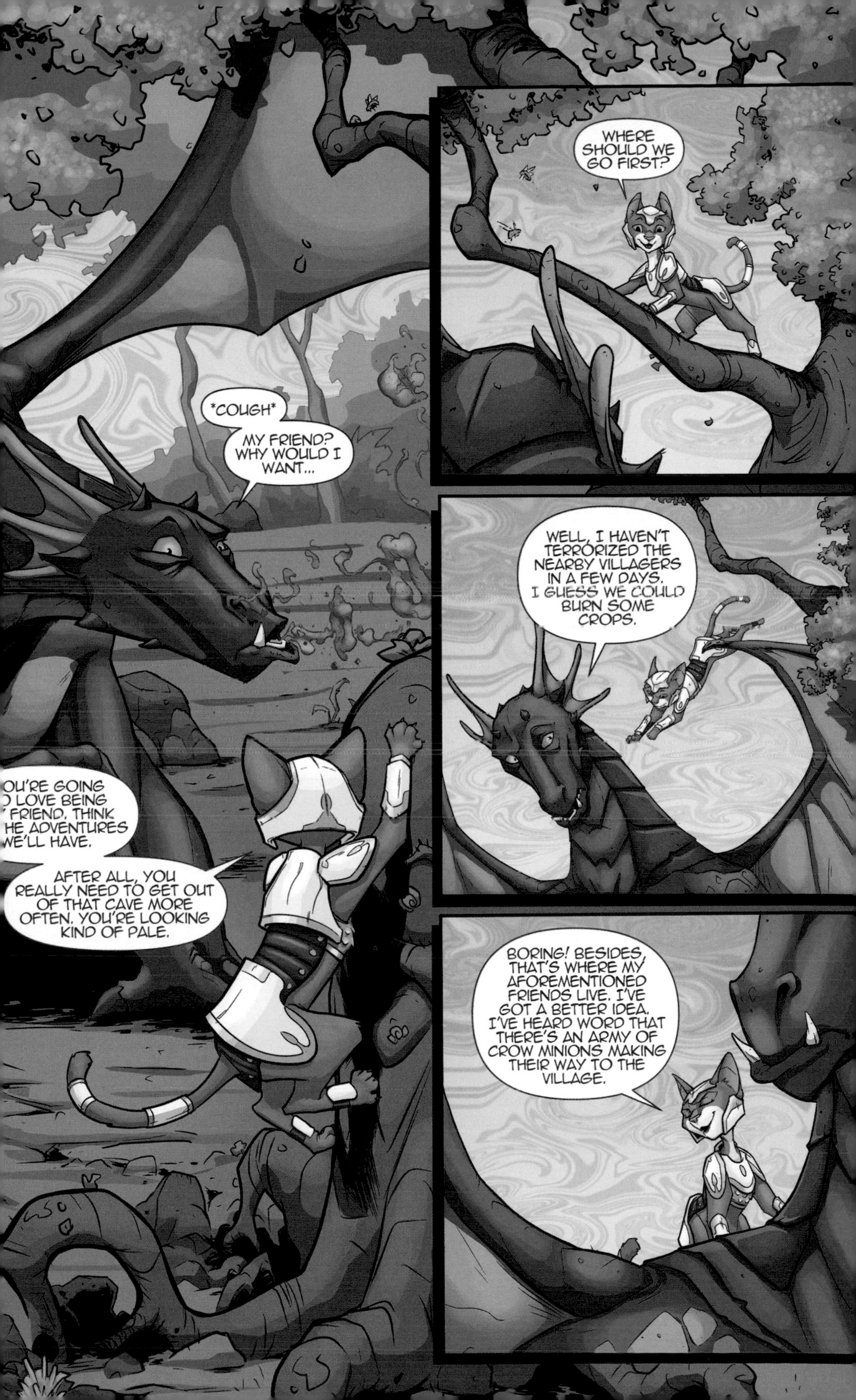
COUGH
MY FRIEND? WHY WOULD I WANT...
OU'RE GOING O LOVE BEING FRIEND. THINK HE ADVENTURES WE'LL HAVE.
AFTER ALL, YOU REALLY NEED TO GET OUT OF THAT CAVE MORE OFTEN. YOU'RE LOOKING KIND OF PALE.
WHERE SHOULD WE GO FIRST?
WELL, I HAVEN'T TERRORIZED THE NEARBY VILLAGERS IN A FEW DAYS. I GUESS WE COULD BURN SOME CROPS.
BORING! BESIDES, THAT'S WHERE MY AFOREMENTIONED FRIENDS LIVE. I'VE GOT A BETTER IDEA. I'VE HEARD WORD THAT THERE'S AN ARMY OF CROW MINIONS MAKING THEIR WAY TO THE VILLAGE.

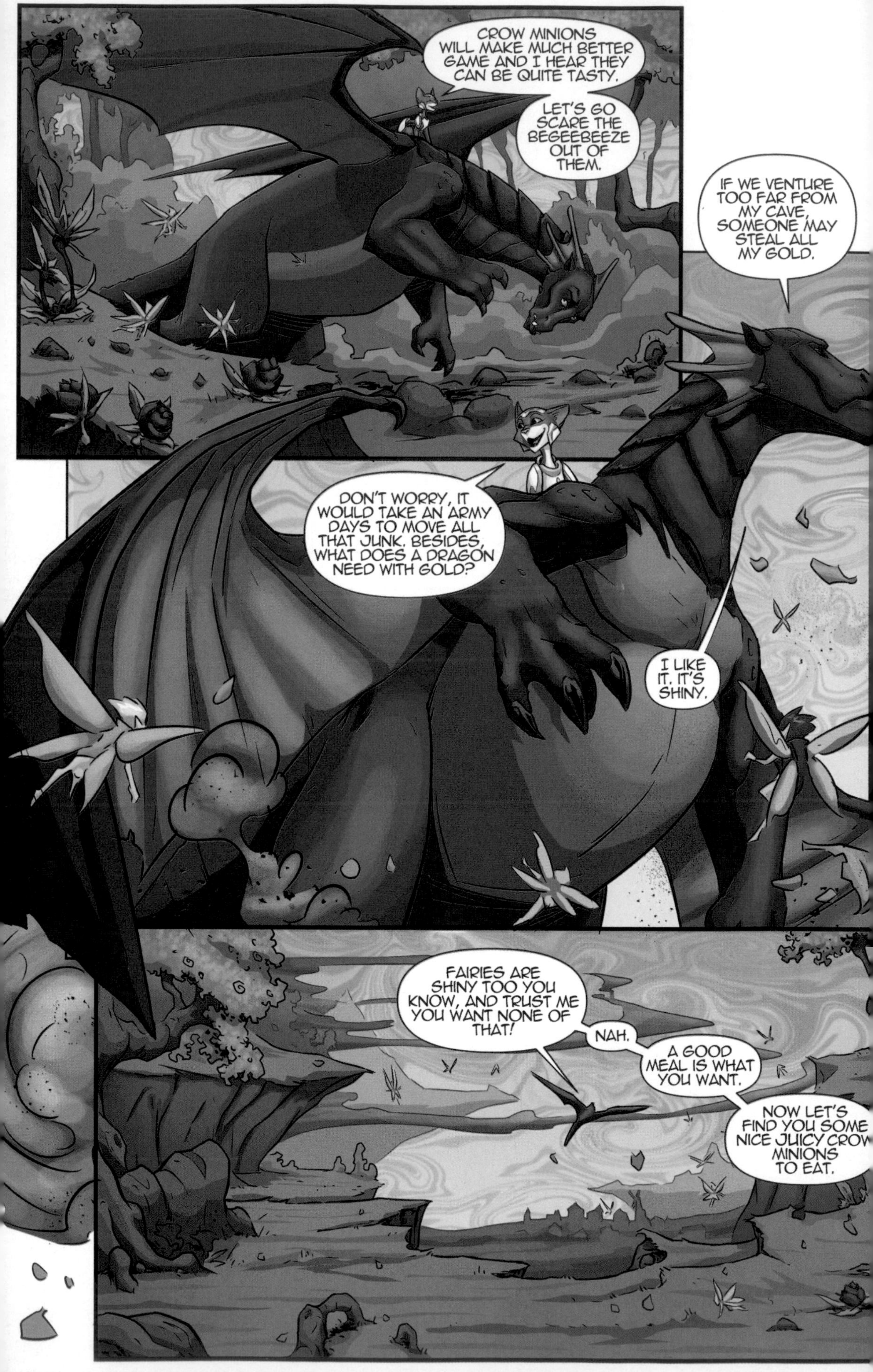
CROW MINIONS WILL MAKE MUCH BETTER GAME AND I HEAR THEY CAN BE QUITE TASTY.
LET'S GO SCARE THE BEGEEBEEZE OUT OF THEM.
IF WE VENTURE TOO FAR FROM MY CAVE, SOMEONE MAY STEAL ALL MY GOLD.
DON'T WORRY, IT WOULD TAKE AN ARMY DAYS TO MOVE ALL THAT JUNK. BESIDES, WHAT DOES A DRAGON NEED WITH GOLD?
I LIKE IT. IT'S SHINY.
FAIRIES ARE SHINY TOO YOU KNOW, AND TRUST ME YOU WANT NONE OF THAT!
NAH.
A GOOD MEAL IS WHAT YOU WANT.
NOW LET'S FIND YOU SOME NICE JUICY CROW MINIONS TO EAT.

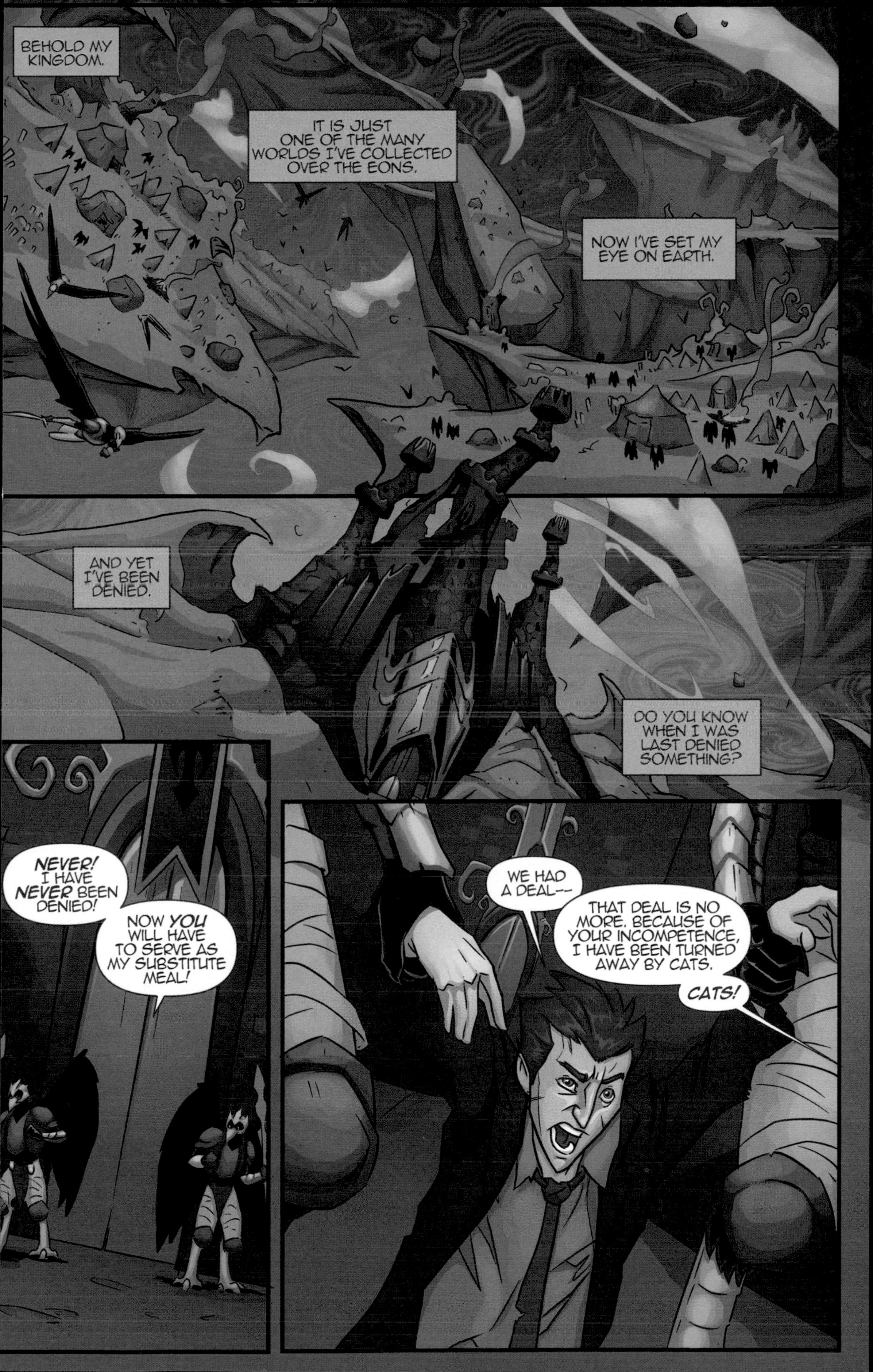

BEHOLD MY KINGDOM.
IT IS JUST ONE OF THE MANY WORLDS I'VE COLLECTED OVER THE EONS.
NOW I'VE SET MY EYE ON EARTH.
AND YET I'VE BEEN DENIED.
DO YOU KNOW WHEN I WAS LAST DENIED SOMETHING?
NEVER! I HAVE NEVER BEEN DENIED!
NOW YOU WILL HAVE TO SERVE AS MY SUBSTITUTE MEAL!
WE HAD A DEAL--
THAT DEAL IS NO MORE. BECAUSE OF YOUR INCOMPETENCE, I HAVE BEEN TURNED AWAY BY CATS.
CATS!

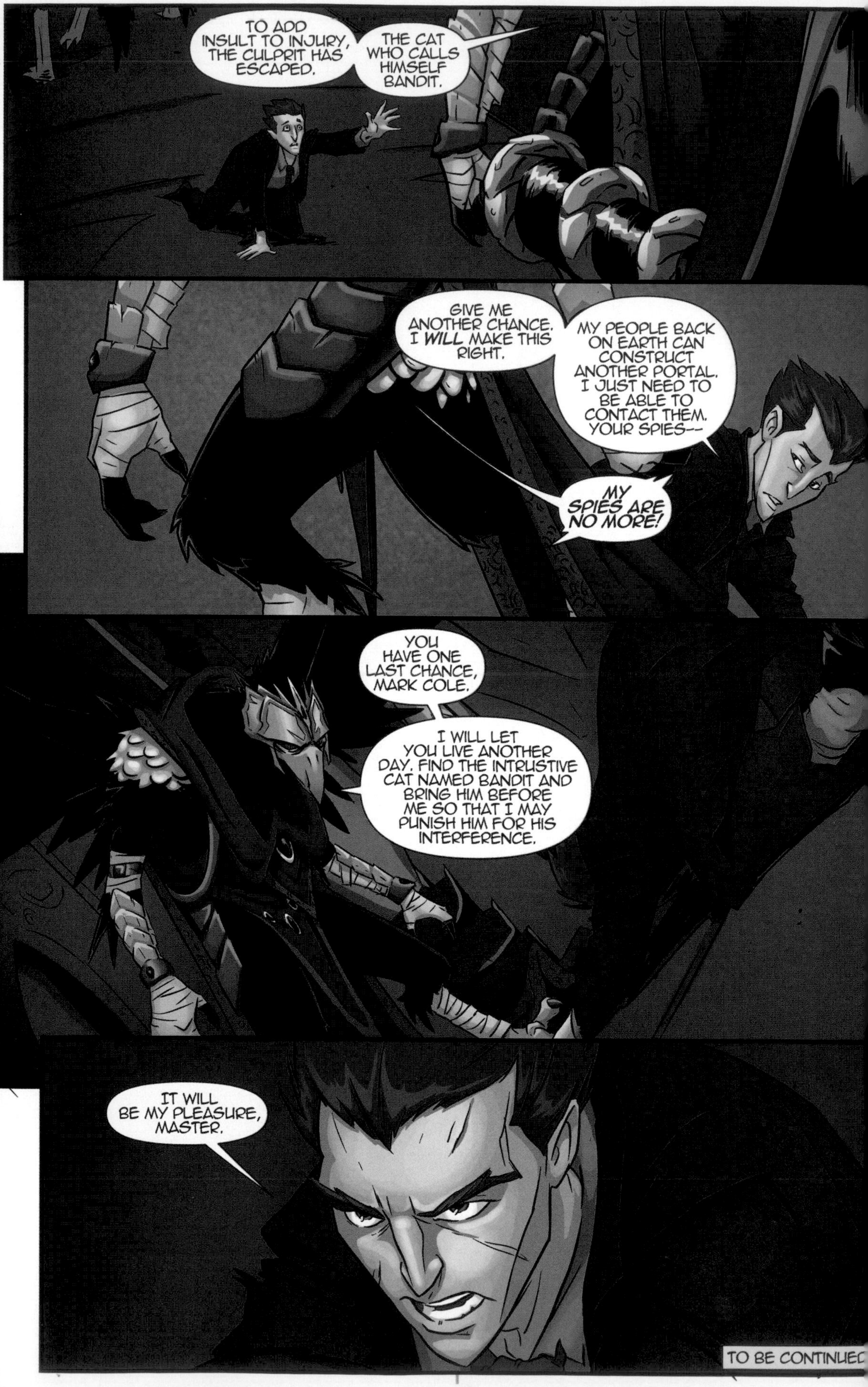

TO ADD INSULT TO INJURY, THE CULPRIT HAS ESCAPED.
THE CAT WHO CALLS HIMSELF BANDIT.
GIVE ME ANOTHER CHANCE. I *WILL* MAKE THIS RIGHT.
MY PEOPLE BACK ON EARTH CAN CONSTRUCT ANOTHER PORTAL. I JUST NEED TO BE ABLE TO CONTACT THEM. YOUR SPIES--
MY SPIES ARE NO MORE!
YOU HAVE ONE LAST CHANCE, MARK COLE.
I WILL LET YOU LIVE ANOTHER DAY. FIND THE INTRUSTIVE CAT NAMED BANDIT AND BRING HIM BEFORE ME SO THAT I MAY PUNISH HIM FOR HIS INTERFERENCE.
IT WILL BE MY PLEASURE, MASTER.
TO BE CONTINUED

HERO CHAT

BANDIT AND THE MYSTERIES OF SKYWORLD!

HEY KIDS & CATS!

A WHOLE NEW BATCH OF HERO CATS? YOU BET YOUR TAILS! BUT DON'T WORRY - ACE, MIDNIGHT, CASSIE, BELLE, ROCKET AND ROCCO WILL RETURN.

THE HERO CATS OF SKYWORLD - LANCELOT, NEWTON, SAPPHIRE AND MADALYN ARE IN FOR A SURPRISE WHEN THEY MEET BANDIT AND TAKE ON THE CROW KING.

WE'RE OFF ON A WHOLE NEW EXCITING JOURNEY!

COLLECT ALL 3 "HERO CATS OF SKYWORLD" CONNECTING COVERS!

UP NEXT:
MISFITS & REBELS!

PART ONE   **PART TWO**   **PART THREE**

HERO CATS #16, May 2017

Bryan Seaton - Publisher
Dave Dwonch - President of Marketing
Shawn Gabborin - Editor in Chief
Jason Martin - Publisher - Danger Zone
Nicole D'Andria - Marketing Director
Jim Dietz - Social Media Manager
Scott Bradley - CFO
Chad Cicconi -Head in the Clouds

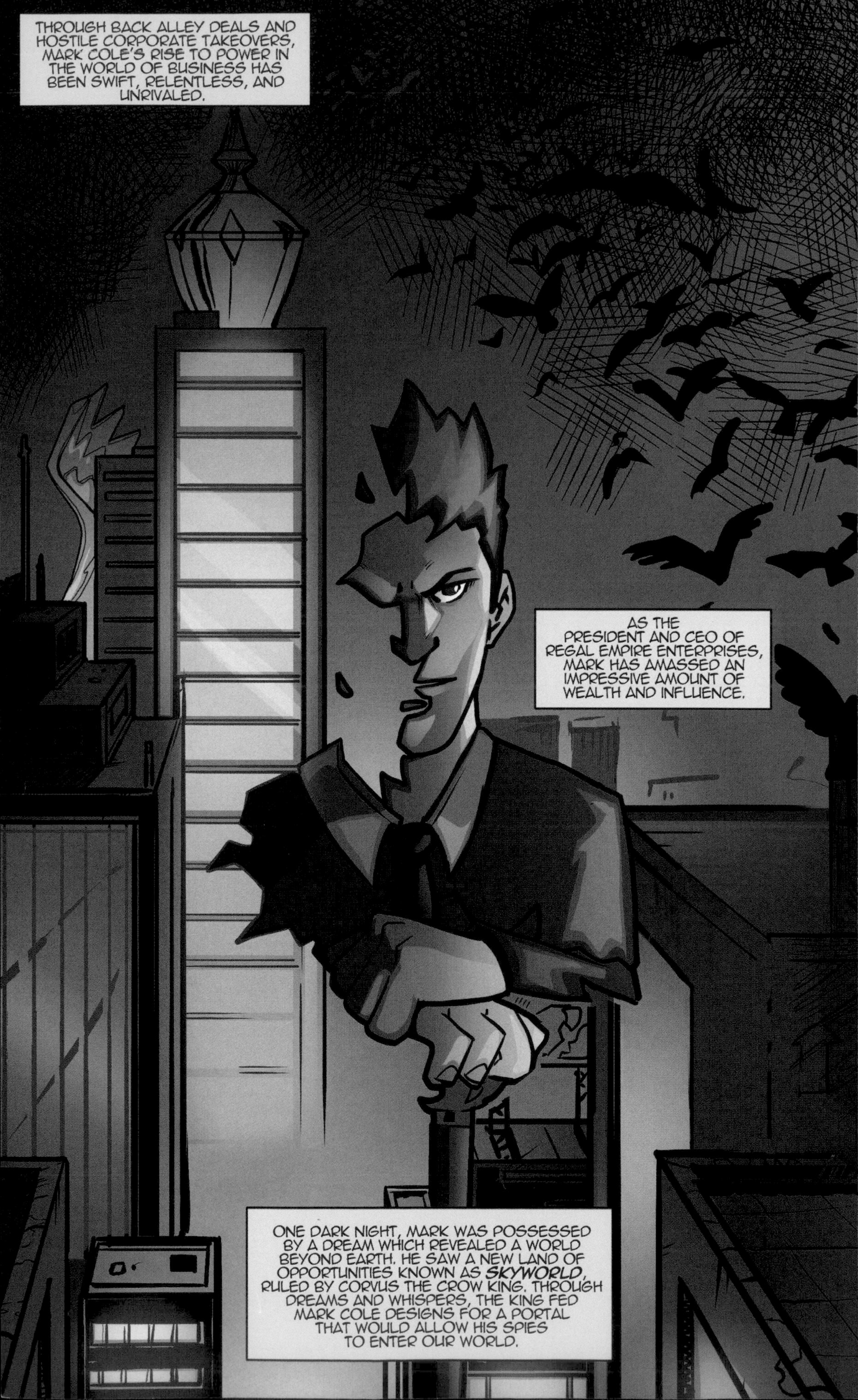
THROUGH BACK ALLEY DEALS AND HOSTILE CORPORATE TAKEOVERS, MARK COLE'S RISE TO POWER IN THE WORLD OF BUSINESS HAS BEEN SWIFT, RELENTLESS, AND UNRIVALED.
AS THE PRESIDENT AND CEO OF REGAL EMPIRE ENTERPRISES, MARK HAS AMASSED AN IMPRESSIVE AMOUNT OF WEALTH AND INFLUENCE.
ONE DARK NIGHT, MARK WAS POSSESSED BY A DREAM WHICH REVEALED A WORLD BEYOND EARTH. HE SAW A NEW LAND OF OPPORTUNITIES KNOWN AS ***SKYWORLD***, RULED BY CORVUS THE CROW KING. THROUGH DREAMS AND WHISPERS, THE KING FED MARK COLE DESIGNS FOR A PORTAL THAT WOULD ALLOW HIS SPIES TO ENTER OUR WORLD.

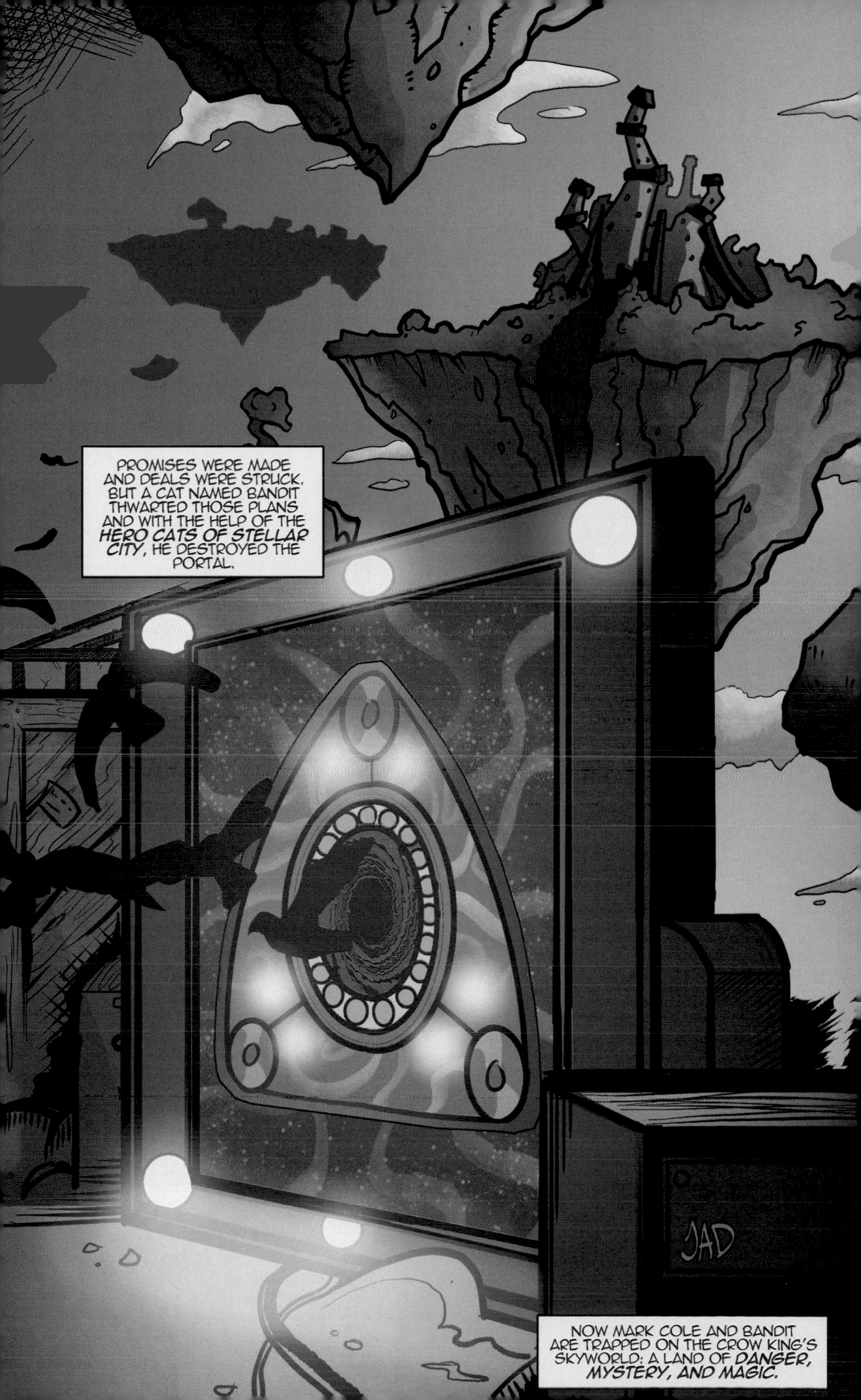
PROMISES WERE MADE AND DEALS WERE STRUCK. BUT A CAT NAMED BANDIT THWARTED THOSE PLANS AND WITH THE HELP OF THE *HERO CATS OF STELLAR CITY*, HE DESTROYED THE PORTAL.
JAD
NOW MARK COLE AND BANDIT ARE TRAPPED ON THE CROW KING'S SKYWORLD: A LAND OF *DANGER, MYSTERY, AND MAGIC.*

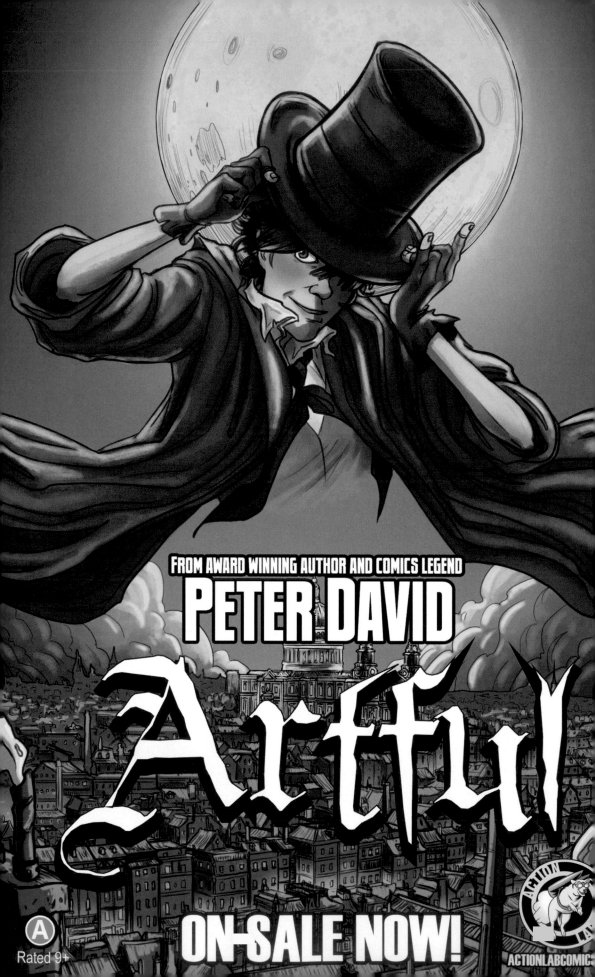

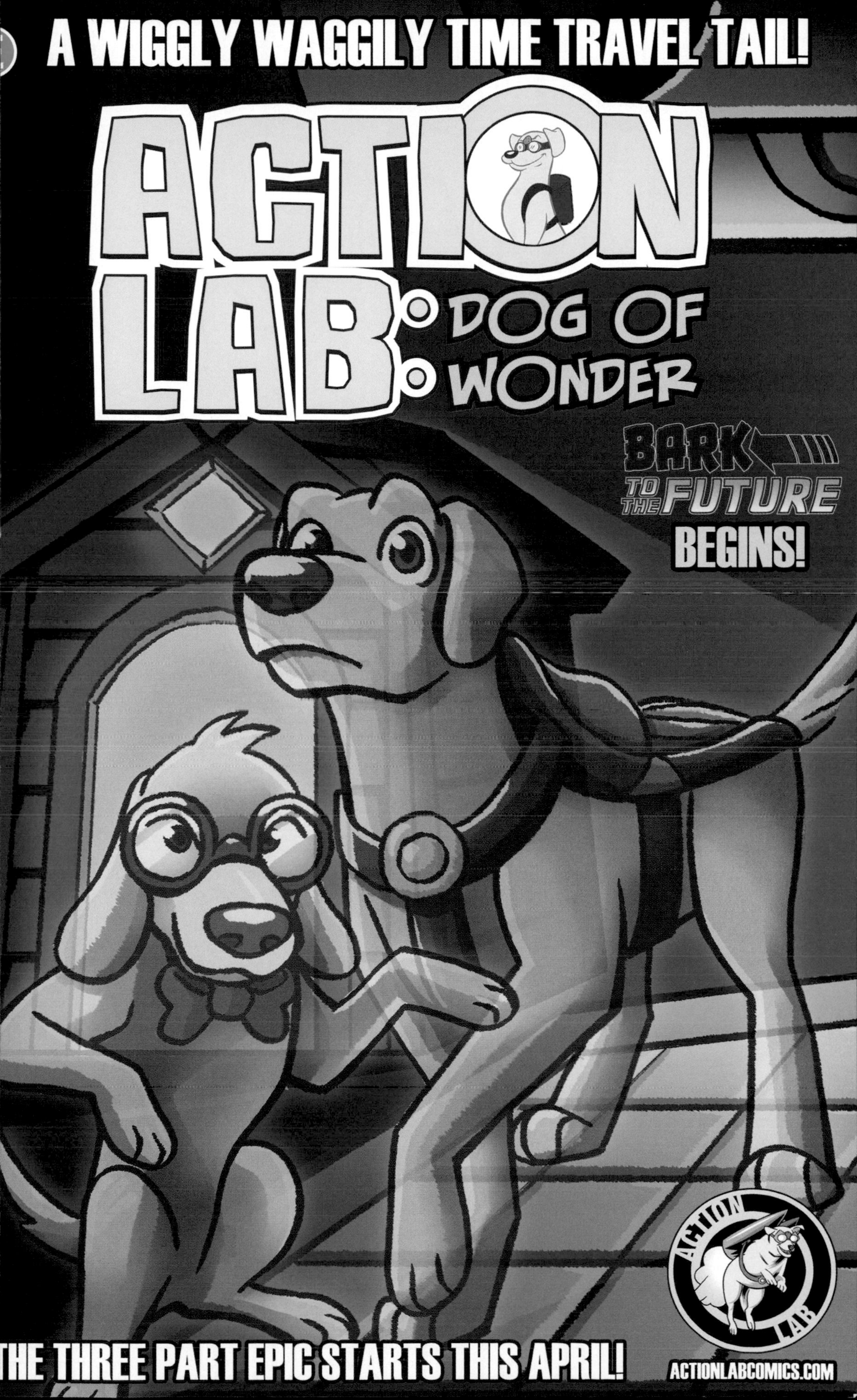
A WIGGLY WAGGILY TIME TRAVEL TAIL!
ACTION LAB: DOG OF WONDER
BARK TO THE FUTURE BEGINS!
ACTION LAB
THE THREE PART EPIC STARTS THIS APRIL!
ACTIONLABCOMICS.COM

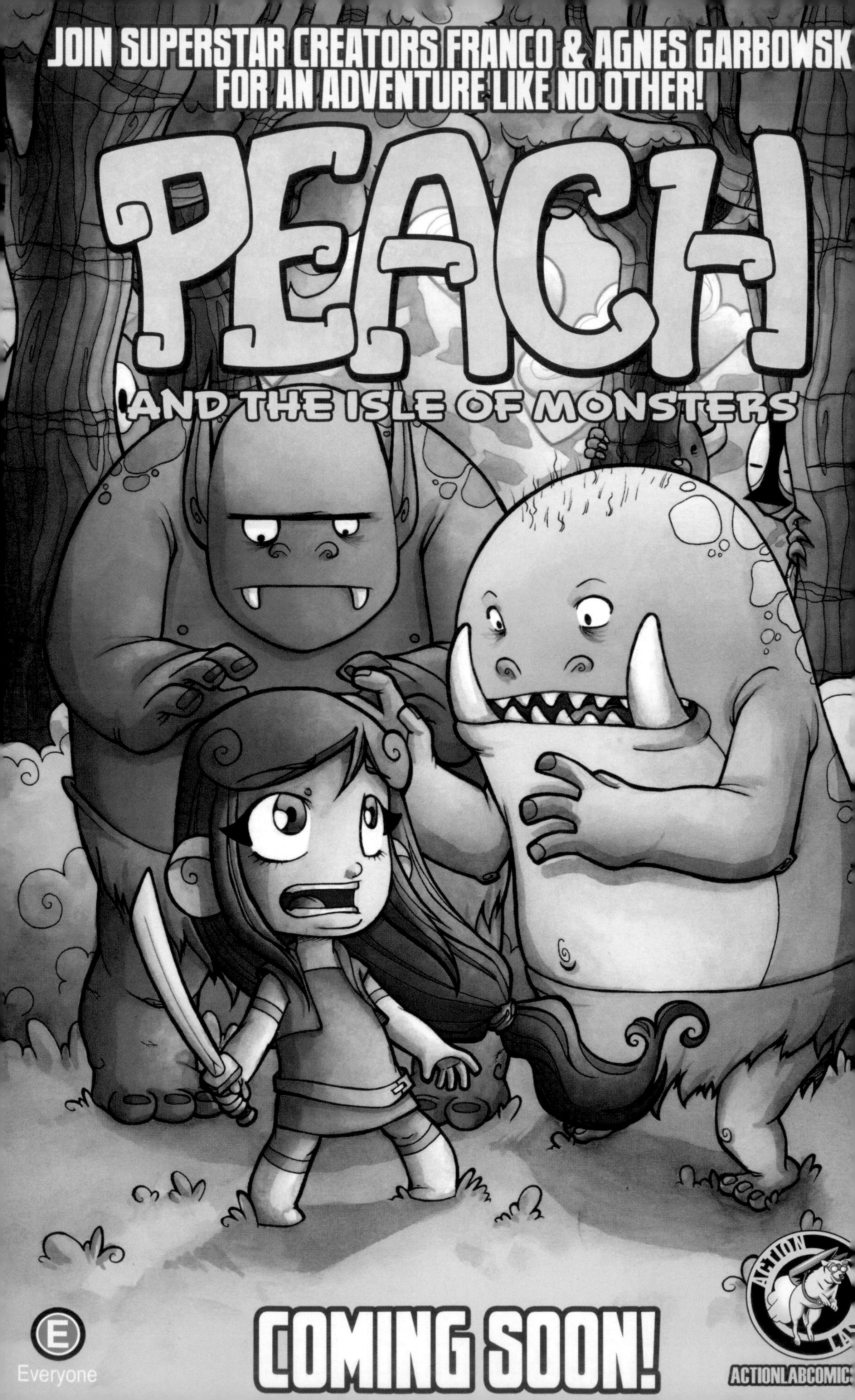
JOIN SUPERSTAR CREATORS FRANCO & AGNES GARBOWSK
FOR AN ADVENTURE LIKE NO OTHER!
PEACH
AND THE ISLE OF MONSTERS
COMING SOON!
E
Everyone
ACTIONLABCOMICS

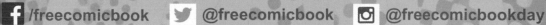

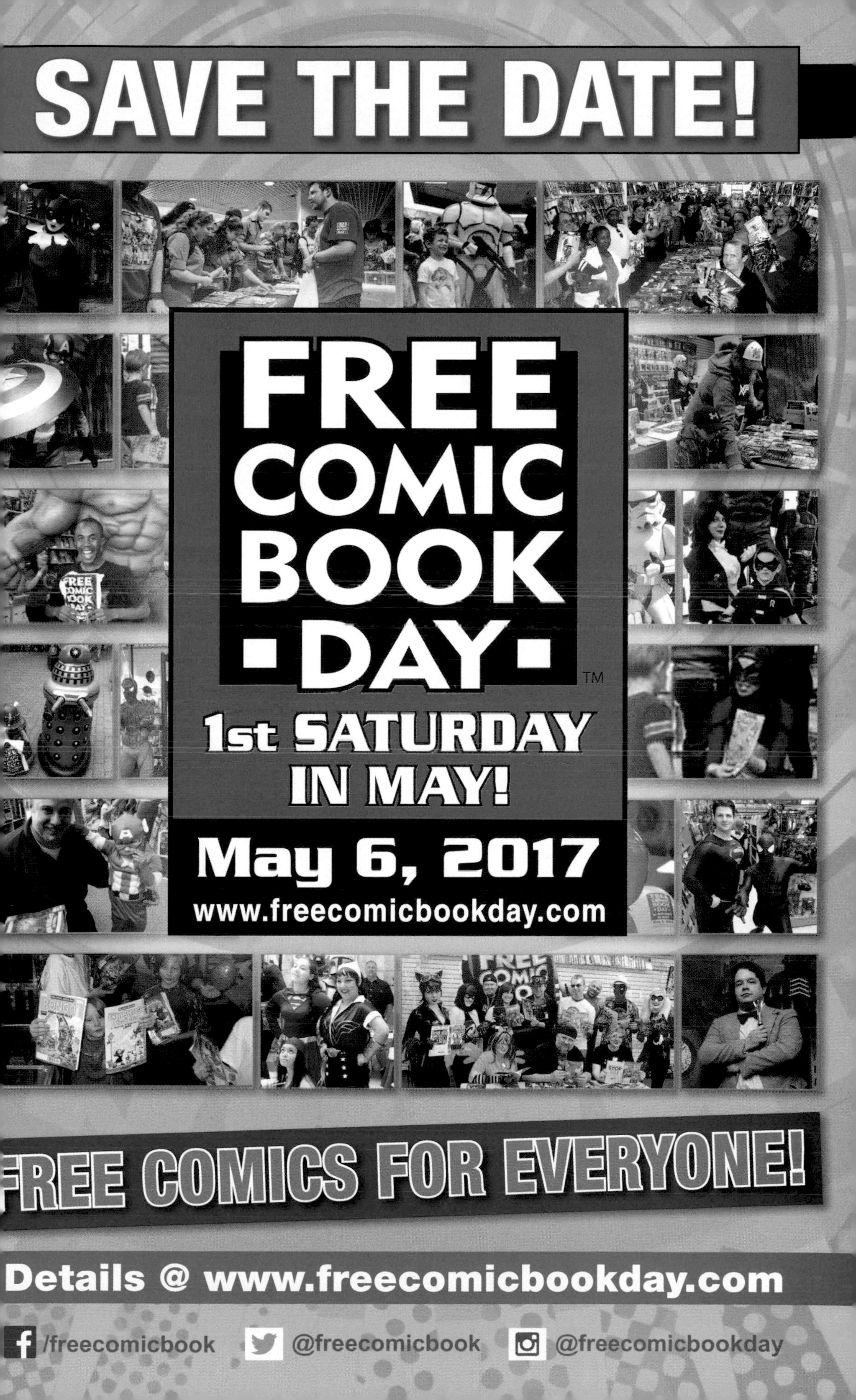

SAVE THE DATE!

FREE COMIC BOOK ·DAY·™

1st SATURDAY IN MAY!

May 6, 2017
www.freecomicbookday.com

FREE COMICS FOR EVERYONE!

Details @ www.freecomicbookday.com

f /freecomicbook 🐦 @freecomicbook 📷 @freecomicbookday

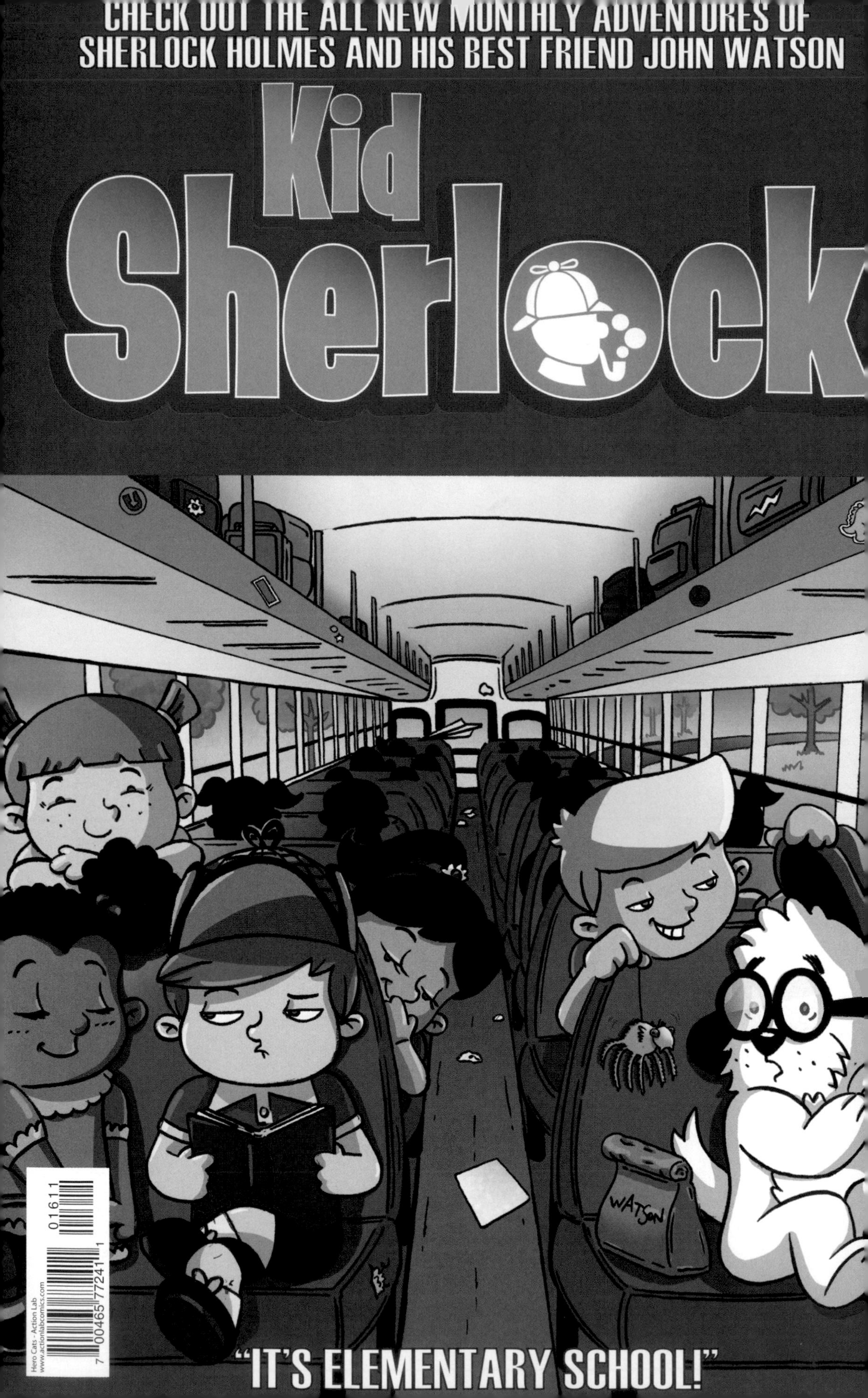

CHECK OUT THE ALL NEW MONTHLY ADVENTURES OF SHERLOCK HOLMES AND HIS BEST FRIEND JOHN WATSON
Kid Sherlock
WATSON
"IT'S ELEMENTARY SCHOOL!"
Hero Cats - Action Lab
www.actionlabcomics.com

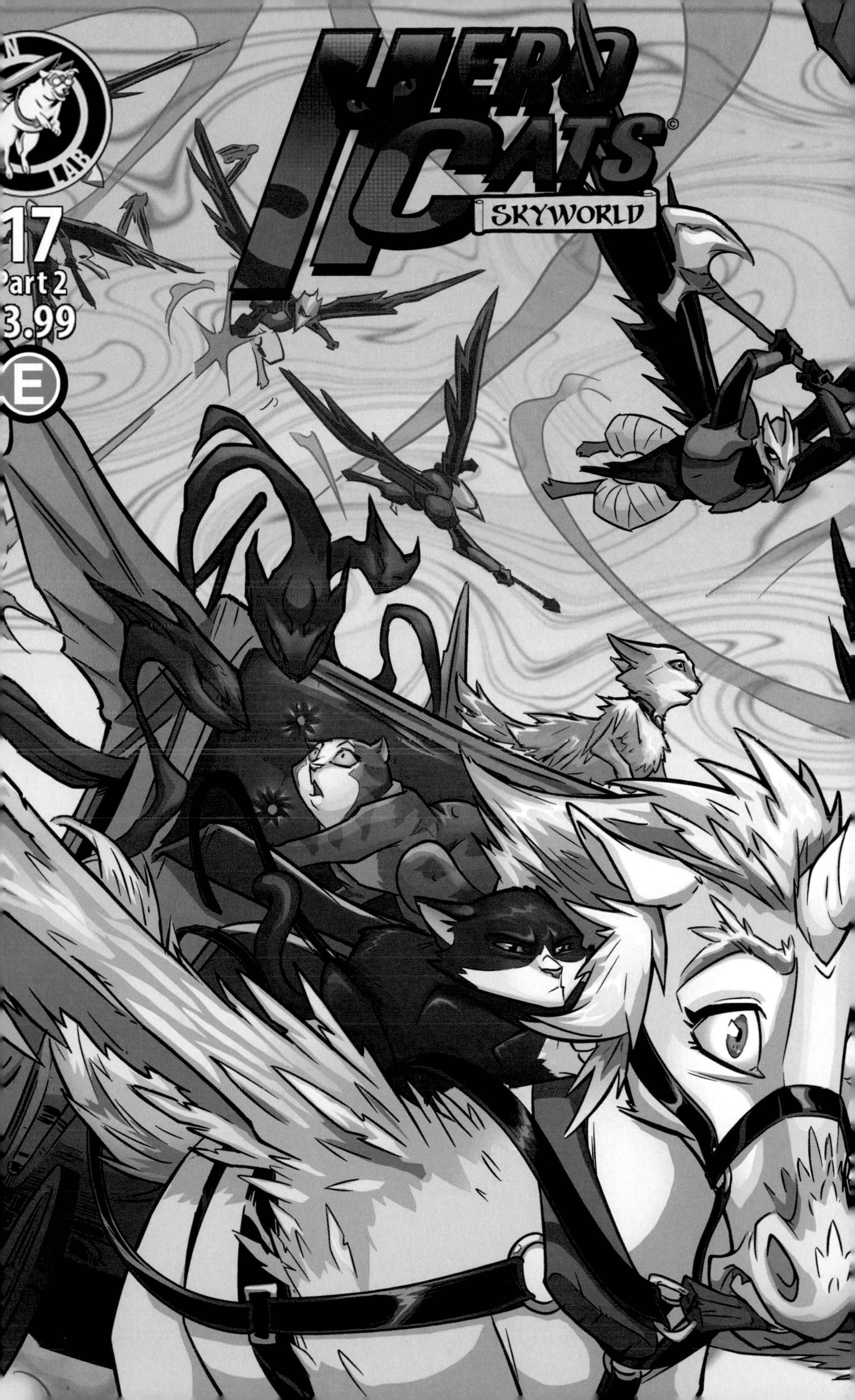

HERO CATS
SKYWORLD
17
Part 2
3.99
E
LAB

FROM ALL-AGES TO MATURE READERS ACTION LAB HAS YOU COVERED.

 **Appropriate for everyone.**

 **Appropriate for age 9 and up. Absent of profanity or adult content.**

Suggested for 12 and Up. Comics with this rating are comparable to a PG-13 movie rating. Recommended for our teen and young adult readers.

 **Appropriate for older teens. Similar to Teen, but featuring more mature themes and/or more graphic imagery.**

 **Contains extreme violence and some nudity. Basically the Rated-R of comics.**

 FIND YOUR NEW FAVORITE COMICS.

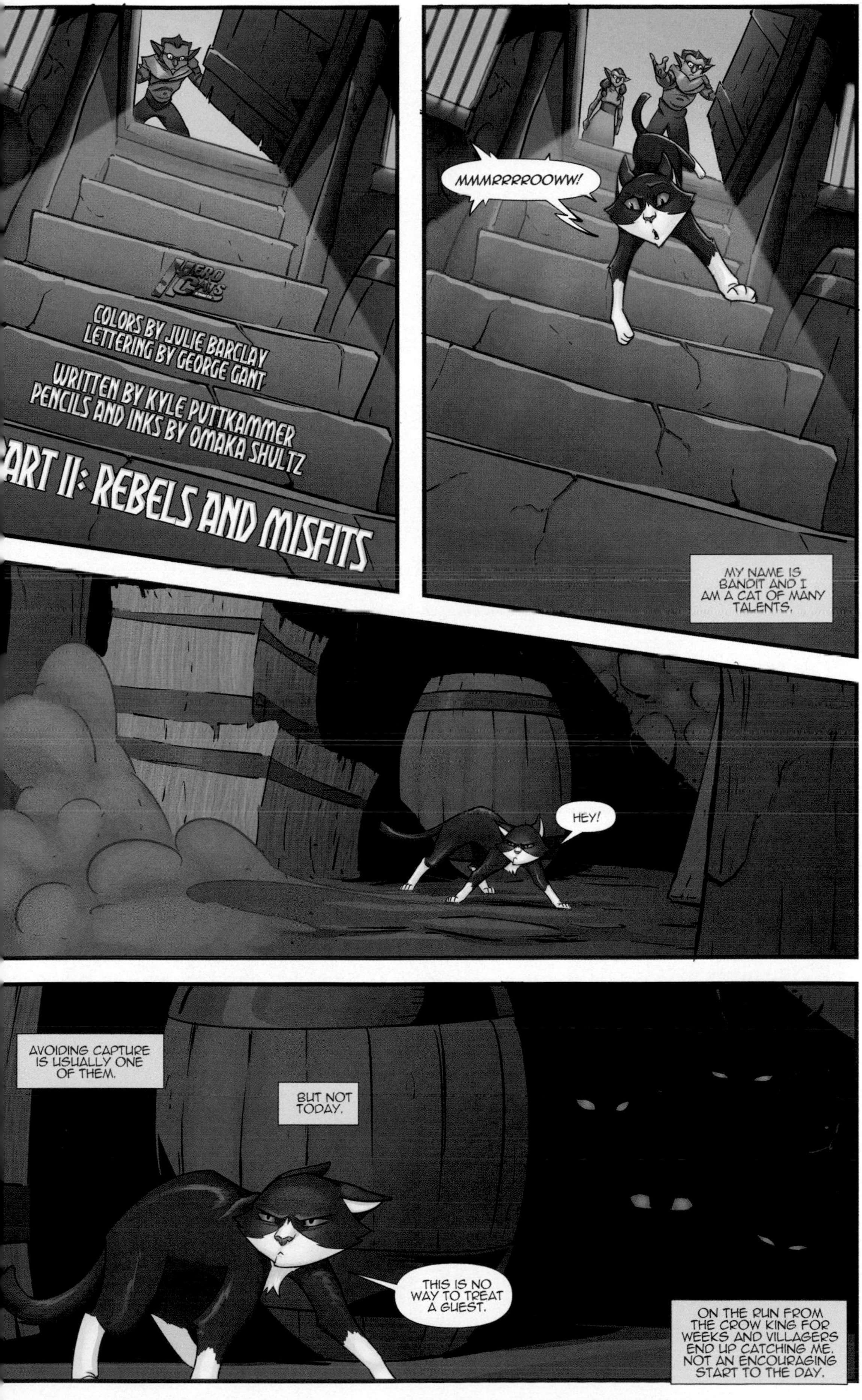
COLORS BY JULIE BARCLAY
LETTERING BY GEORGE GANT
WRITTEN BY KYLE PUTTKAMMER
PENCILS AND INKS BY OMAKA SHULTZ
ART II: REBELS AND MISFITS
MMMRRRROOWW!
MY NAME IS BANDIT AND I AM A CAT OF MANY TALENTS.
HEY!
AVOIDING CAPTURE IS USUALLY ONE OF THEM.
BUT NOT TODAY.
THIS IS NO WAY TO TREAT A GUEST.
ON THE RUN FROM THE CROW KING FOR WEEKS AND VILLAGERS END UP CATCHING ME. NOT AN ENCOURAGING START TO THE DAY.

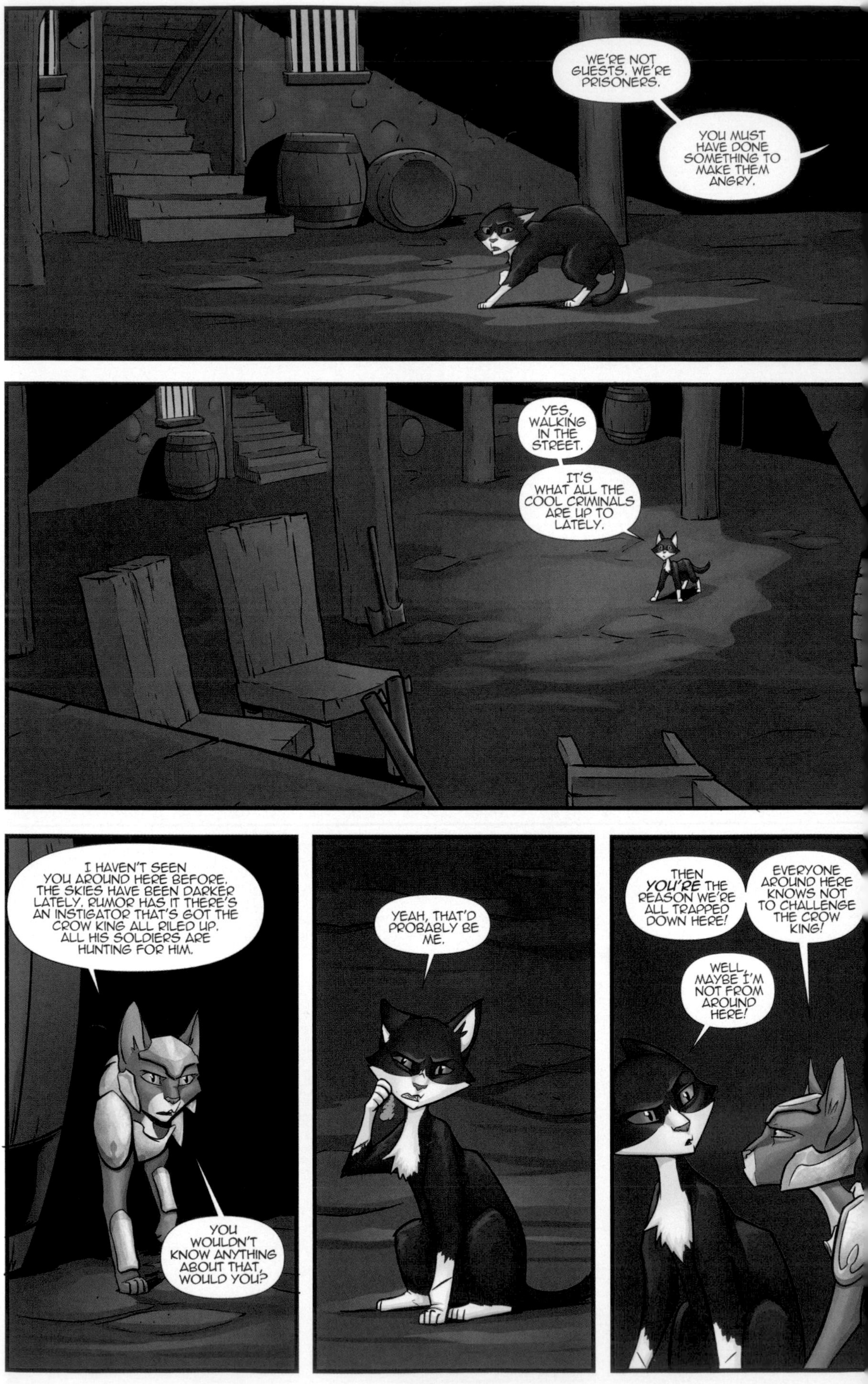
WE'RE NOT GUESTS. WE'RE PRISONERS.
YOU MUST HAVE DONE SOMETHING TO MAKE THEM ANGRY.
YES, WALKING IN THE STREET.
IT'S WHAT ALL THE COOL CRIMINALS ARE UP TO LATELY.
I HAVEN'T SEEN YOU AROUND HERE BEFORE. THE SKIES HAVE BEEN DARKER LATELY. RUMOR HAS IT THERE'S AN INSTIGATOR THAT'S GOT THE CROW KING ALL RILED UP. ALL HIS SOLDIERS ARE HUNTING FOR HIM.
YOU WOULDN'T KNOW ANYTHING ABOUT THAT, WOULD YOU?
YEAH, THAT'D PROBABLY BE ME.
EVERYONE AROUND HERE KNOWS NOT TO CHALLENGE THE CROW KING!
THEN *YOU'RE* THE REASON WE'RE ALL TRAPPED DOWN HERE!
WELL, MAYBE I'M NOT FROM AROUND HERE!

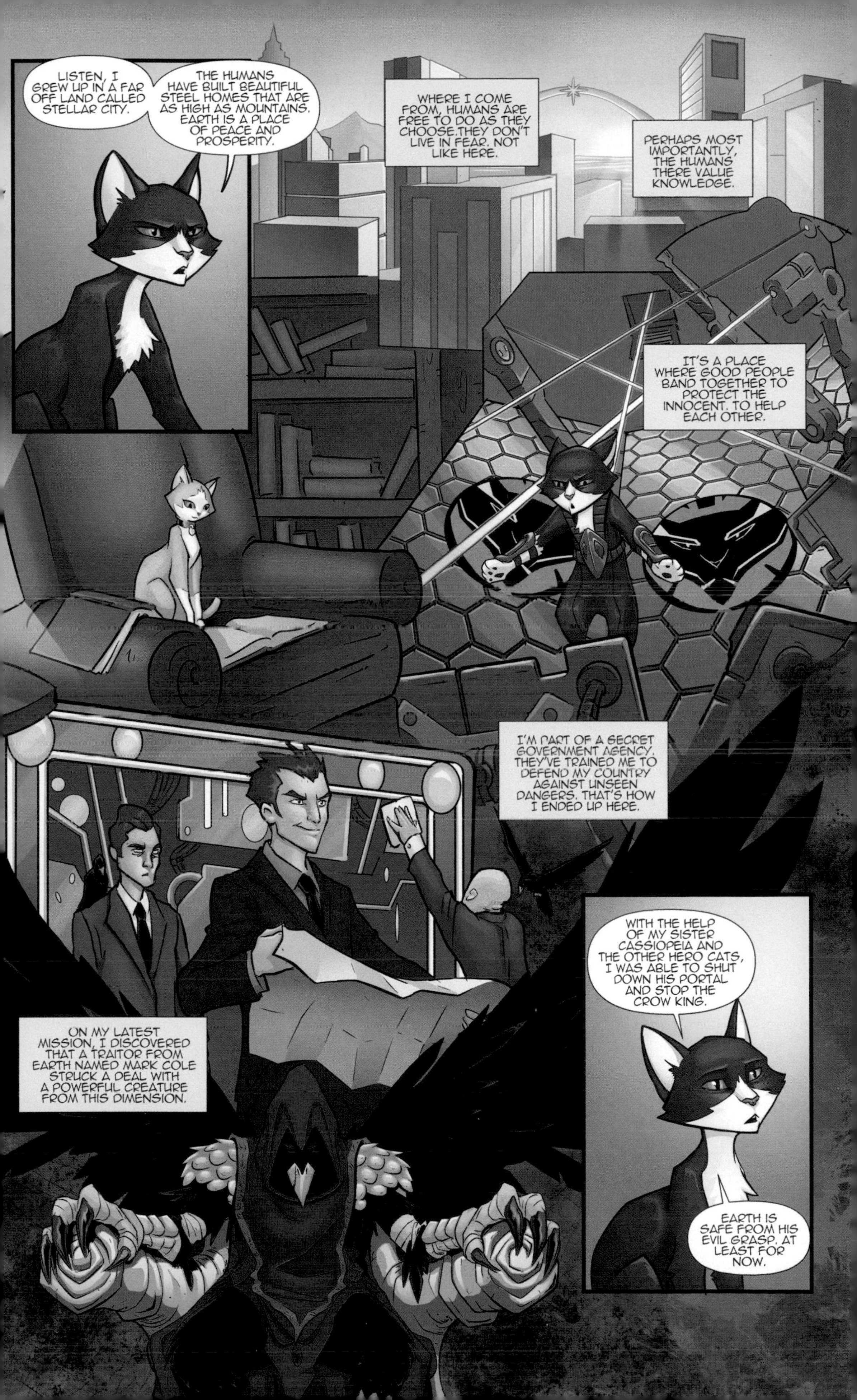
LISTEN, I GREW UP IN A FAR OFF LAND CALLED STELLAR CITY.
THE HUMANS HAVE BUILT BEAUTIFUL STEEL HOMES THAT ARE AS HIGH AS MOUNTAINS. EARTH IS A PLACE OF PEACE AND PROSPERITY.
WHERE I COME FROM, HUMANS ARE FREE TO DO AS THEY CHOOSE.THEY DON'T LIVE IN FEAR. NOT LIKE HERE.
PERHAPS MOST IMPORTANTLY, THE HUMANS THERE VALUE KNOWLEDGE.
IT'S A PLACE WHERE GOOD PEOPLE BAND TOGETHER TO PROTECT THE INNOCENT. TO HELP EACH OTHER.
I'M PART OF A SECRET GOVERNMENT AGENCY. THEY'VE TRAINED ME TO DEFEND MY COUNTRY AGAINST UNSEEN DANGERS. THAT'S HOW I ENDED UP HERE.
ON MY LATEST MISSION, I DISCOVERED THAT A TRAITOR FROM EARTH NAMED MARK COLE STRUCK A DEAL WITH A POWERFUL CREATURE FROM THIS DIMENSION.
WITH THE HELP OF MY SISTER CASSIOPEIA AND THE OTHER HERO CATS, I WAS ABLE TO SHUT DOWN HIS PORTAL AND STOP THE CROW KING.
EARTH IS SAFE FROM HIS EVIL GRASP. AT LEAST FOR NOW.

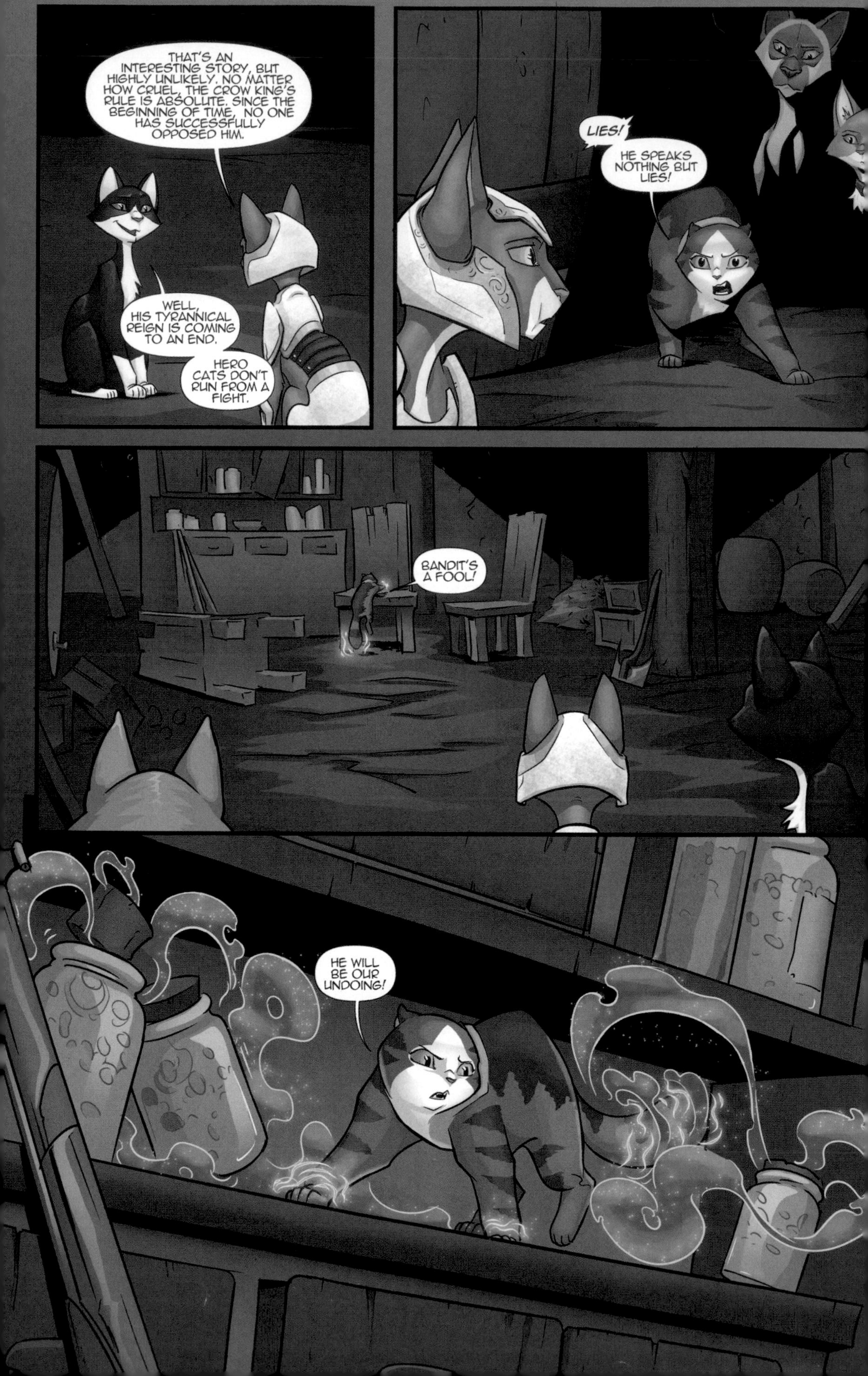
THAT'S AN INTERESTING STORY, BUT HIGHLY UNLIKELY. NO MATTER HOW CRUEL, THE CROW KING'S RULE IS ABSOLUTE. SINCE THE BEGINNING OF TIME, NO ONE HAS SUCCESSFULLY OPPOSED HIM.
WELL, HIS TYRANNICAL REIGN IS COMING TO AN END.
HERO CATS DON'T RUN FROM A FIGHT.
LIES!
HE SPEAKS NOTHING BUT LIES!
BANDIT'S A FOOL!
HE WILL BE OUR UNDOING!

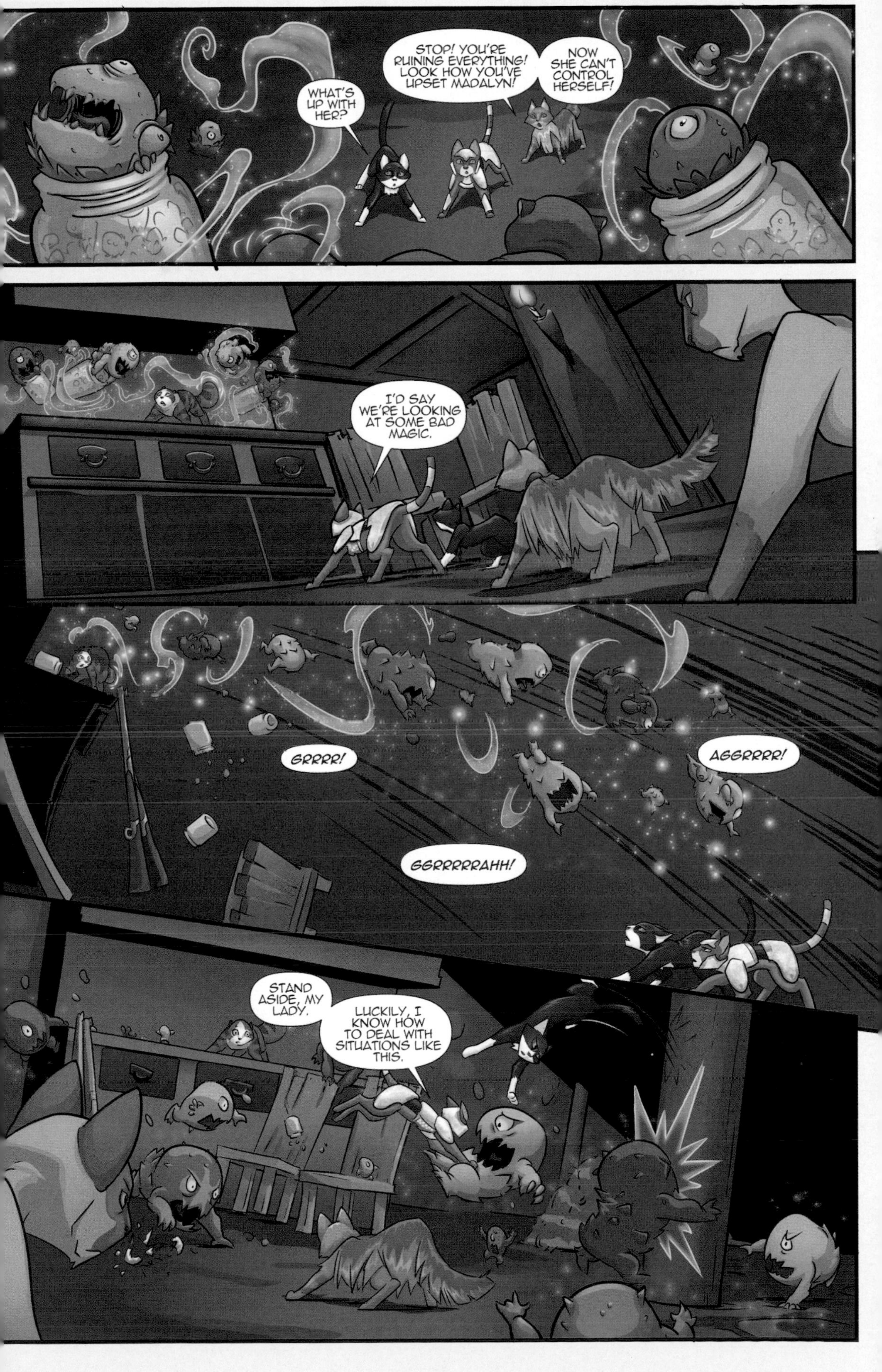
WHAT'S UP WITH HER?
STOP! YOU'RE RUINING EVERYTHING! LOOK HOW YOU'VE UPSET MADALYN!
NOW SHE CAN'T CONTROL HERSELF!
I'D SAY WE'RE LOOKING AT SOME BAD MAGIC.
GRRRR!
AGGRRRR!
GGRRRRRAHH!
STAND ASIDE, MY LADY.
LUCKILY, I KNOW HOW TO DEAL WITH SITUATIONS LIKE THIS.

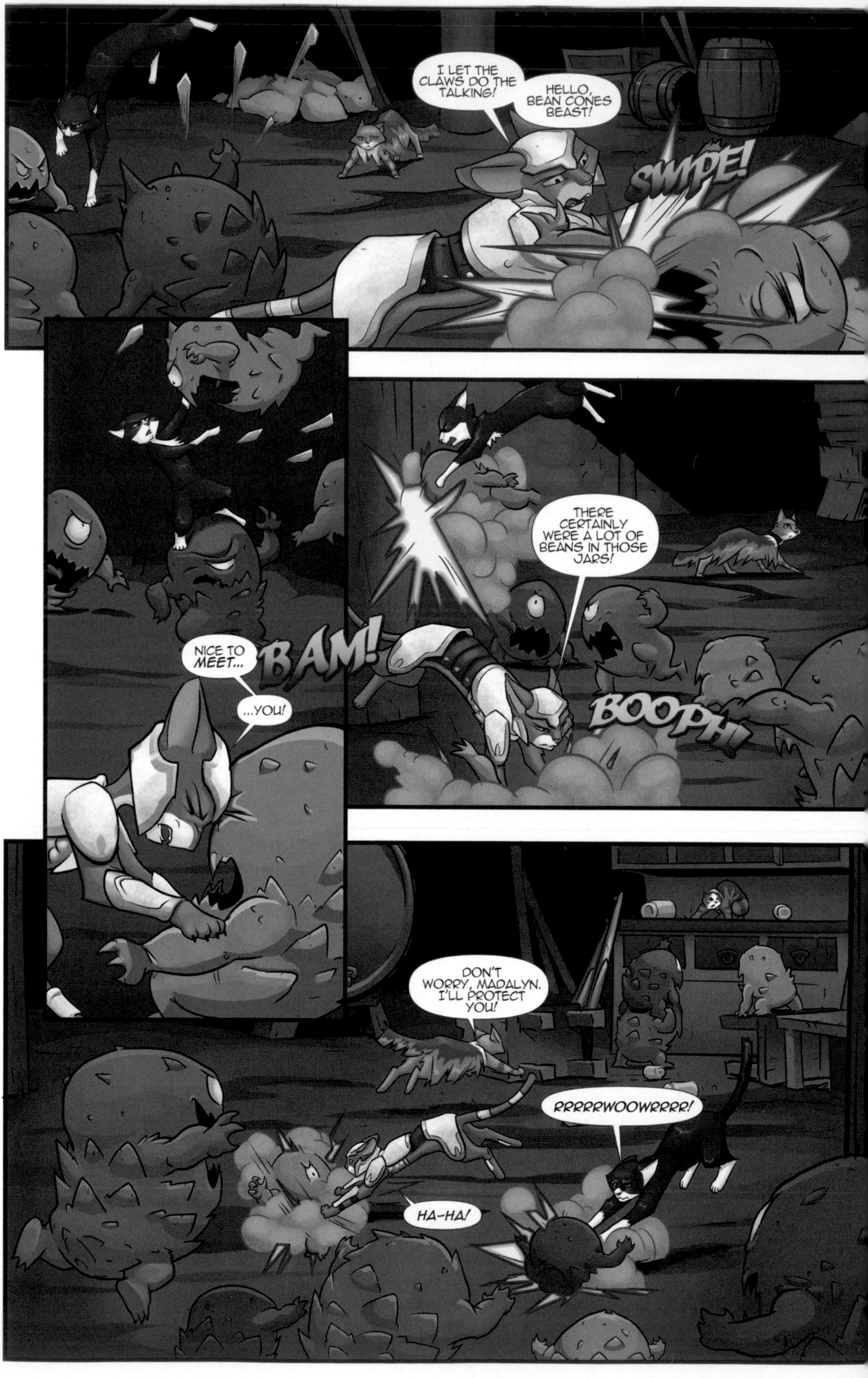
I LET THE CLAWS DO THE TALKING!
HELLO, BEAN CONES BEAST!
SWIPE!
NICE TO MEET...
BAM!
...YOU!
THERE CERTAINLY WERE A LOT OF BEANS IN THOSE JARS!
BOOPH!
DON'T WORRY, MADALYN. I'LL PROTECT YOU!
RRRRRWOOWRRRR!
HA-HA!

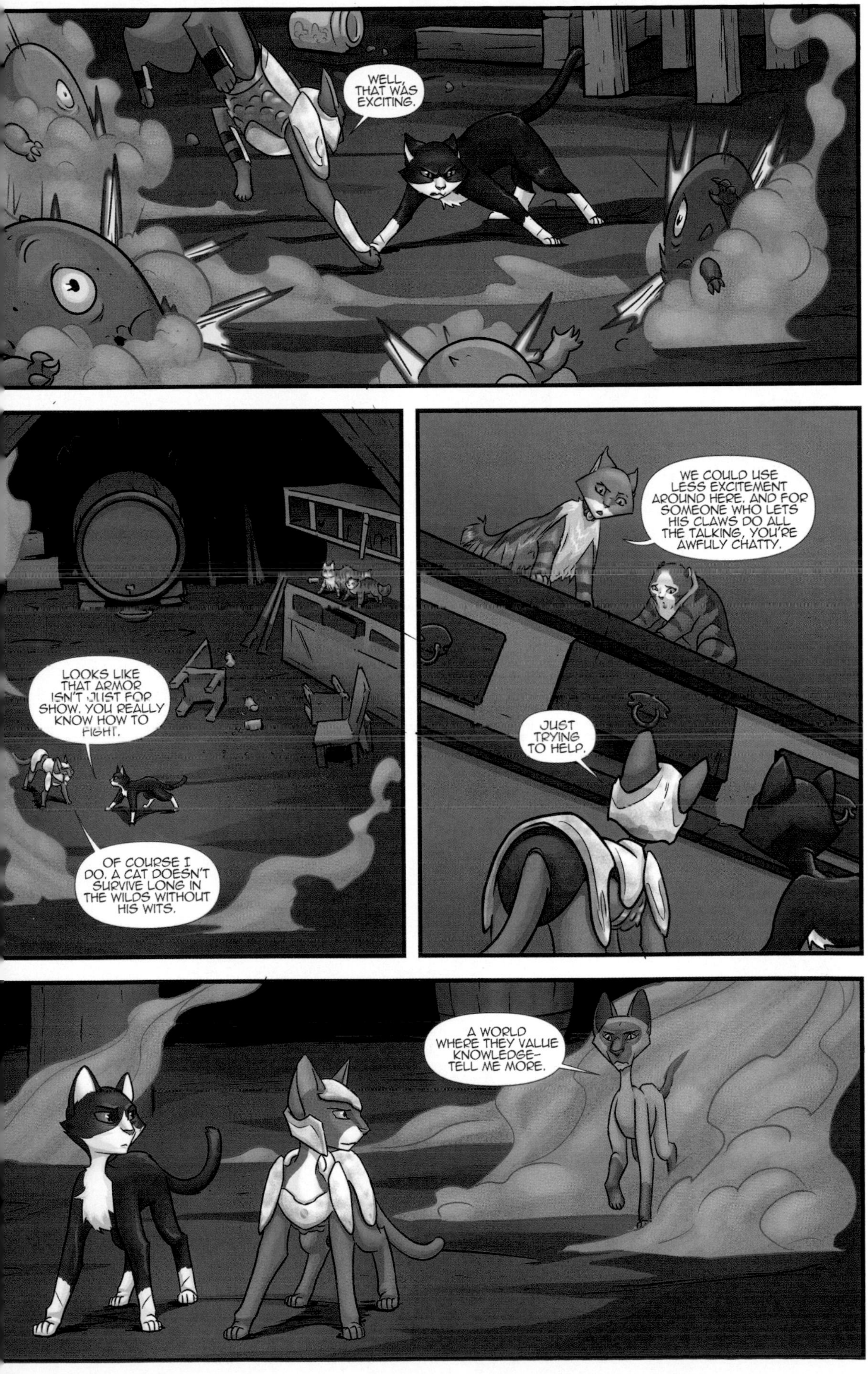
WELL, THAT WAS EXCITING.
LOOKS LIKE THAT ARMOR ISN'T JUST FOR SHOW. YOU REALLY KNOW HOW TO FIGHT.
OF COURSE I DO. A CAT DOESN'T SURVIVE LONG IN THE WILDS WITHOUT HIS WITS.
WE COULD USE LESS EXCITEMENT AROUND HERE. AND FOR SOMEONE WHO LETS HIS CLAWS DO ALL THE TALKING, YOU'RE AWFULY CHATTY.
JUST TRYING TO HELP.
A WORLD WHERE THEY VALUE KNOWLEDGE-TELL ME MORE.

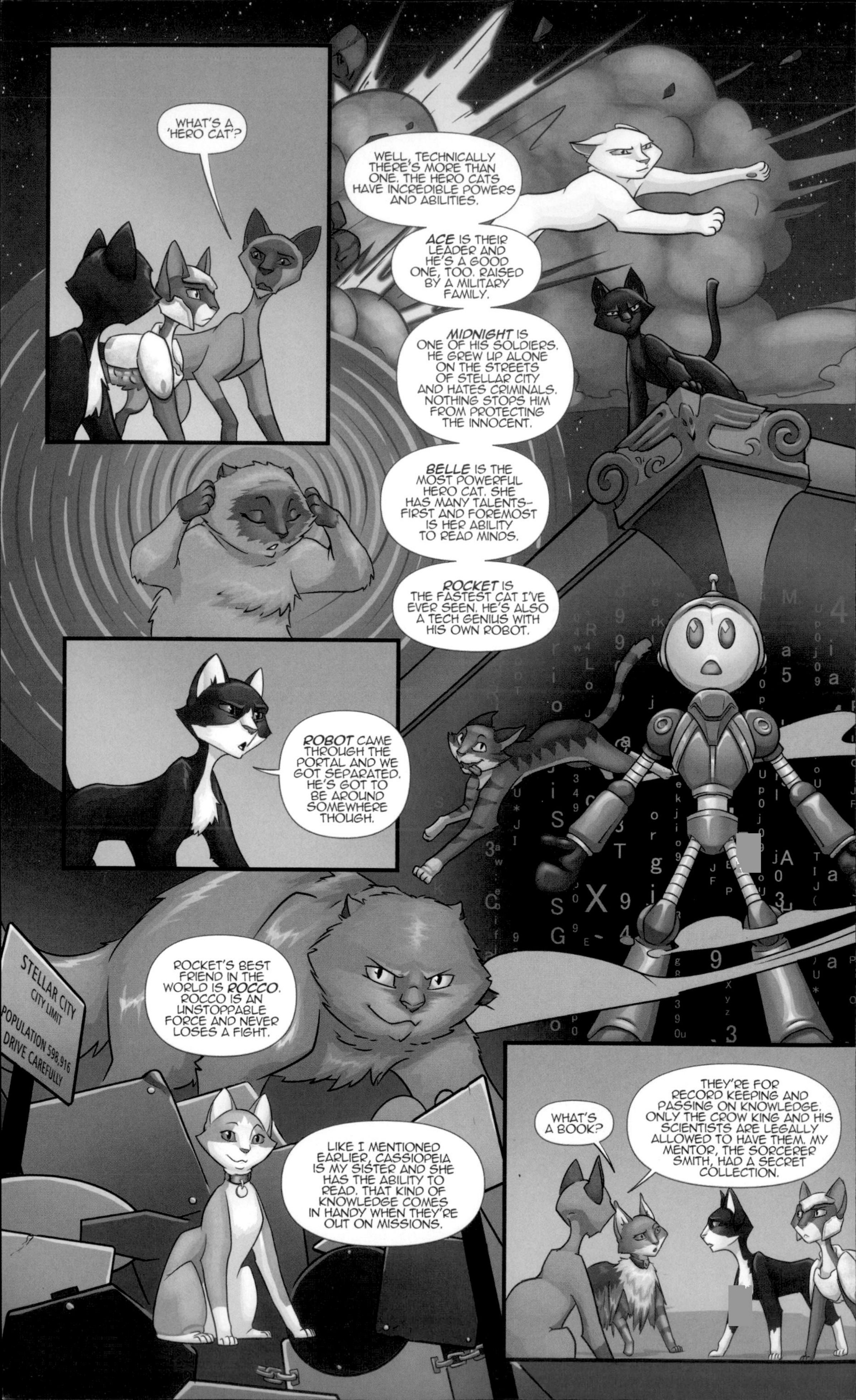
WHAT'S A 'HERO CAT'?
WELL, TECHNICALLY THERE'S MORE THAN ONE. THE HERO CATS HAVE INCREDIBLE POWERS AND ABILITIES.
ACE IS THEIR LEADER AND HE'S A GOOD ONE, TOO. RAISED BY A MILITARY FAMILY.
MIDNIGHT IS ONE OF HIS SOLDIERS. HE GREW UP ALONE ON THE STREETS OF STELLAR CITY AND HATES CRIMINALS. NOTHING STOPS HIM FROM PROTECTING THE INNOCENT.
BELLE IS THE MOST POWERFUL HERO CAT. SHE HAS MANY TALENTS-FIRST AND FOREMOST IS HER ABILITY TO READ MINDS.
ROCKET IS THE FASTEST CAT I'VE EVER SEEN. HE'S ALSO A TECH GENIUS WITH HIS OWN ROBOT.
ROBOT CAME THROUGH THE PORTAL AND WE GOT SEPARATED. HE'S GOT TO BE AROUND SOMEWHERE THOUGH.
ROCKET'S BEST FRIEND IN THE WORLD IS ROCCO. ROCCO IS AN UNSTOPPABLE FORCE AND NEVER LOSES A FIGHT.
STELLAR CITY
CITY LIMIT
POPULATION 598,916
DRIVE CAREFULLY
LIKE I MENTIONED EARLIER, CASSIOPEIA IS MY SISTER AND SHE HAS THE ABILITY TO READ. THAT KIND OF KNOWLEDGE COMES IN HANDY WHEN THEY'RE OUT ON MISSIONS.
WHAT'S A BOOK?
THEY'RE FOR RECORD KEEPING AND PASSING ON KNOWLEDGE. ONLY THE CROW KING AND HIS SCIENTISTS ARE LEGALLY ALLOWED TO HAVE THEM. MY MENTOR, THE SORCERER SMITH, HAD A SECRET COLLECTION.

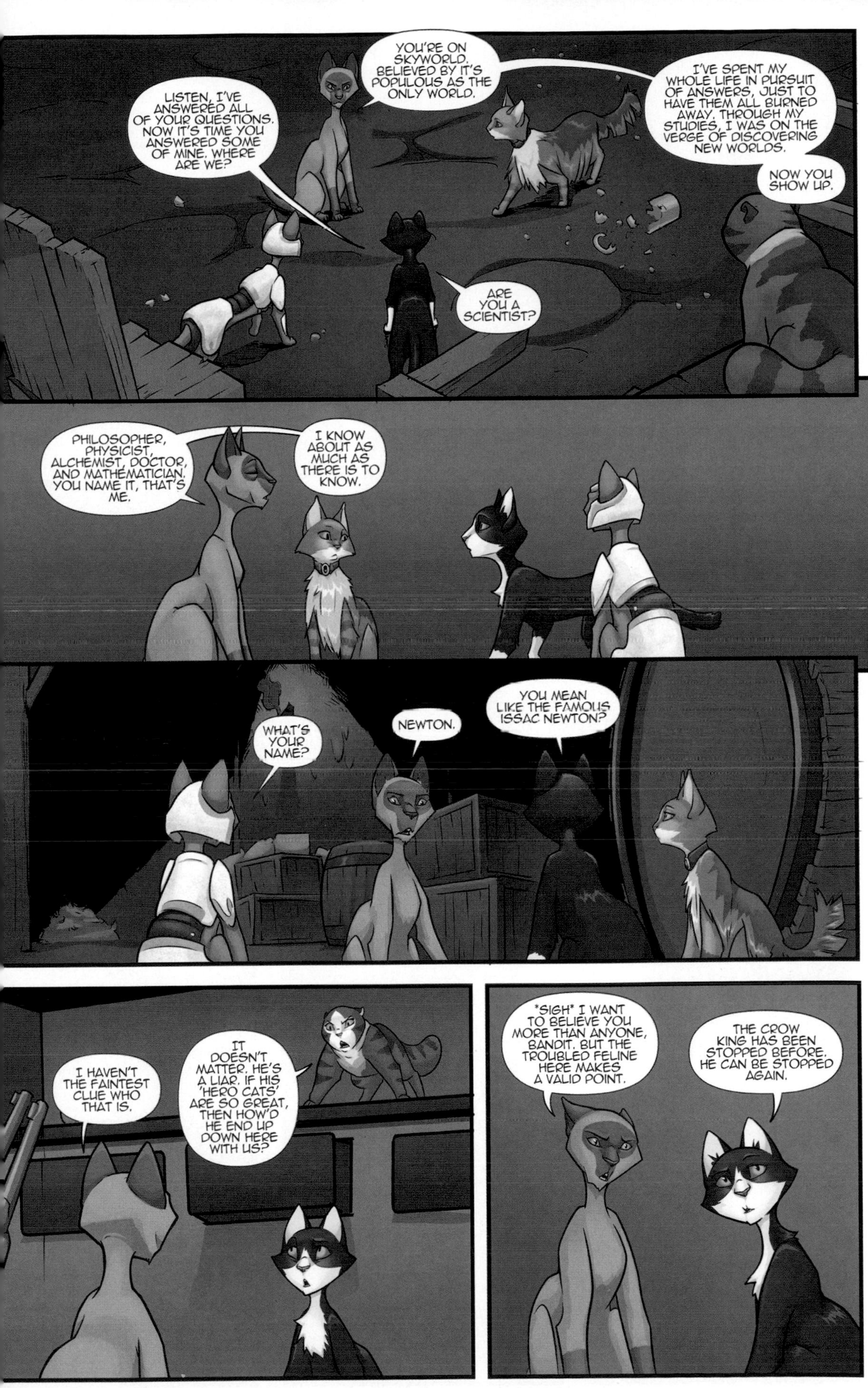

LISTEN, I'VE ANSWERED ALL OF YOUR QUESTIONS. NOW IT'S TIME YOU ANSWERED SOME OF MINE. WHERE ARE WE?
YOU'RE ON SKYWORLD. BELIEVED BY IT'S POPULOUS AS THE ONLY WORLD.
I'VE SPENT MY WHOLE LIFE IN PURSUIT OF ANSWERS, JUST TO HAVE THEM ALL BURNED AWAY. THROUGH MY STUDIES, I WAS ON THE VERGE OF DISCOVERING NEW WORLDS.
NOW YOU SHOW UP.
ARE YOU A SCIENTIST?
PHILOSOPHER, PHYSICIST, ALCHEMIST, DOCTOR, AND MATHEMATICIAN. YOU NAME IT, THAT'S ME.
I KNOW ABOUT AS MUCH AS THERE IS TO KNOW.
WHAT'S YOUR NAME?
NEWTON.
YOU MEAN LIKE THE FAMOUS ISSAC NEWTON?
I HAVEN'T THE FAINTEST CLUE WHO THAT IS.
IT DOESN'T MATTER. HE'S A LIAR. IF HIS 'HERO CATS' ARE SO GREAT, THEN HOW'D HE END UP DOWN HERE WITH US?
SIGH I WANT TO BELIEVE YOU MORE THAN ANYONE, BANDIT. BUT THE TROUBLED FELINE HERE MAKES A VALID POINT.
THE CROW KING HAS BEEN STOPPED BEFORE. HE CAN BE STOPPED AGAIN.

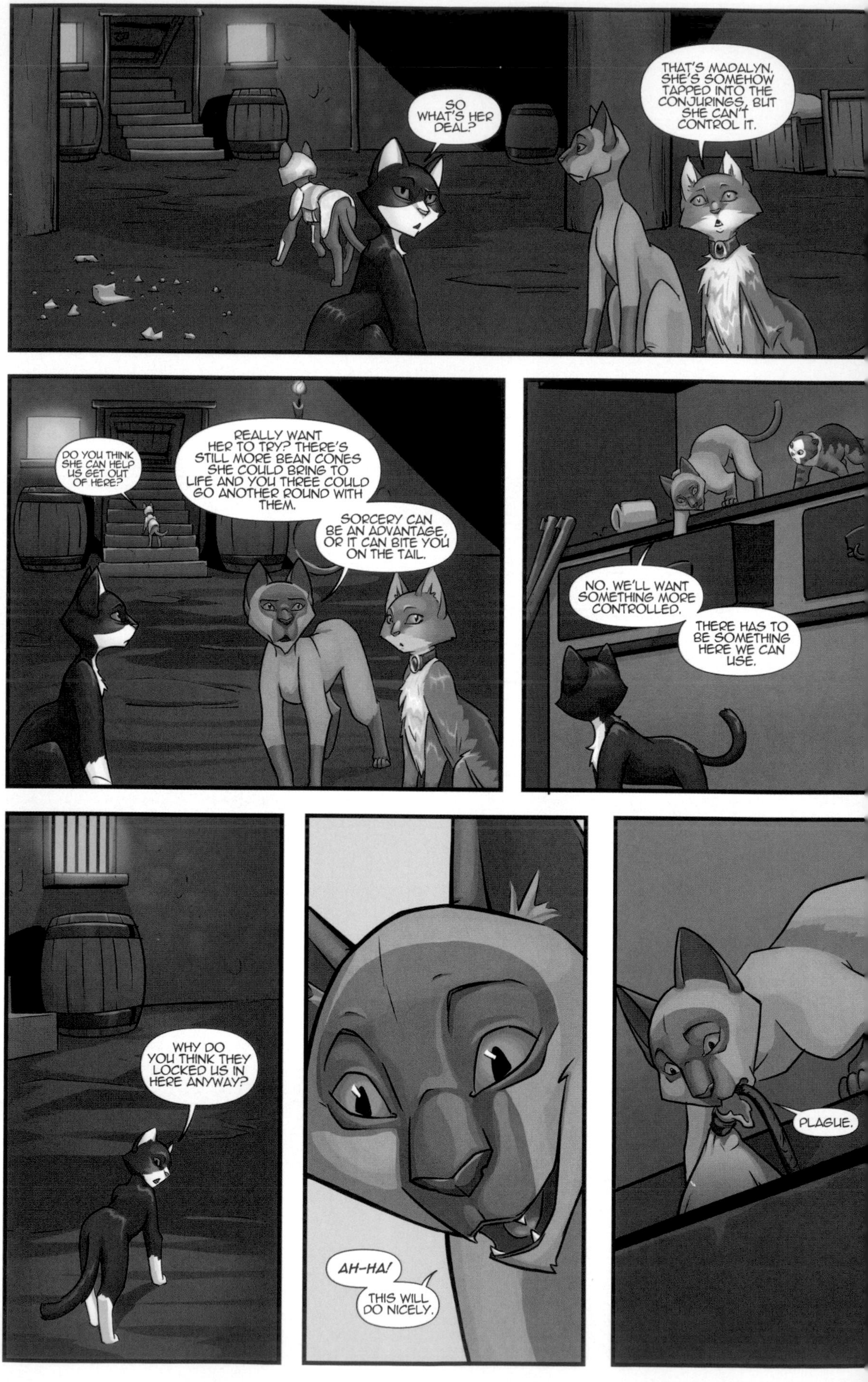
SO WHAT'S HER DEAL?
THAT'S MADALYN. SHE'S SOMEHOW TAPPED INTO THE CONJURINGS, BUT SHE CAN'T CONTROL IT.
DO YOU THINK SHE CAN HELP US GET OUT OF HERE?
REALLY WANT HER TO TRY? THERE'S STILL MORE BEAN CONES SHE COULD BRING TO LIFE AND YOU THREE COULD GO ANOTHER ROUND WITH THEM.
SORCERY CAN BE AN ADVANTAGE, OR IT CAN BITE YOU ON THE TAIL.
NO. WE'LL WANT SOMETHING MORE CONTROLLED.
THERE HAS TO BE SOMETHING HERE WE CAN USE.
WHY DO YOU THINK THEY LOCKED US IN HERE ANYWAY?
AH-HA!
THIS WILL DO NICELY.
PLAGUE.

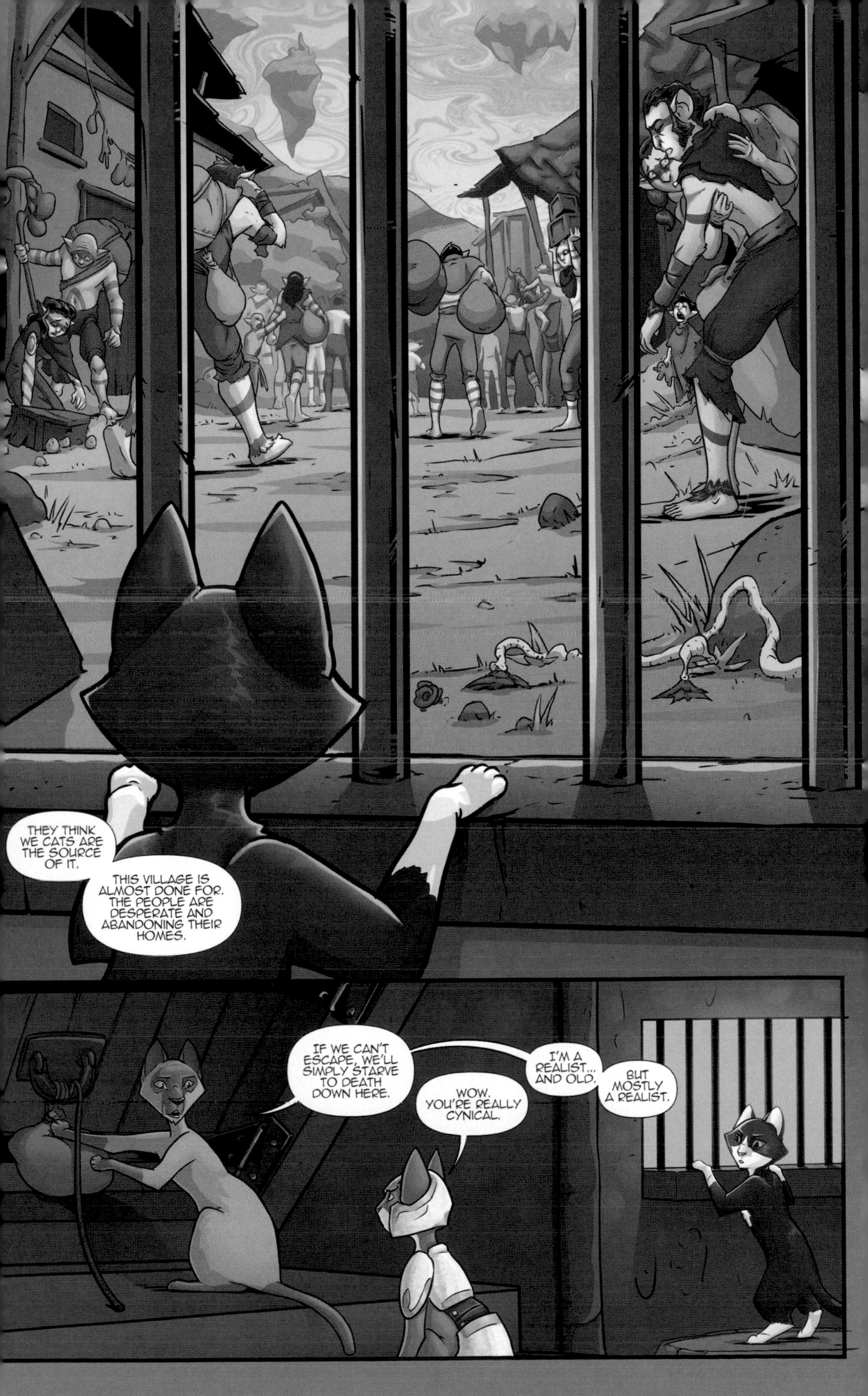
THEY THINK WE CATS ARE THE SOURCE OF IT.
THIS VILLAGE IS ALMOST DONE FOR. THE PEOPLE ARE DESPERATE AND ABANDONING THEIR HOMES.
IF WE CAN'T ESCAPE, WE'LL SIMPLY STARVE TO DEATH DOWN HERE.
WOW. YOU'RE REALLY CYNICAL.
I'M A REALIST... AND OLD.
BUT MOSTLY A REALIST.

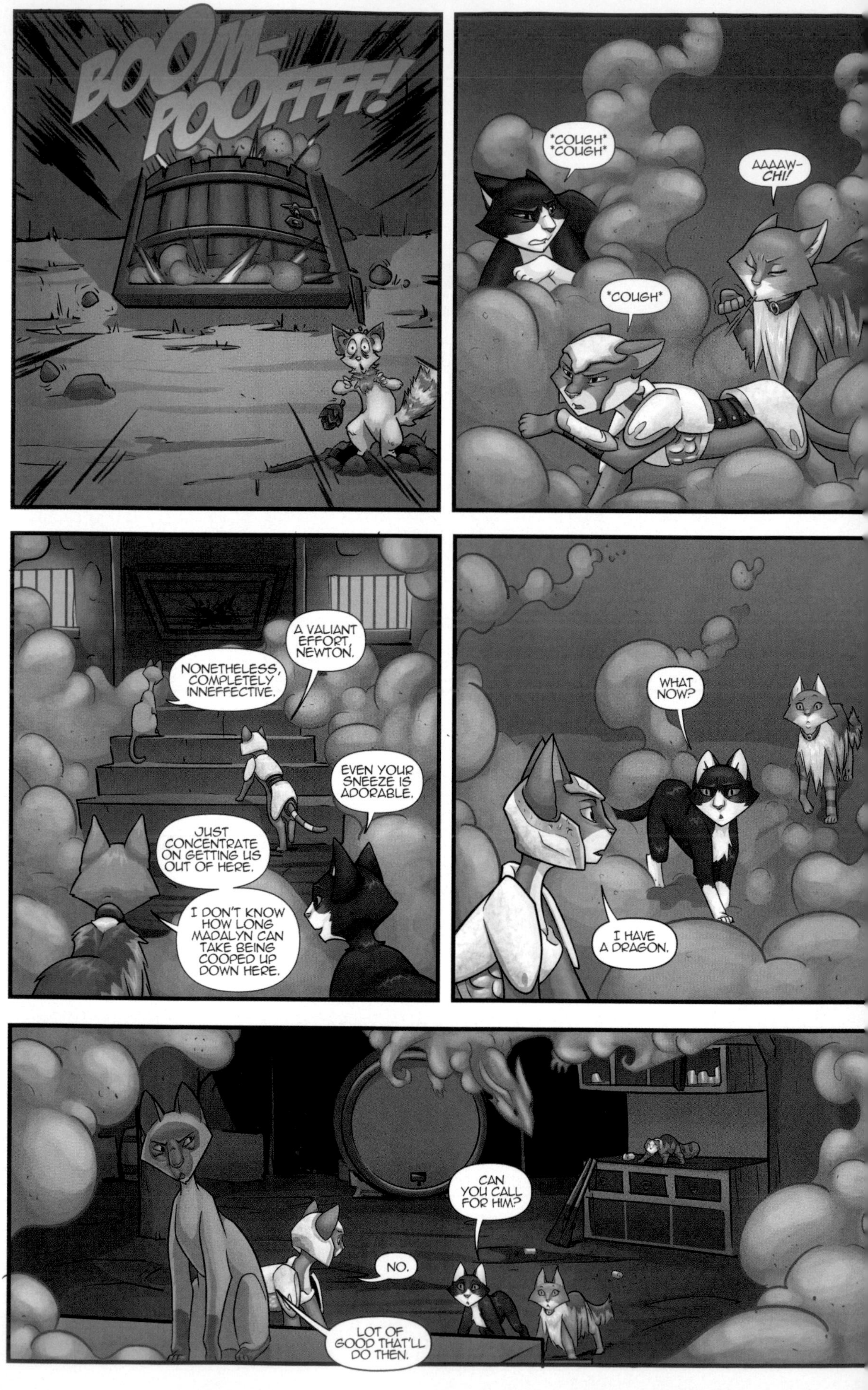
BOOM-POOFFFF!
COUGH *COUGH*
AAAAW-CHI!
COUGH
A VALIANT EFFORT, NEWTON.
NONETHELESS, COMPLETELY INNEFFECTIVE.
EVEN YOUR SNEEZE IS ADORABLE.
JUST CONCENTRATE ON GETTING US OUT OF HERE.
I DON'T KNOW HOW LONG MADALYN CAN TAKE BEING COOPED UP DOWN HERE.
WHAT NOW?
I HAVE A DRAGON.
CAN YOU CALL FOR HIM?
NO.
LOT OF GOOD THAT'LL DO THEN.

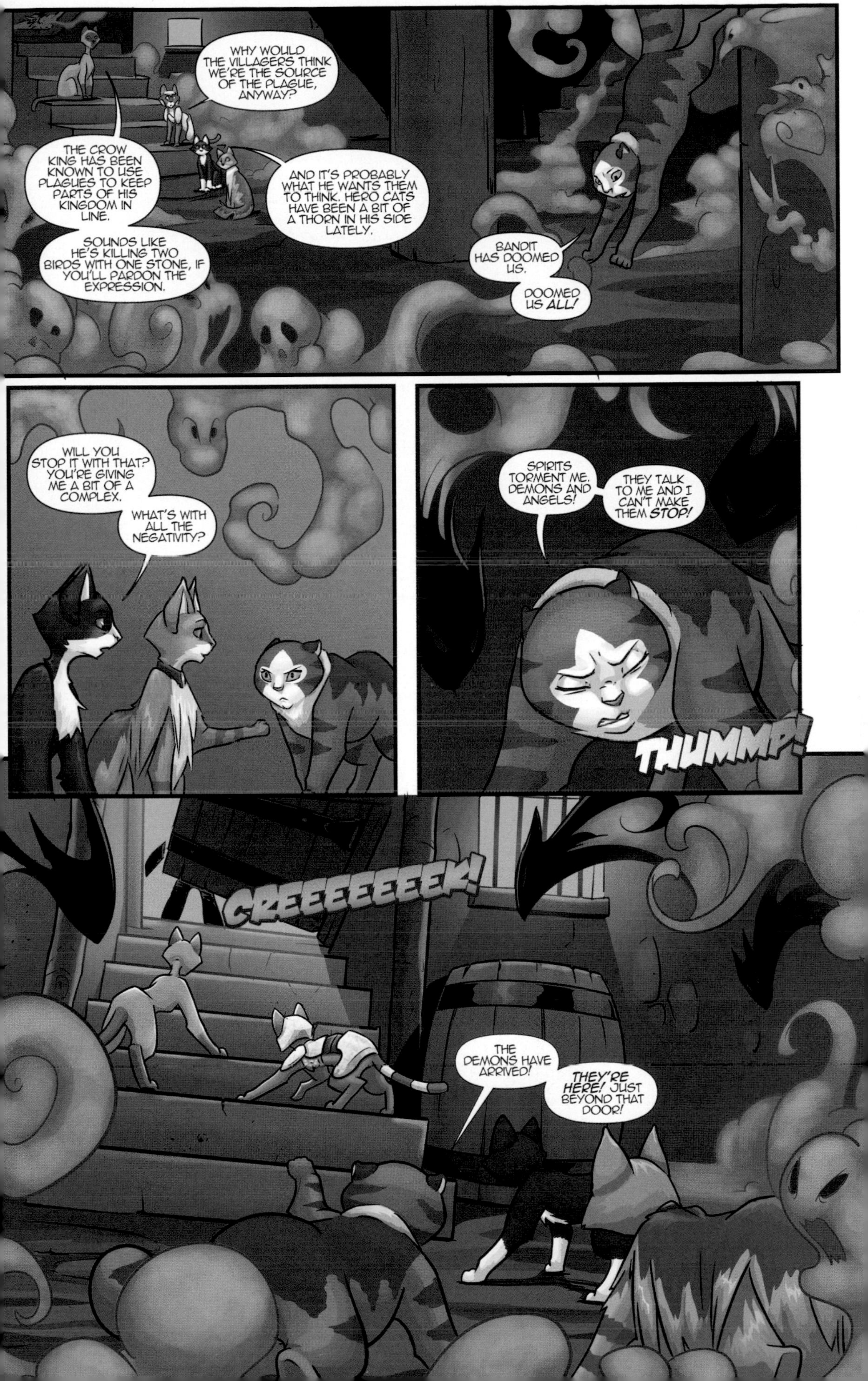
WHY WOULD THE VILLAGERS THINK WE'RE THE SOURCE OF THE PLAGUE, ANYWAY?
THE CROW KING HAS BEEN KNOWN TO USE PLAGUES TO KEEP PARTS OF HIS KINGDOM IN LINE.
SOUNDS LIKE HE'S KILLING TWO BIRDS WITH ONE STONE, IF YOU'LL PARDON THE EXPRESSION.
AND IT'S PROBABLY WHAT HE WANTS THEM TO THINK. HERO CATS HAVE BEEN A BIT OF A THORN IN HIS SIDE LATELY.
BANDIT HAS DOOMED US.
DOOMED US ALL!
WILL YOU STOP IT WITH THAT? YOU'RE GIVING ME A BIT OF A COMPLEX.
WHAT'S WITH ALL THE NEGATIVITY?
SPIRITS TORMENT ME. DEMONS AND ANGELS!
THEY TALK TO ME AND I CAN'T MAKE THEM STOP!
THUMMP!
CREEEEEEEEK!
THE DEMONS HAVE ARRIVED!
THEY'RE HERE! JUST BEYOND THAT DOOR!

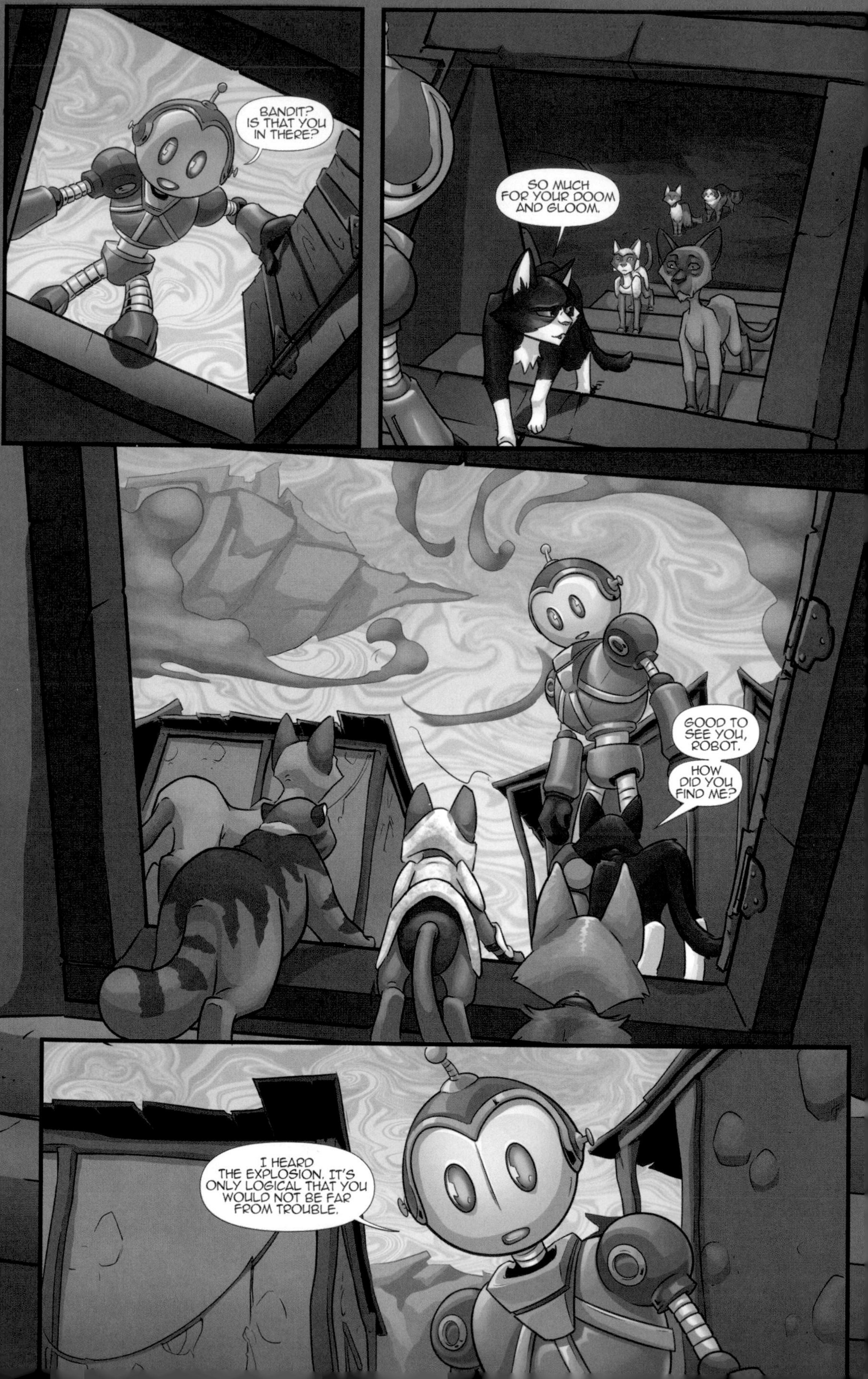
BANDIT? IS THAT YOU IN THERE?
SO MUCH FOR YOUR DOOM AND GLOOM.
GOOD TO SEE YOU, ROBOT.
HOW DID YOU FIND ME?
I HEARD THE EXPLOSION. IT'S ONLY LOGICAL THAT YOU WOULD NOT BE FAR FROM TROUBLE.

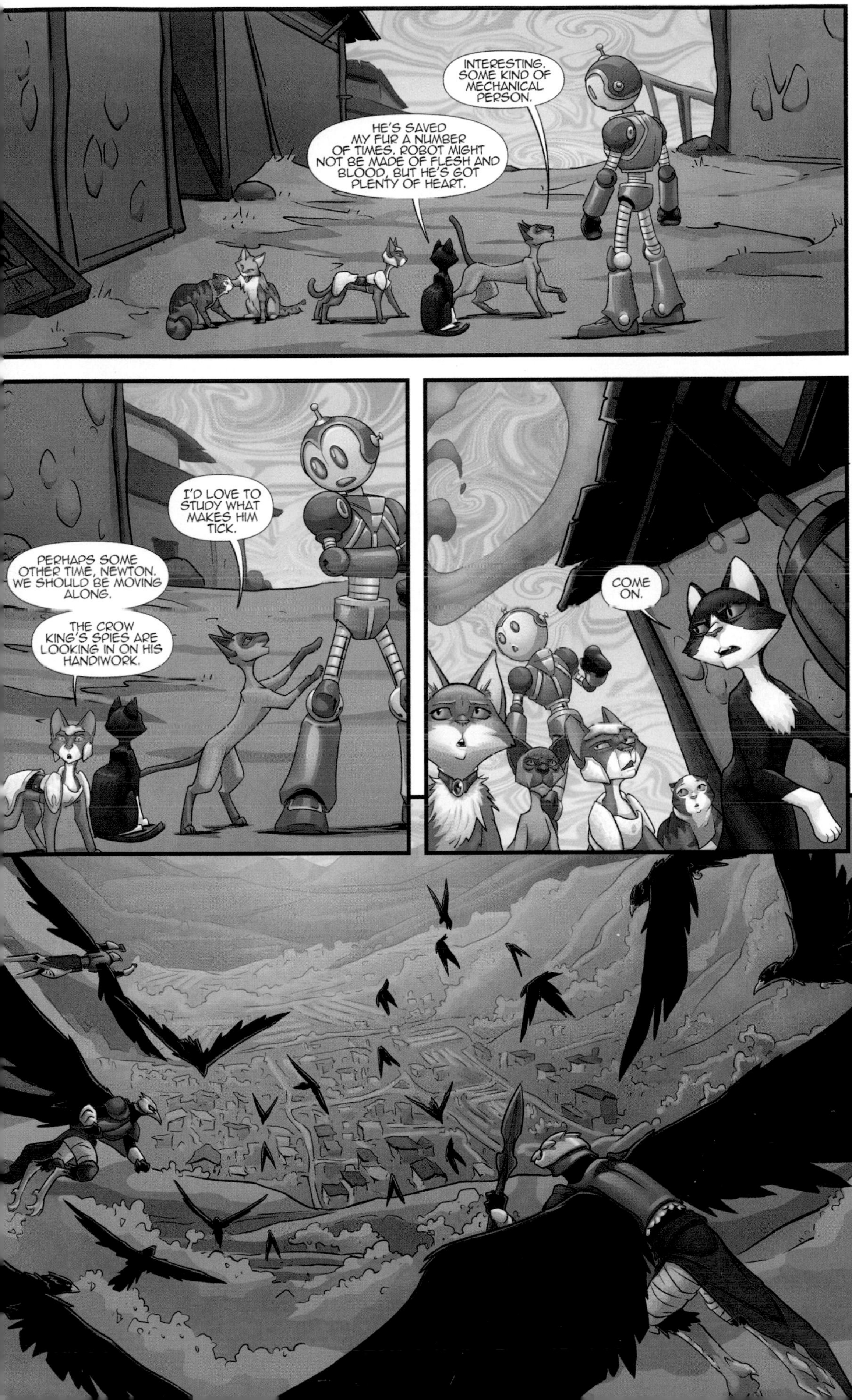
INTERESTING. SOME KIND OF MECHANICAL PERSON.
HE'S SAVED MY FUR A NUMBER OF TIMES. ROBOT MIGHT NOT BE MADE OF FLESH AND BLOOD, BUT HE'S GOT PLENTY OF HEART.
I'D LOVE TO STUDY WHAT MAKES HIM TICK.
PERHAPS SOME OTHER TIME, NEWTON. WE SHOULD BE MOVING ALONG.
THE CROW KING'S SPIES ARE LOOKING IN ON HIS HANDIWORK.
COME ON.

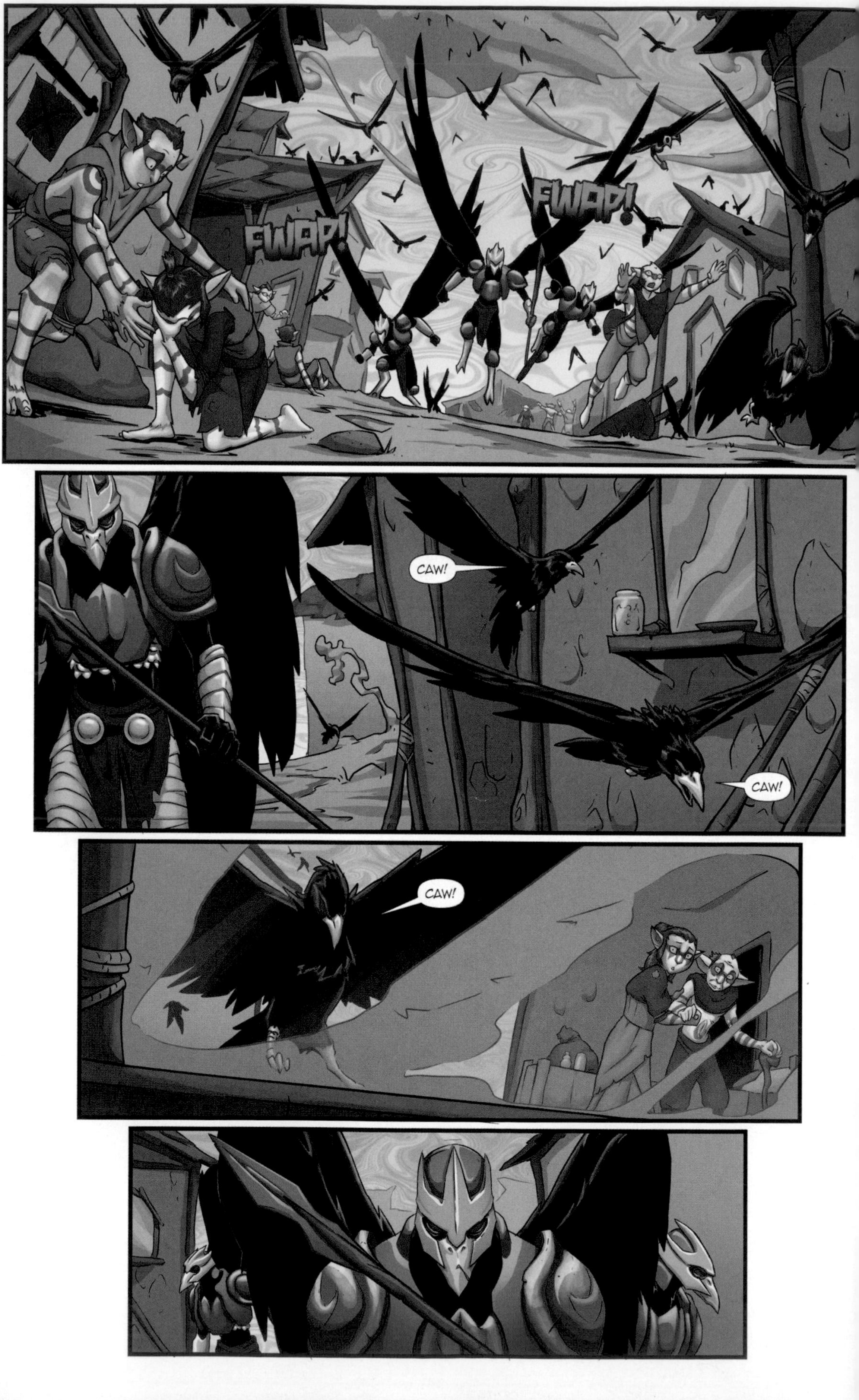
FWAP!
FWAP!
CAW!
CAW!
CAW!

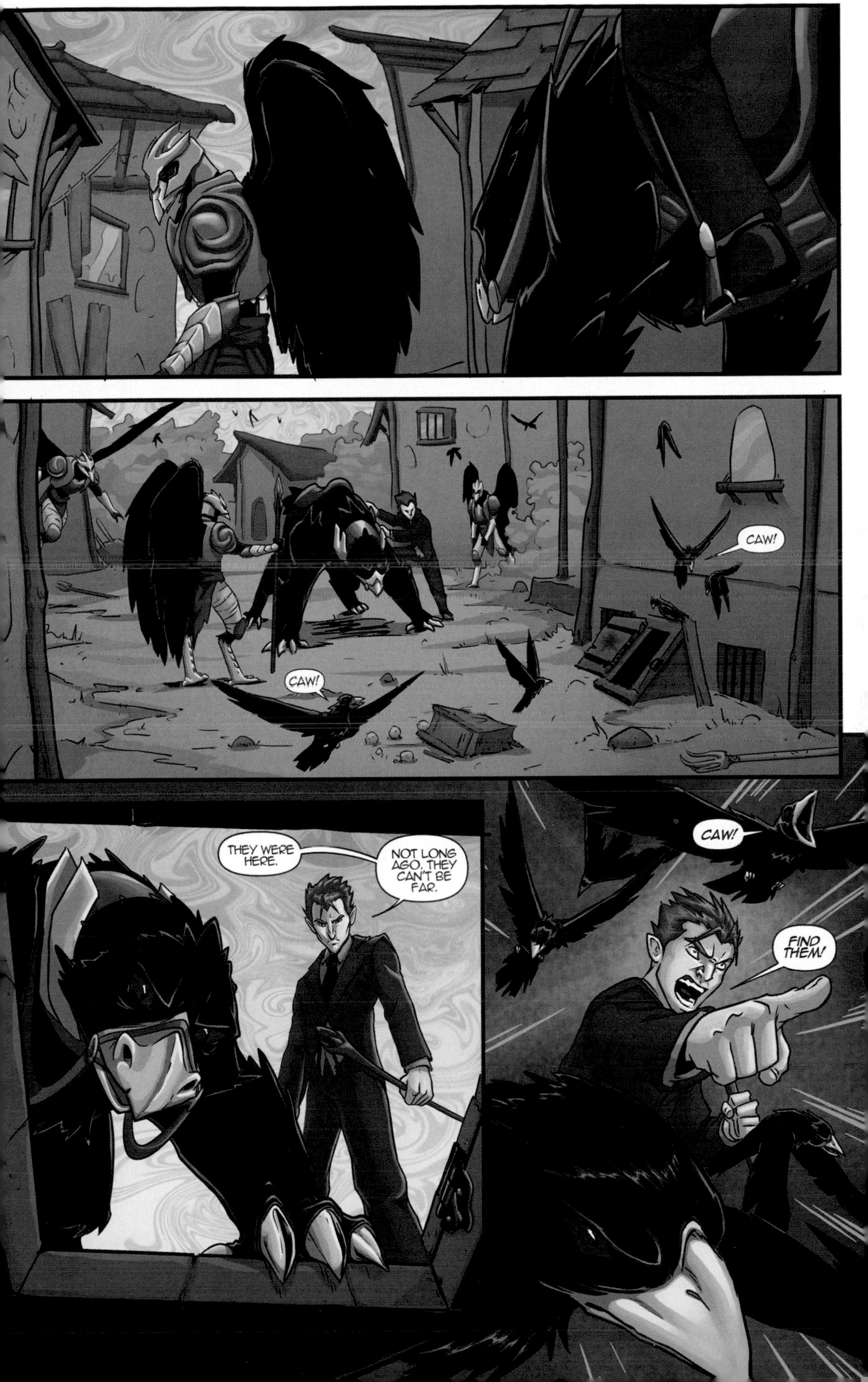
CAW!
CAW!
THEY WERE HERE.
NOT LONG AGO. THEY CAN'T BE FAR.
CAW!
FIND THEM!

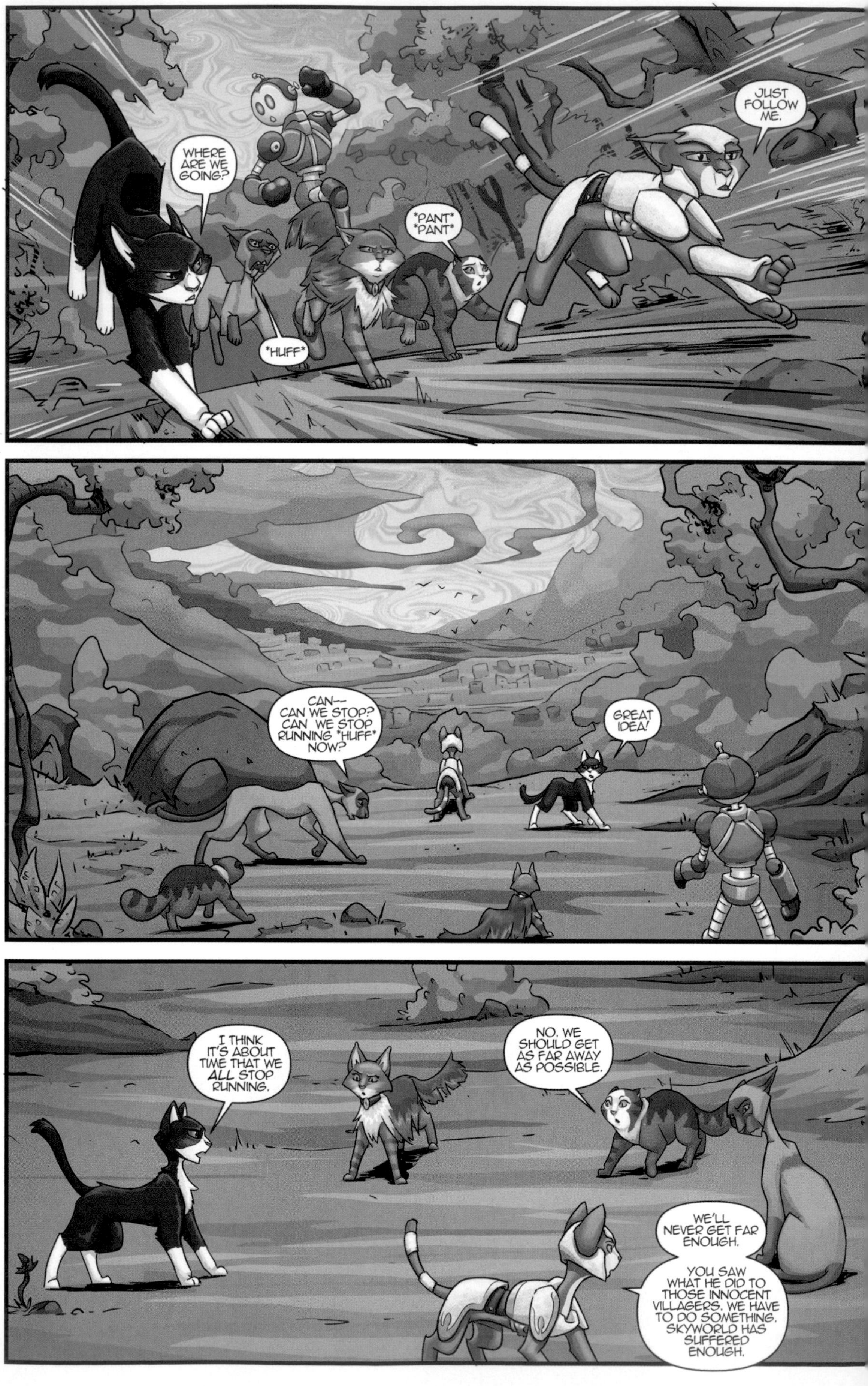
WHERE ARE WE GOING?
HUFF
PANT *PANT*
JUST FOLLOW ME.
CAN-- CAN WE STOP? CAN WE STOP RUNNING *HUFF* NOW?
GREAT IDEA!
I THINK IT'S ABOUT TIME THAT WE ALL STOP RUNNING.
NO, WE SHOULD GET AS FAR AWAY AS POSSIBLE.
WE'LL NEVER GET FAR ENOUGH.
YOU SAW WHAT HE DID TO THOSE INNOCENT VILLAGERS. WE HAVE TO DO SOMETHING. SKYWORLD HAS SUFFERED ENOUGH.

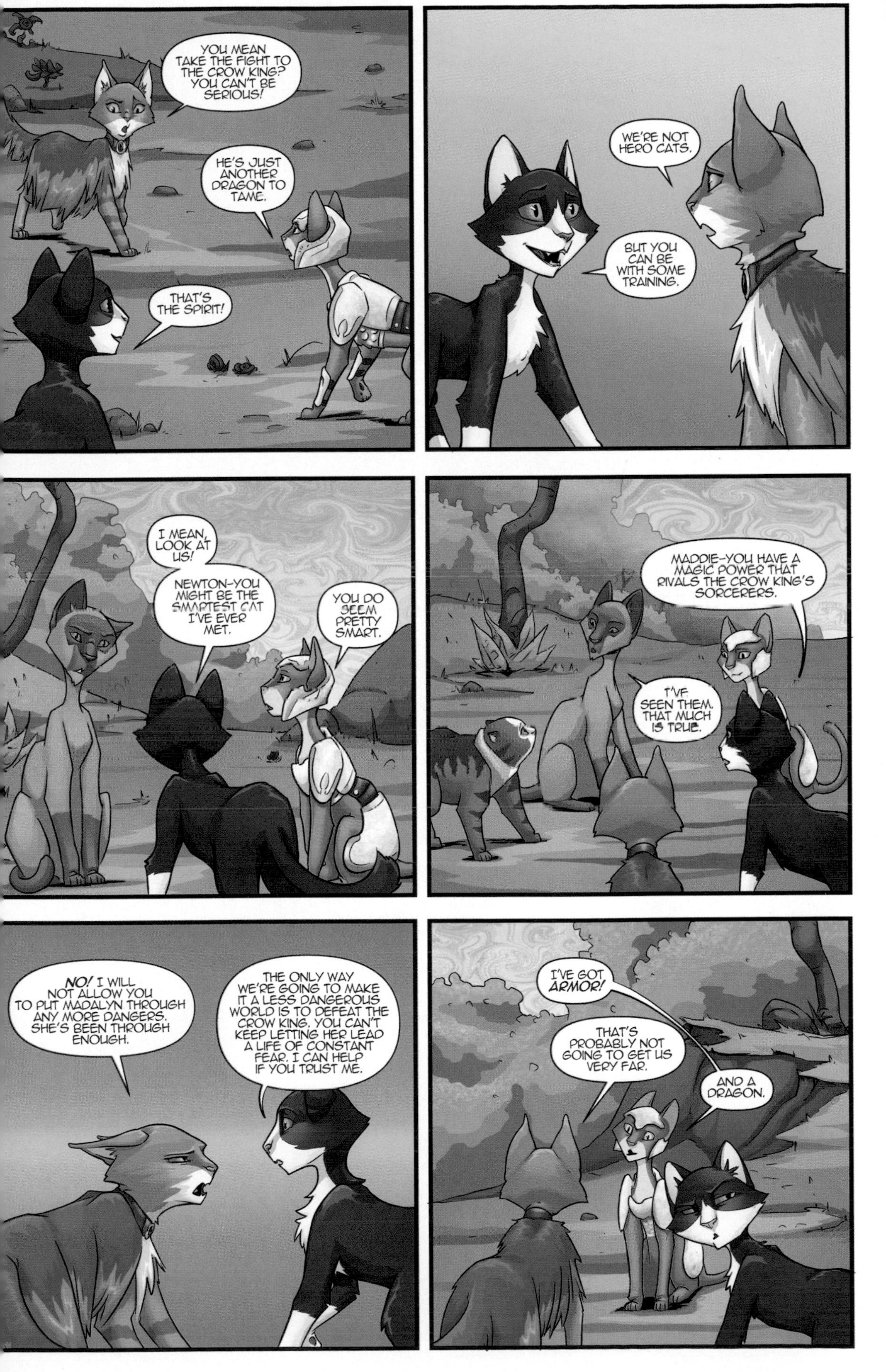
YOU MEAN TAKE THE FIGHT TO THE CROW KING? YOU CAN'T BE SERIOUS!
HE'S JUST ANOTHER DRAGON TO TAME.
THAT'S THE SPIRIT!
WE'RE NOT HERO CATS.
BUT YOU CAN BE WITH SOME TRAINING.
I MEAN, LOOK AT US!
NEWTON-YOU MIGHT BE THE SMARTEST CAT I'VE EVER MET.
YOU DO SEEM PRETTY SMART.
MADDIE-YOU HAVE A MAGIC POWER THAT RIVALS THE CROW KING'S SORCERERS.
I'VE SEEN THEM. THAT MUCH IS TRUE.
NO! I WILL NOT ALLOW YOU TO PUT MADALYN THROUGH ANY MORE DANGERS. SHE'S BEEN THROUGH ENOUGH.
THE ONLY WAY WE'RE GOING TO MAKE IT A LESS DANGEROUS WORLD IS TO DEFEAT THE CROW KING. YOU CAN'T KEEP LETTING HER LEAD A LIFE OF CONSTANT FEAR. I CAN HELP IF YOU TRUST ME.
I'VE GOT ARMOR!
THAT'S PROBABLY NOT GOING TO GET US VERY FAR.
AND A DRAGON.

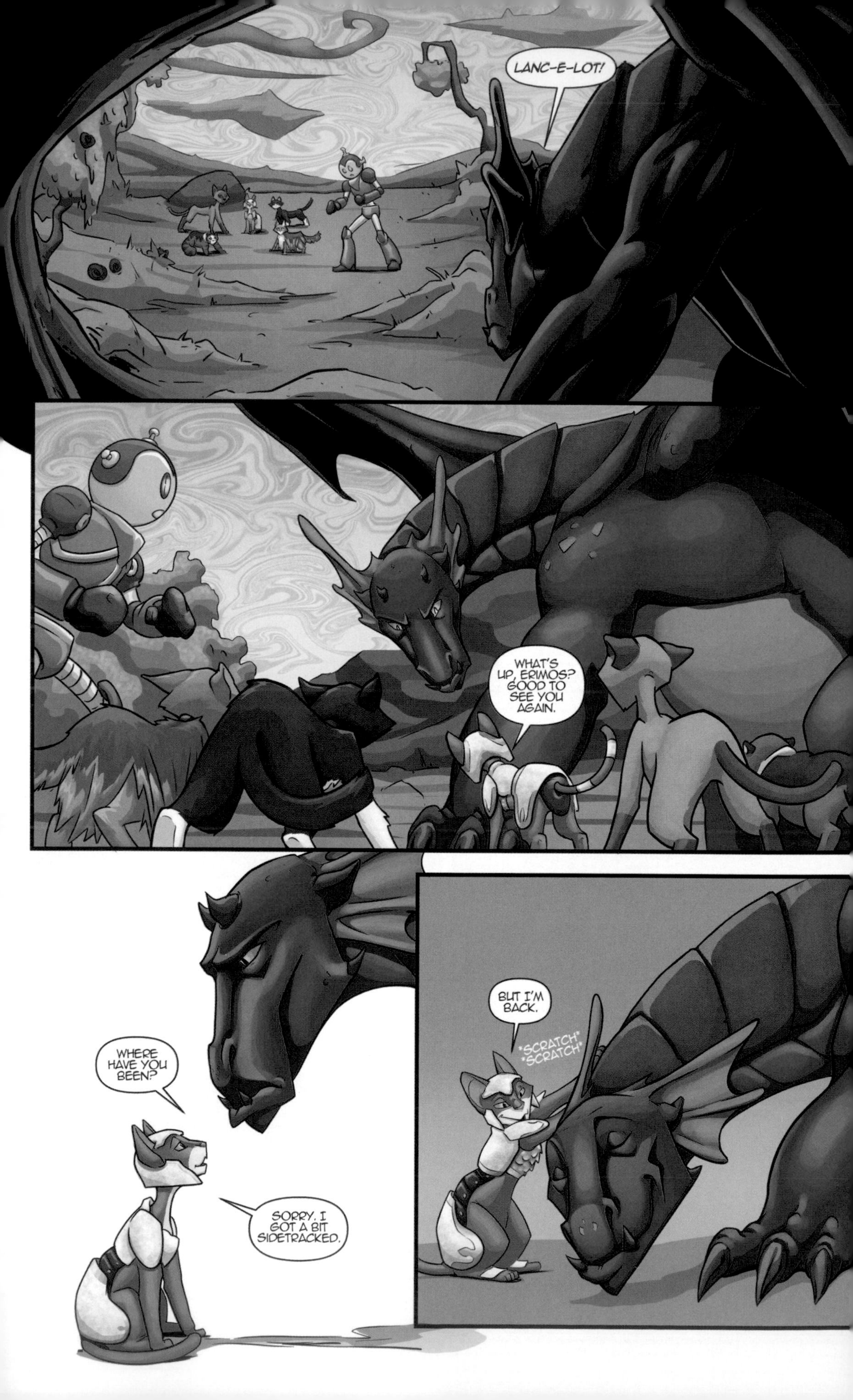
LANC-E-LOT!
WHAT'S UP, ERIMOS? GOOD TO SEE YOU AGAIN.
WHERE HAVE YOU BEEN?
SORRY. I GOT A BIT SIDETRACKED.
BUT I'M BACK.
SCRATCH *SCRATCH*

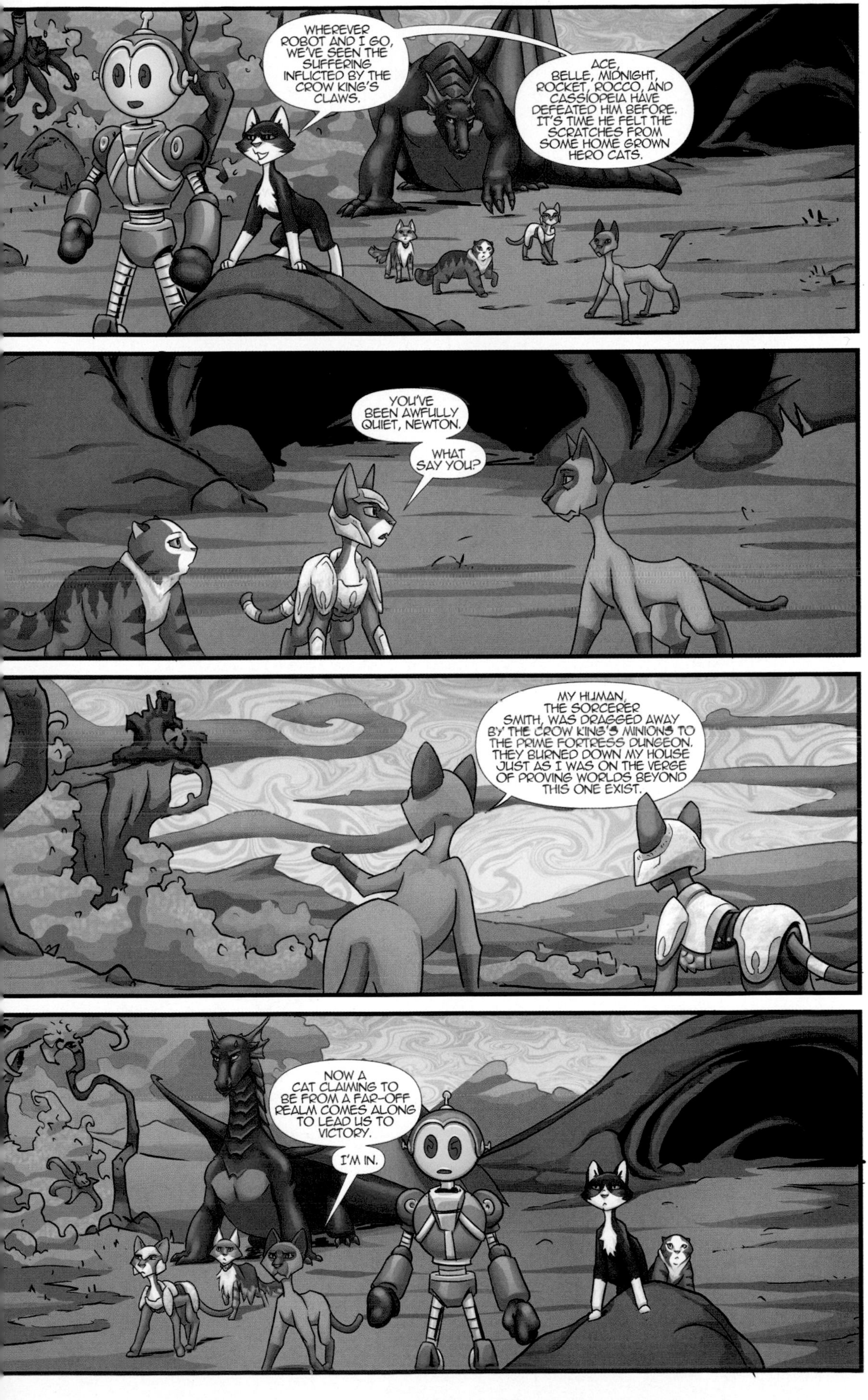
WHEREVER ROBOT AND I GO, WE'VE SEEN THE SUFFERING INFLICTED BY THE CROW KING'S CLAWS.
ACE, BELLE, MIDNIGHT, ROCKET, ROCCO, AND CASSIOPEIA HAVE DEFEATED HIM BEFORE. IT'S TIME HE FELT THE SCRATCHES FROM SOME HOME GROWN HERO CATS.
YOU'VE BEEN AWFULLY QUIET, NEWTON.
WHAT SAY YOU?
MY HUMAN, THE SORCERER SMITH, WAS DRAGGED AWAY BY THE CROW KING'S MINIONS TO THE PRIME FORTRESS DUNGEON. THEY BURNED DOWN MY HOUSE JUST AS I WAS ON THE VERGE OF PROVING WORLDS BEYOND THIS ONE EXIST.
NOW A CAT CLAIMING TO BE FROM A FAR-OFF REALM COMES ALONG TO LEAD US TO VICTORY.
I'M IN.

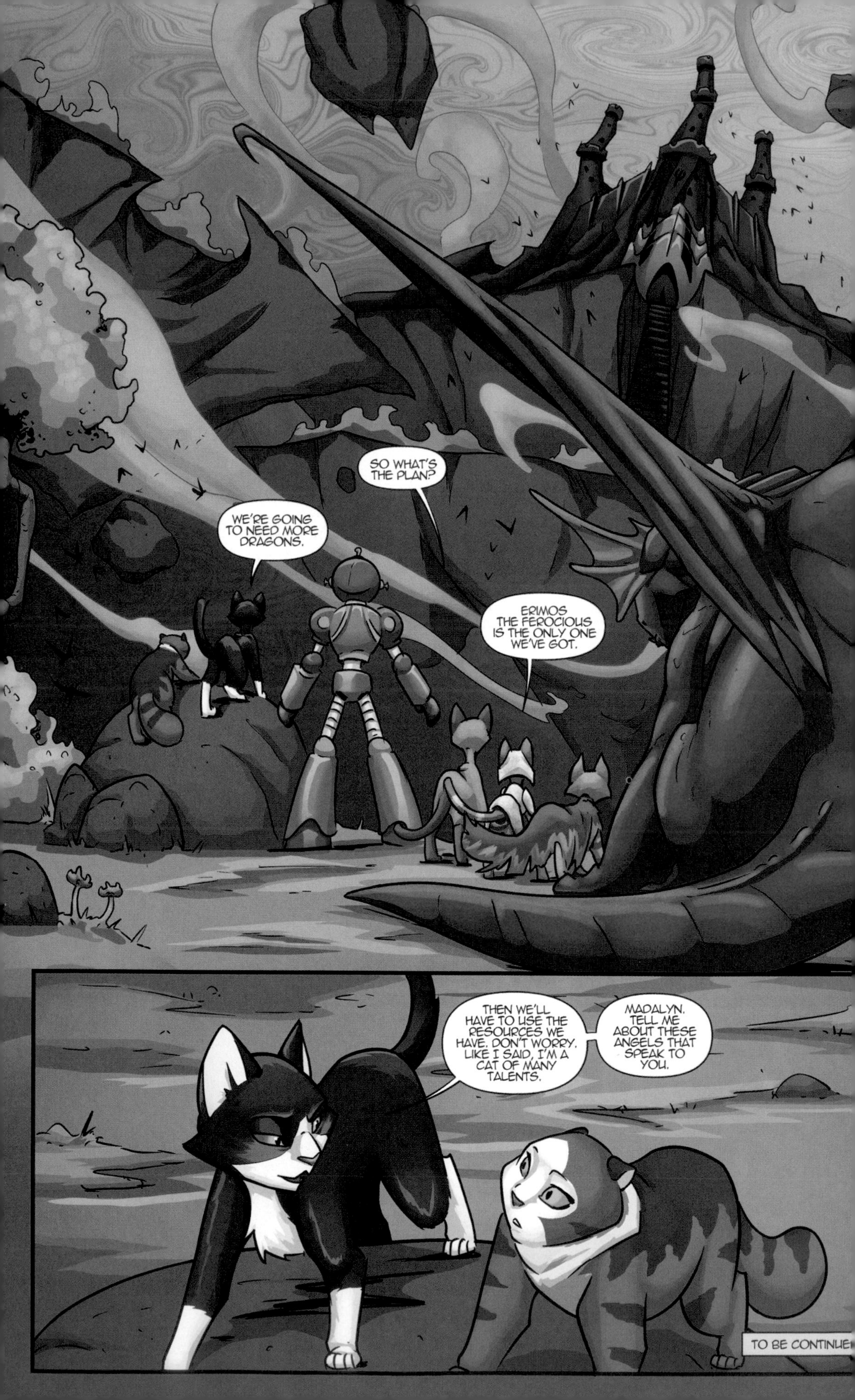
SO WHAT'S THE PLAN?
WE'RE GOING TO NEED MORE DRAGONS.
ERIMOS THE FEROCIOUS IS THE ONLY ONE WE'VE GOT.
THEN WE'LL HAVE TO USE THE RESOURCES WE HAVE. DON'T WORRY. LIKE I SAID, I'M A CAT OF MANY TALENTS.
MADALYN. TELL ME ABOUT THESE ANGELS THAT SPEAK TO YOU.
TO BE CONTINUE

HERO CHAT

BANDIT AND THE HERO CATS
OF SKYWORLD UNITED!

HEY KIDS & CATS!

IT TIME TO TRAIN FOR THE BATTLE AHEAD. BANDIT WILL HAVE HIS PAWS FULL AS HE BRINGS OUT THE BEST IN THIS NEW TEAM OF MISFITS AND RENEGADES.

WHEN WE NEXT SEE LANCELOT, SAPPHIRE, MADDIE & NEWTON THEY'LL BE READY FOR ACTION!

THE CROW KING MUST FALL!

COLLECT ALL 3
"HERO CATS OF
SKYWORLD"
CONNECTING COVERS!

UP NEXT:

COSMIC
SHOWDOWN!

Please note: Due to an unfortunate printer error, some copies of Hero Cats Graphic Novel 5 "New Visions" contained issue #16 instead of issue #13. If you find you have one, please return it to your local comic shop and they should exchange it for you.

And if you are a collector who likes those kind of anomalies, happy hunting.

PART ONE   PART TWO   PART THREE

Bryan Seaton - Publisher
Dave Dwonch - President of Marketing
Shawn Gabborin - Editor in Chief
Jason Martin - Publisher - Danger Zone
Nicole D'Andria - Marketing Director
Jim Dietz - Social Media Manager
Chad Cicconi -Head in the Clouds

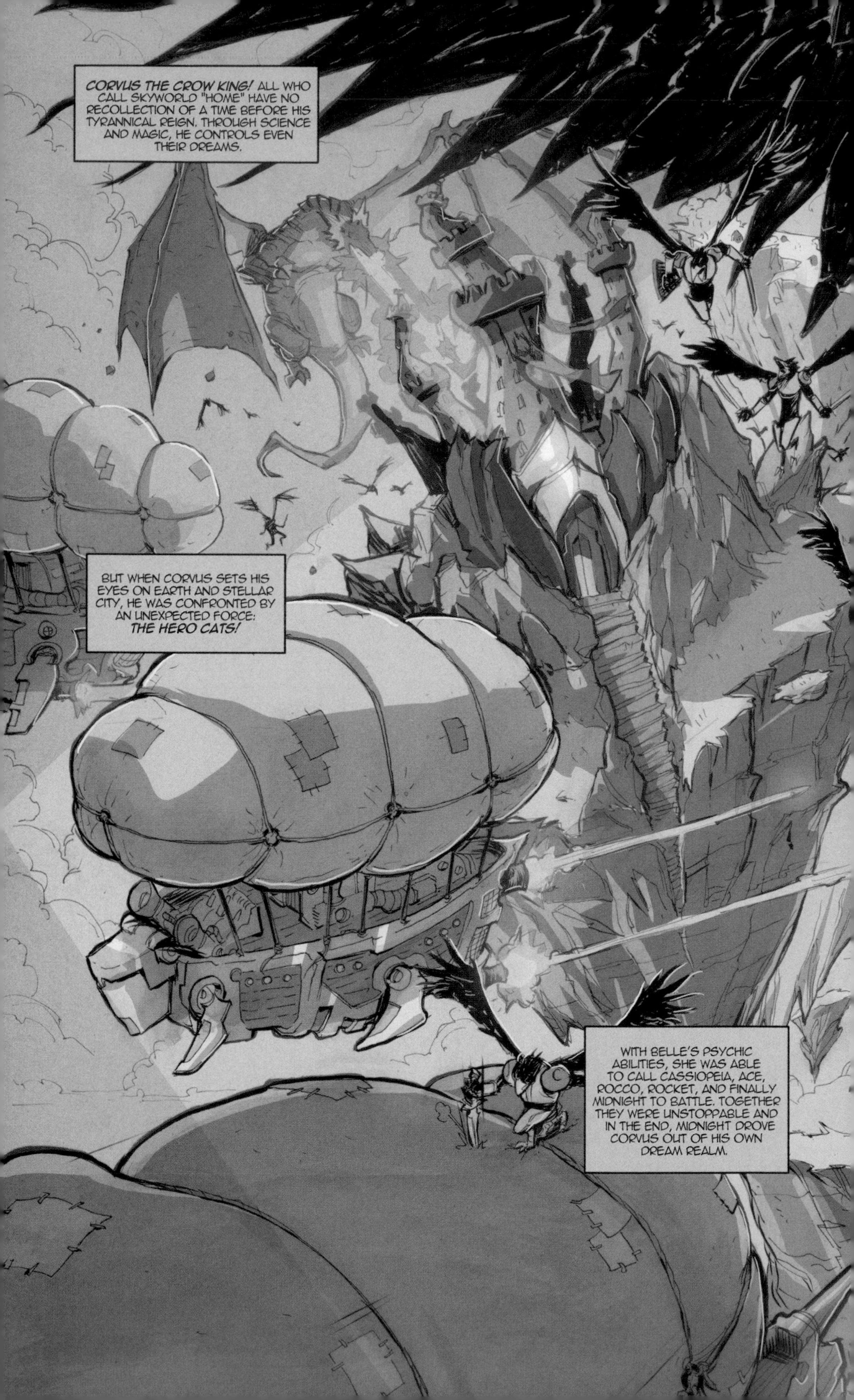
CORVUS THE CROW KING! ALL WHO CALL SKYWORLD "HOME" HAVE NO RECOLLECTION OF A TIME BEFORE HIS TYRANNICAL REIGN. THROUGH SCIENCE AND MAGIC, HE CONTROLS EVEN THEIR DREAMS.
BUT WHEN CORVUS SETS HIS EYES ON EARTH AND STELLAR CITY, HE WAS CONFRONTED BY AN UNEXPECTED FORCE: THE HERO CATS!
WITH BELLE'S PSYCHIC ABILITIES, SHE WAS ABLE TO CALL CASSIOPEIA, ACE, ROCCO, ROCKET, AND FINALLY MIDNIGHT TO BATTLE. TOGETHER THEY WERE UNSTOPPABLE AND IN THE END, MIDNIGHT DROVE CORVUS OUT OF HIS OWN DREAM REALM.

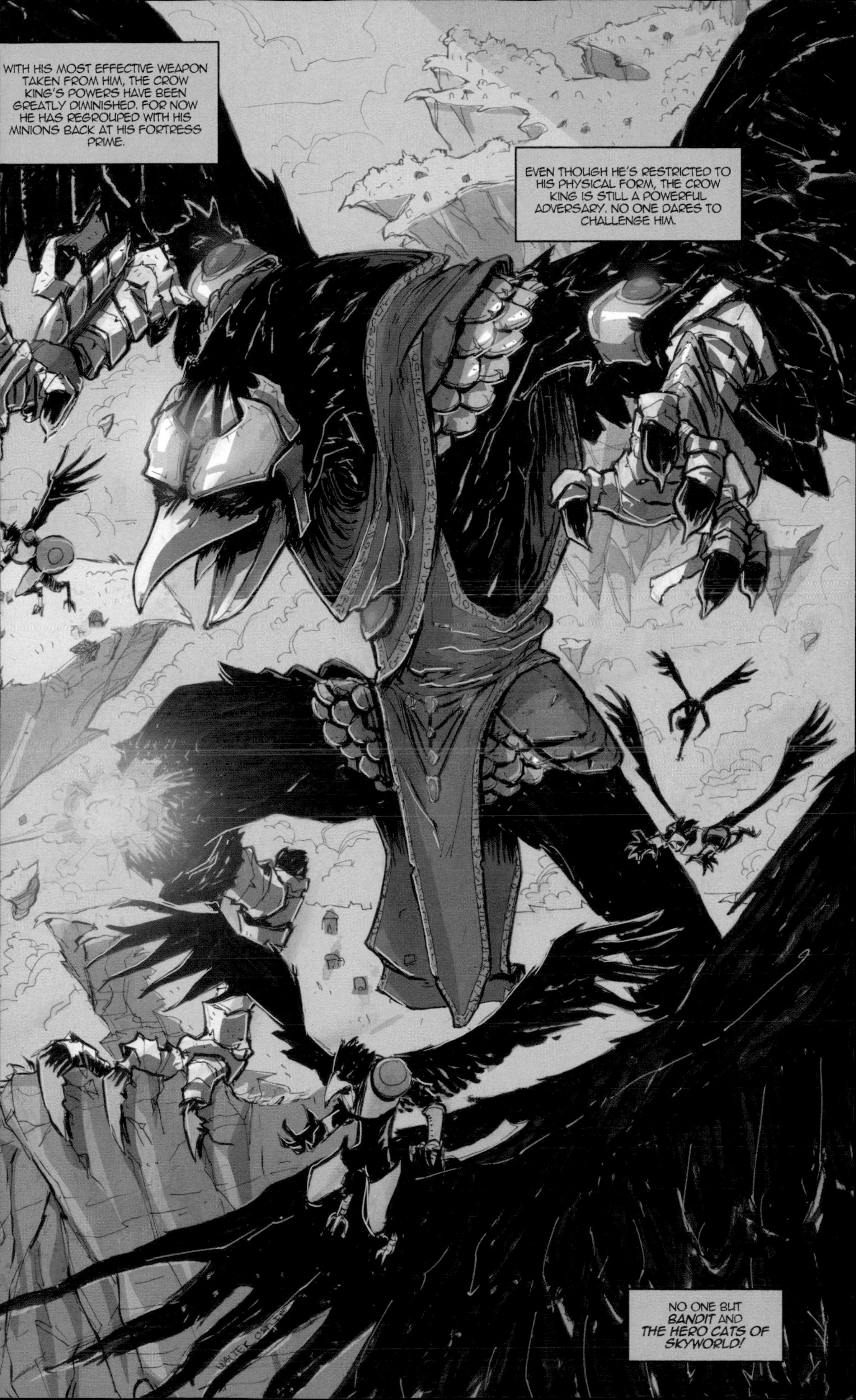
WITH HIS MOST EFFECTIVE WEAPON TAKEN FROM HIM, THE CROW KING'S POWERS HAVE BEEN GREATLY DIMINISHED. FOR NOW HE HAS REGROUPED WITH HIS MINIONS BACK AT HIS FORTRESS PRIME.
EVEN THOUGH HE'S RESTRICTED TO HIS PHYSICAL FORM, THE CROW KING IS STILL A POWERFUL ADVERSARY. NO ONE DARES TO CHALLENGE HIM.
NO ONE BUT *BANDIT* AND *THE HERO CATS OF SKYWORLD!*

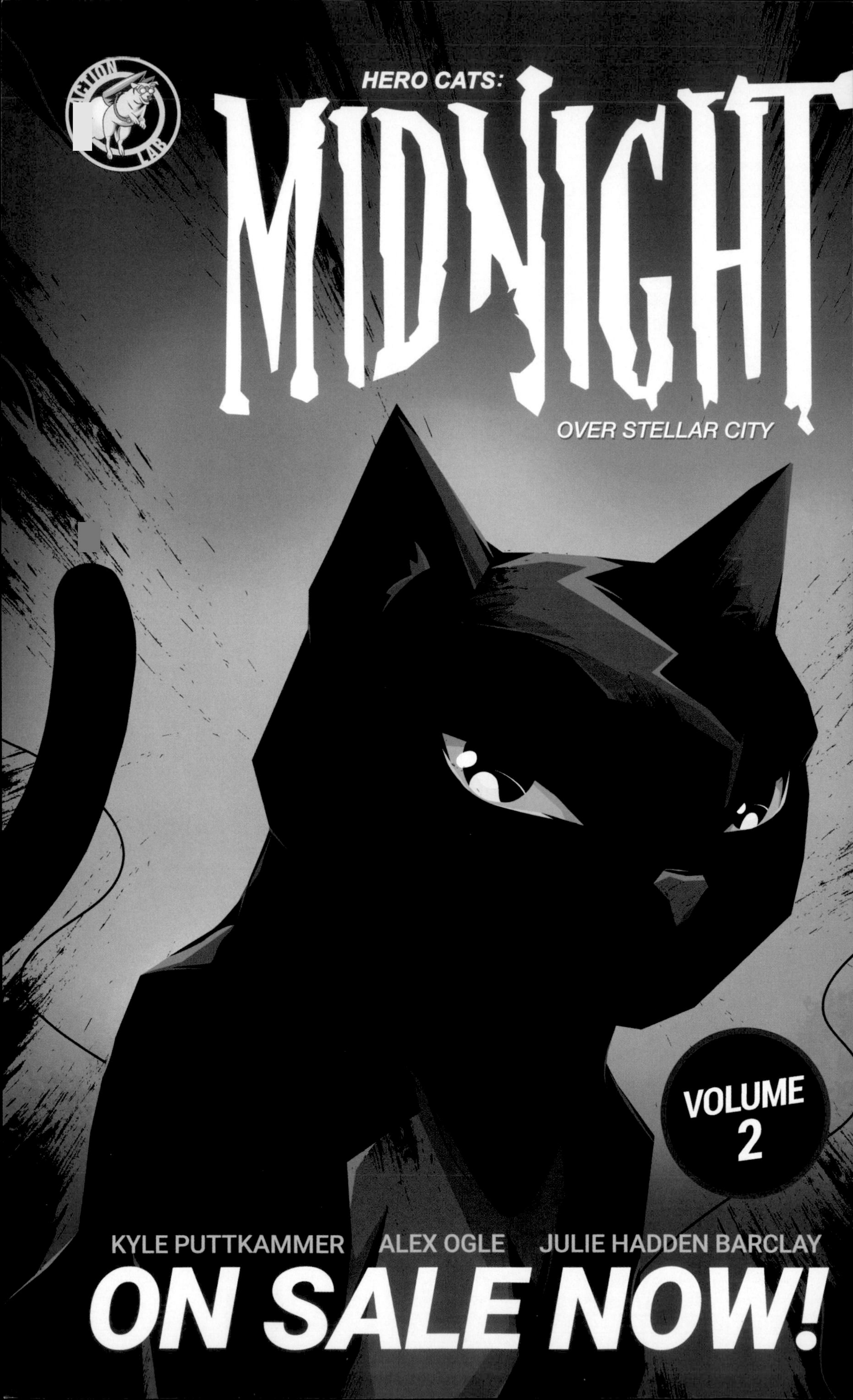
HERO CATS:
MIDNIGHT
OVER STELLAR CITY
VOLUME 2
KYLE PUTTKAMMER
ALEX OGLE
JULIE HADDEN BARCLAY
ON SALE NOW!

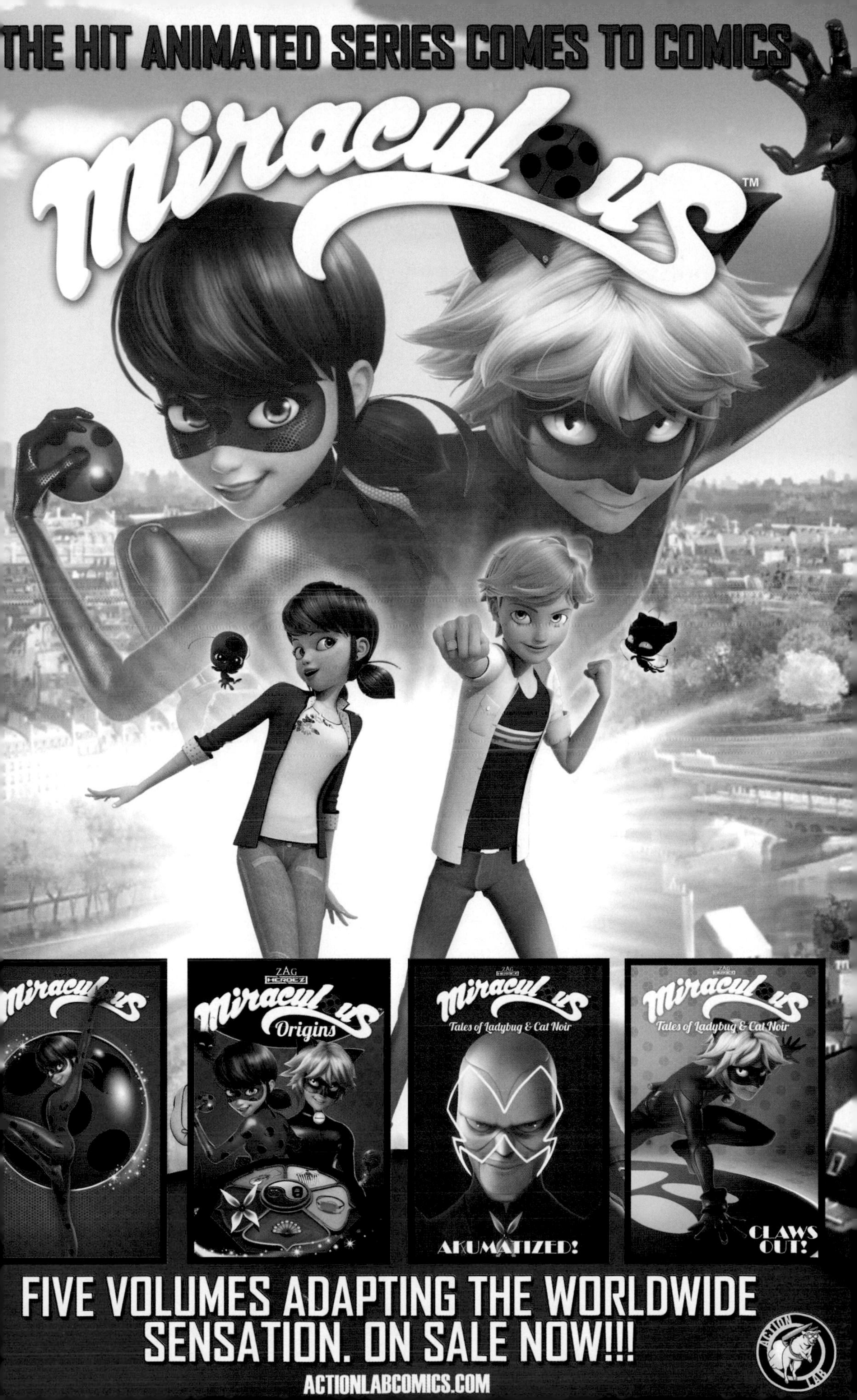
THE HIT ANIMATED SERIES COMES TO COMICS
Miraculous™
Miraculous
ZAG HEROEZ
Miraculous Origins
ZAG HEROEZ
Miraculous
Tales of Ladybug & Cat Noir
AKUMATIZED!
ZAG HEROEZ
Miraculous
Tales of Ladybug & Cat Noir
CLAWS OUT!
FIVE VOLUMES ADAPTING THE WORLDWIDE
SENSATION. ON SALE NOW!!!
ACTIONLABCOMICS.COM
ACTION LAB

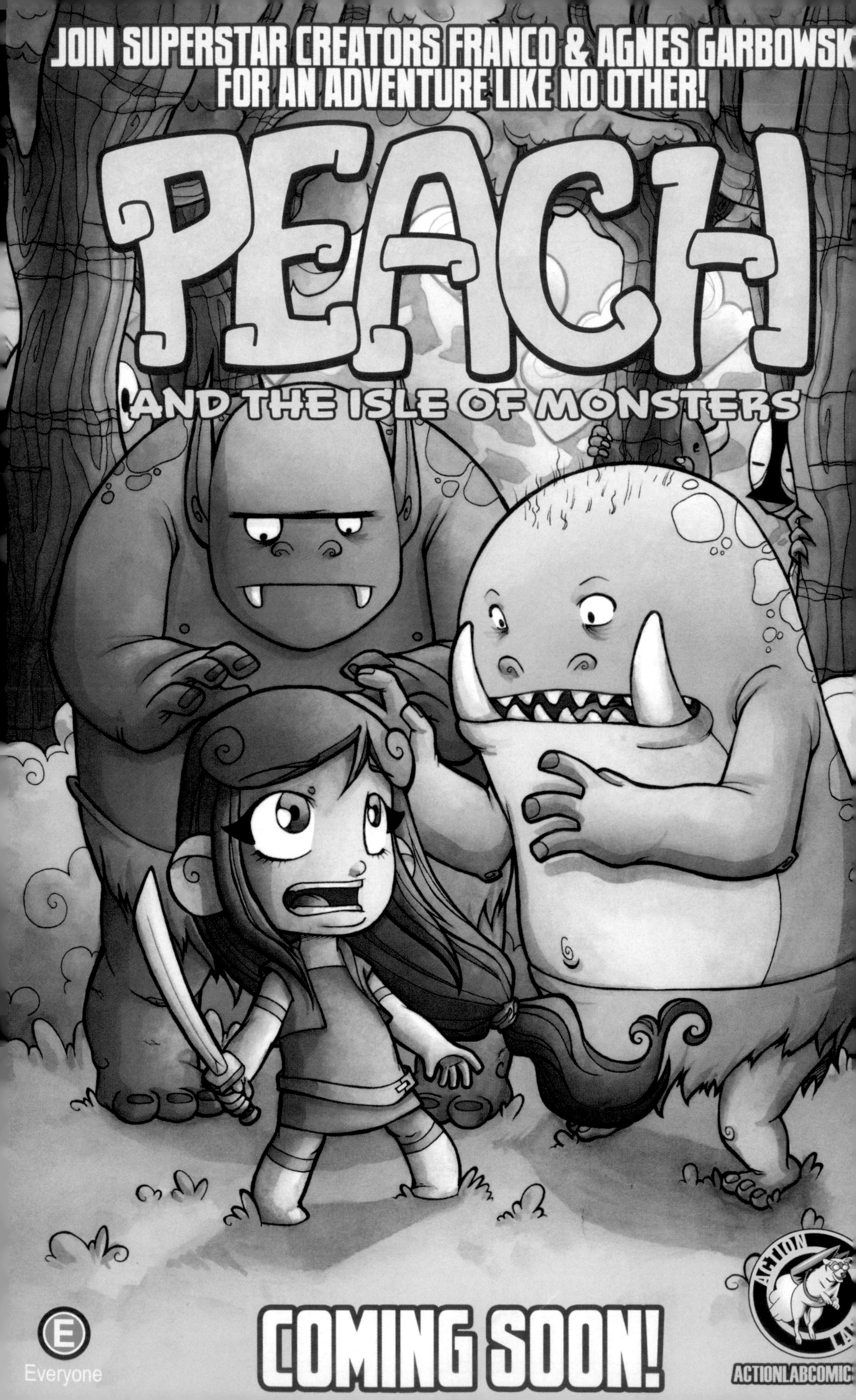
JOIN SUPERSTAR CREATORS FRANCO & AGNES GARBOWSKI
FOR AN ADVENTURE LIKE NO OTHER!
PEACH
AND THE ISLE OF MONSTERS
COMING SOON!
E
Everyone

COMIC COLLECTOR LIVE

COMIC MARKETPLACE

UR FAVORITE

BUY.
SELL.
ORGANIZE.

TRY IT FREE!

WW.COMICCOLLECTORLIVE.COM

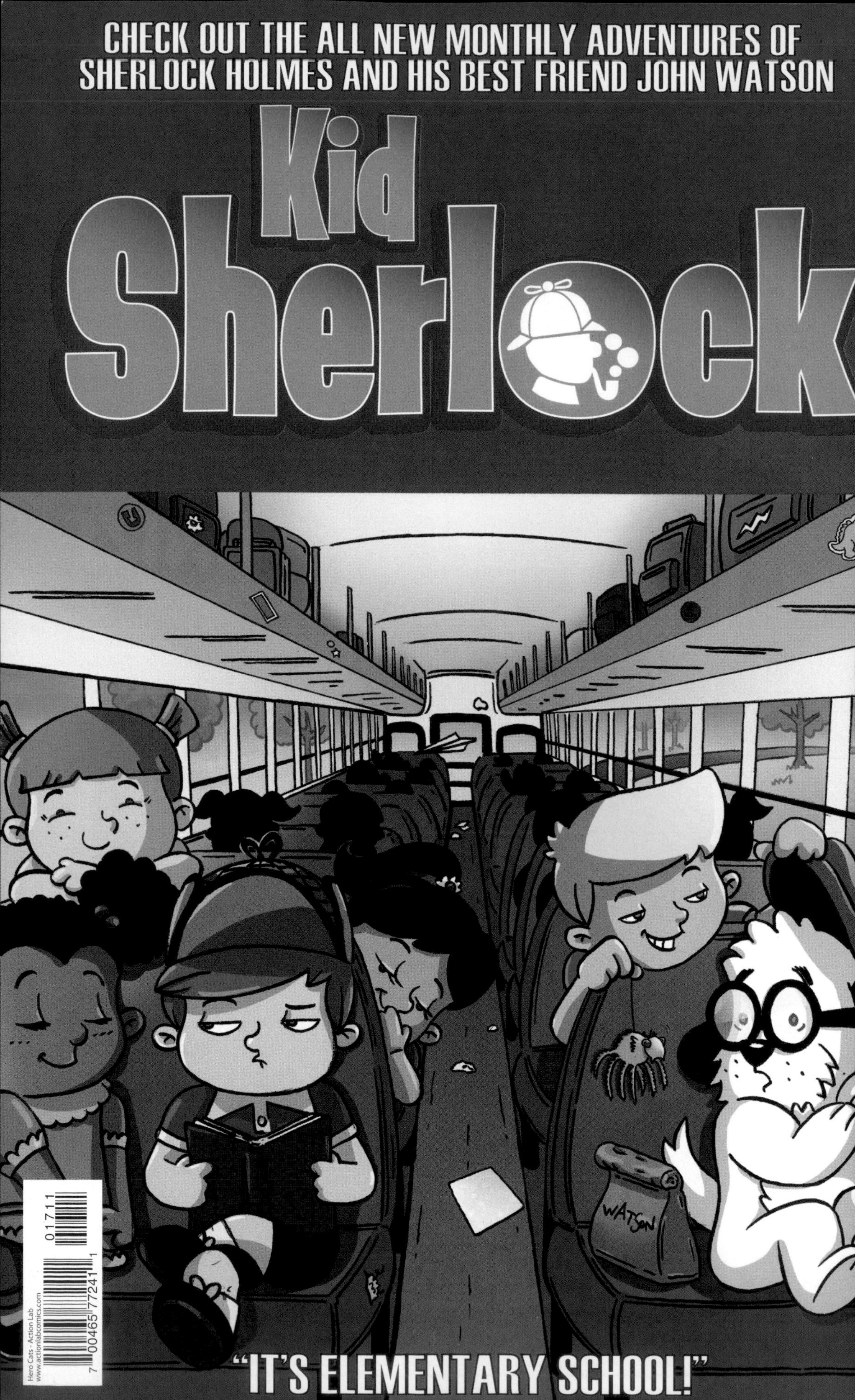
CHECK OUT THE ALL NEW MONTHLY ADVENTURES OF
SHERLOCK HOLMES AND HIS BEST FRIEND JOHN WATSON
Kid
Sherlock
WATSON
"IT'S ELEMENTARY SCHOOL!"
Hero Cats - Action Lab
www.actionlabcomics.com

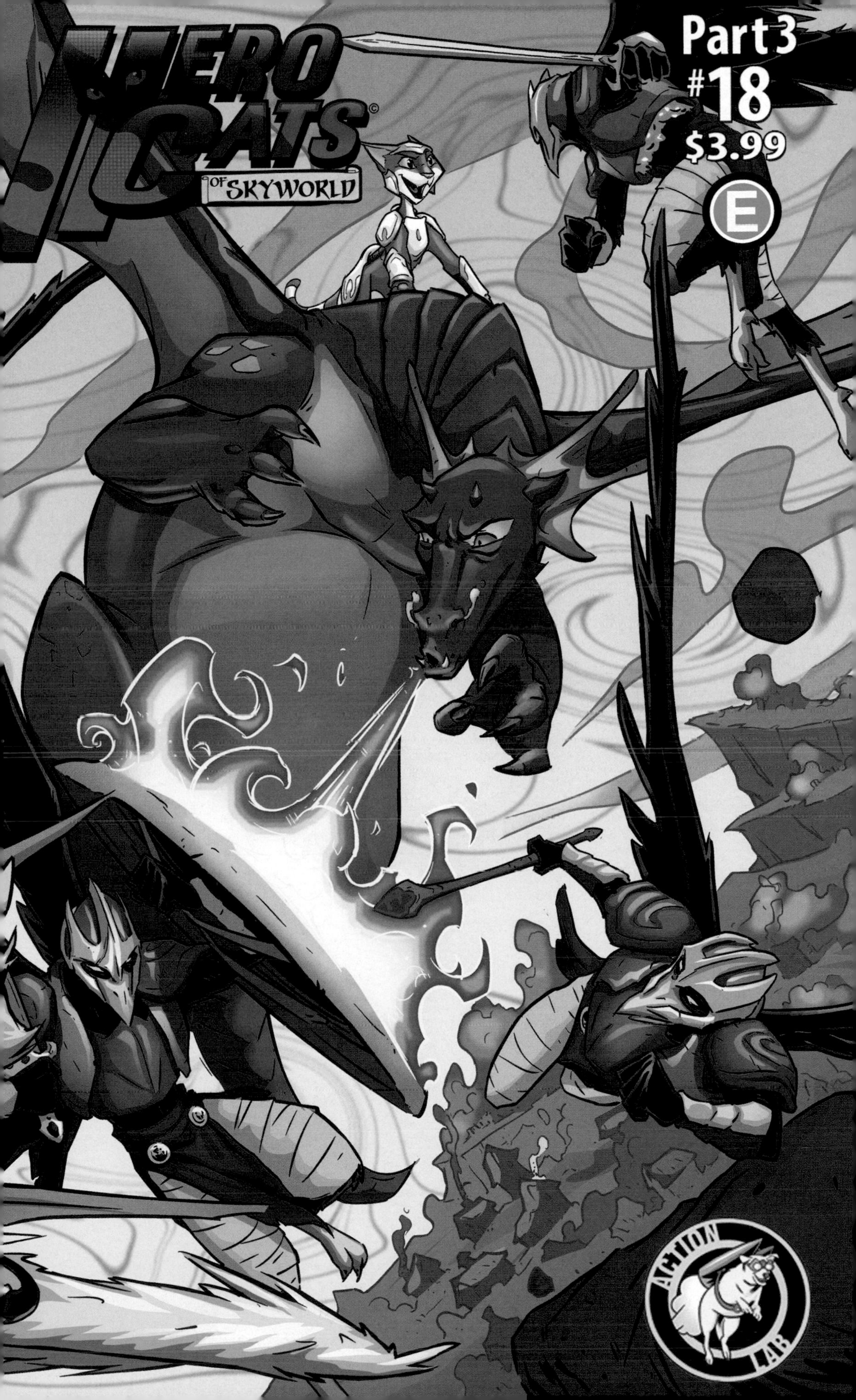
HERO CATS©
OF SKYWORLD
Part 3
#18
$3.99
E
ACTION LAB

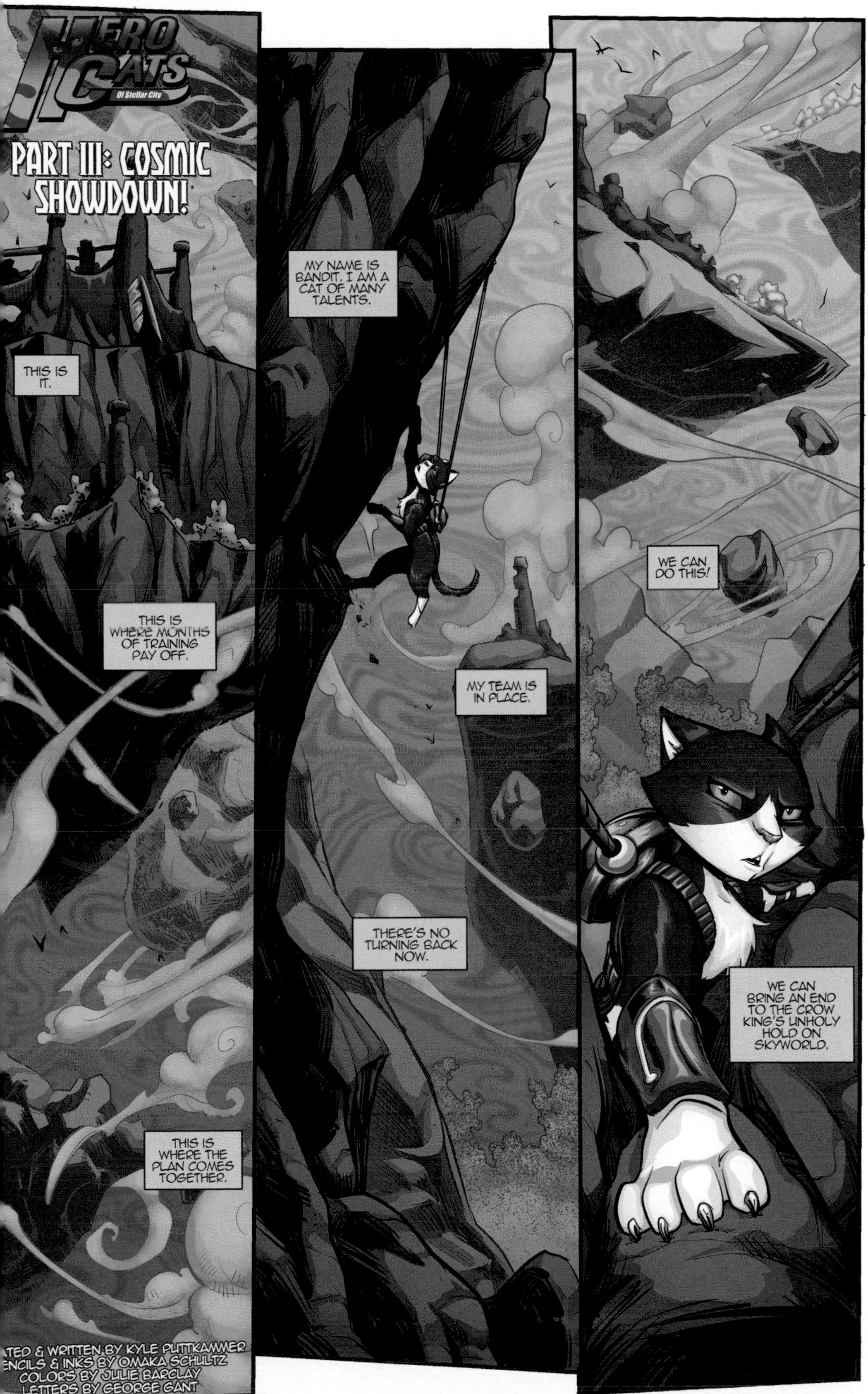

HERO CATS Of Stellar City
PART III: COSMIC SHOWDOWN!
THIS IS IT.
THIS IS WHERE MONTHS OF TRAINING PAY OFF.
THIS IS WHERE THE PLAN COMES TOGETHER.
MY NAME IS BANDIT. I AM A CAT OF MANY TALENTS.
MY TEAM IS IN PLACE.
THERE'S NO TURNING BACK NOW.
WE CAN DO THIS!
WE CAN BRING AN END TO THE CROW KING'S UNHOLY HOLD ON SKYWORLD.
ATED & WRITTEN BY KYLE PUTTKAMMER
ENCILS & INKS BY OMAKA SCHULTZ
COLORS BY JULIE BARCLAY
LETTERS BY GEORGE GANT

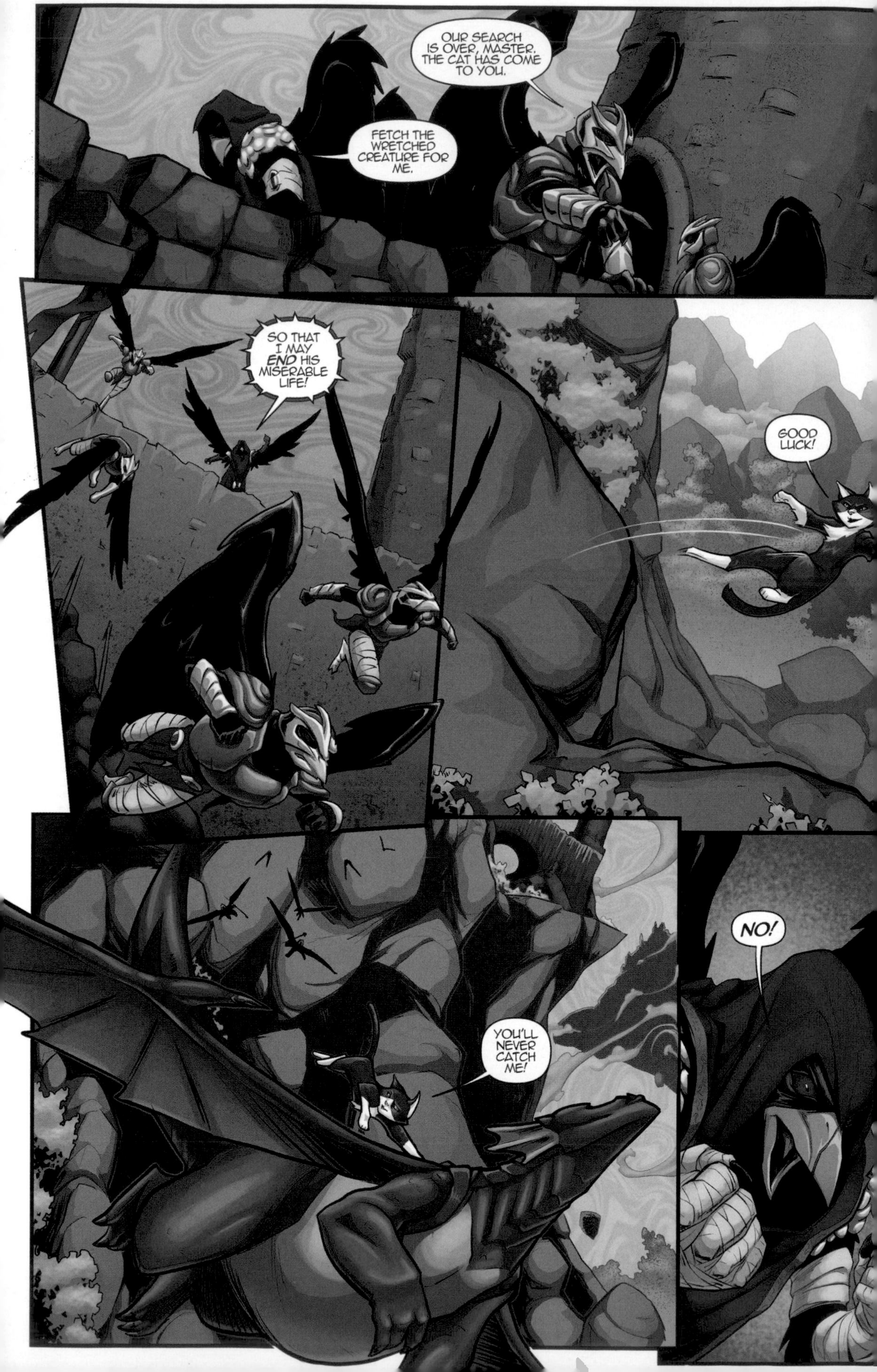
OUR SEARCH IS OVER, MASTER. THE CAT HAS COME TO YOU.
FETCH THE WRETCHED CREATURE FOR ME.
SO THAT I MAY END HIS MISERABLE LIFE!
GOOD LUCK!
YOU'LL NEVER CATCH ME!
NO!

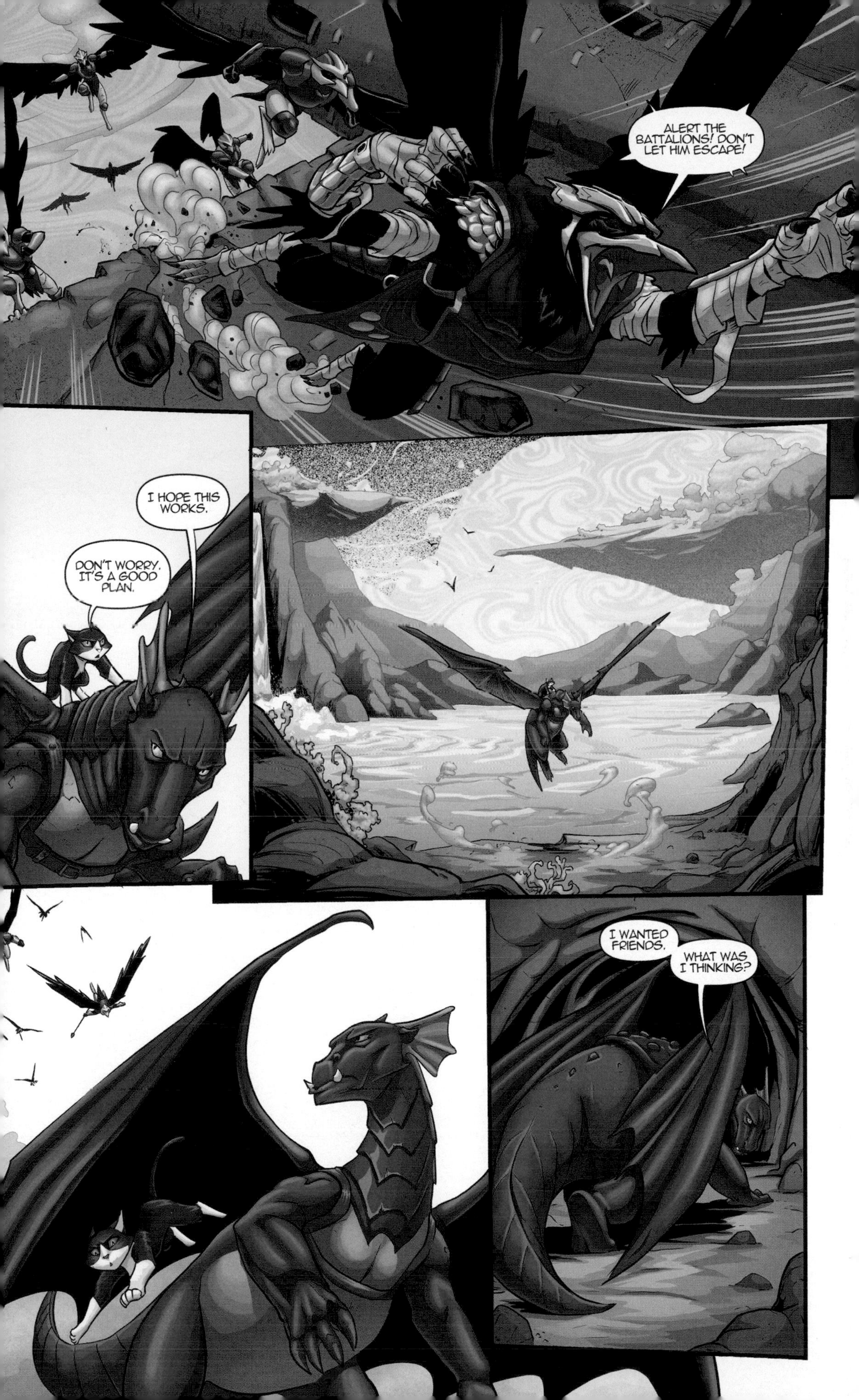
ALERT THE BATTALIONS! DON'T LET HIM ESCAPE!
I HOPE THIS WORKS.
DON'T WORRY. IT'S A GOOD PLAN.
I WANTED FRIENDS.
WHAT WAS I THINKING?

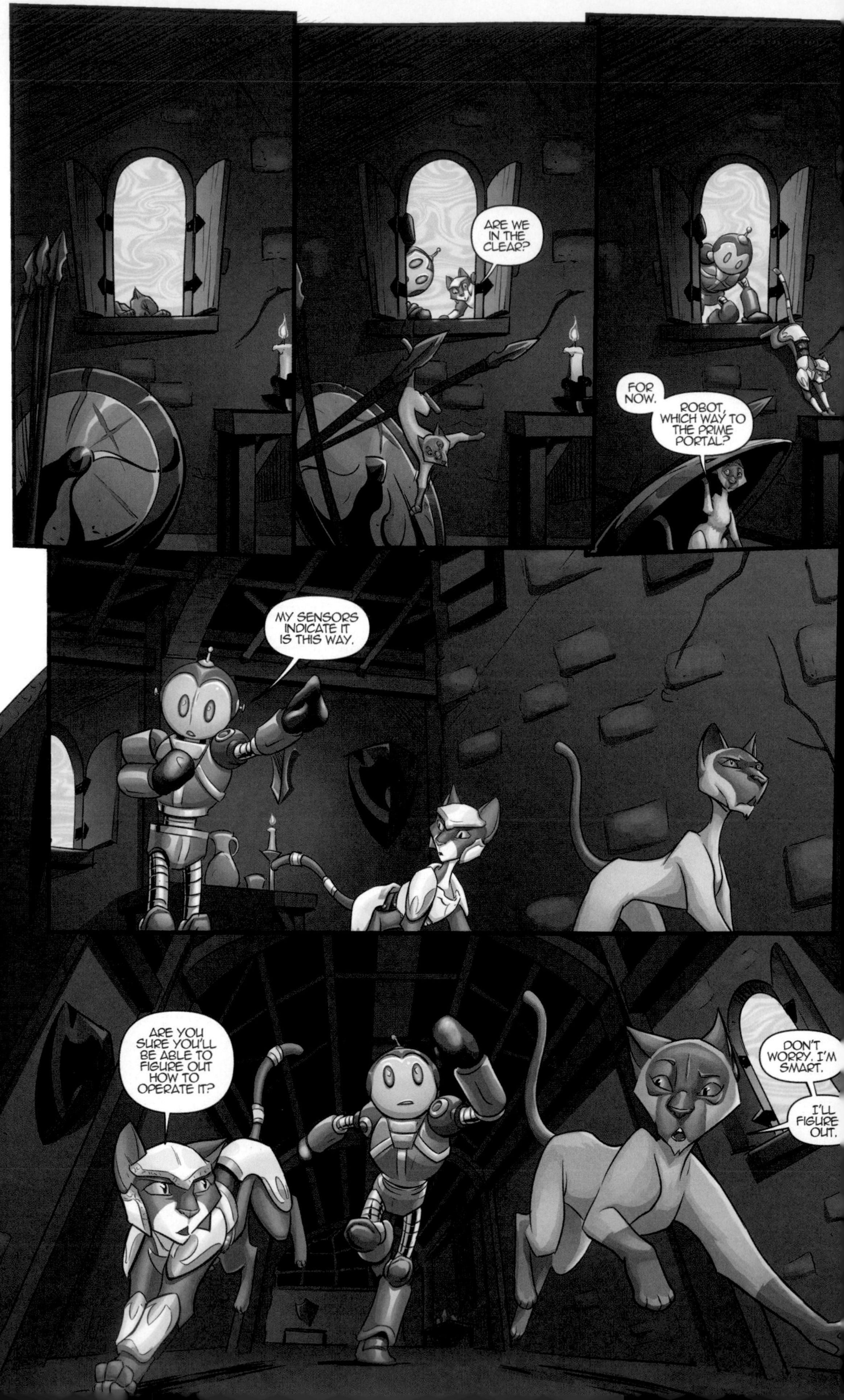
ARE WE IN THE CLEAR?
FOR NOW.
ROBOT, WHICH WAY TO THE PRIME PORTAL?
MY SENSORS INDICATE IT IS THIS WAY.
ARE YOU SURE YOU'LL BE ABLE TO FIGURE OUT HOW TO OPERATE IT?
DON'T WORRY. I'M SMART.
I'LL FIGURE OUT.

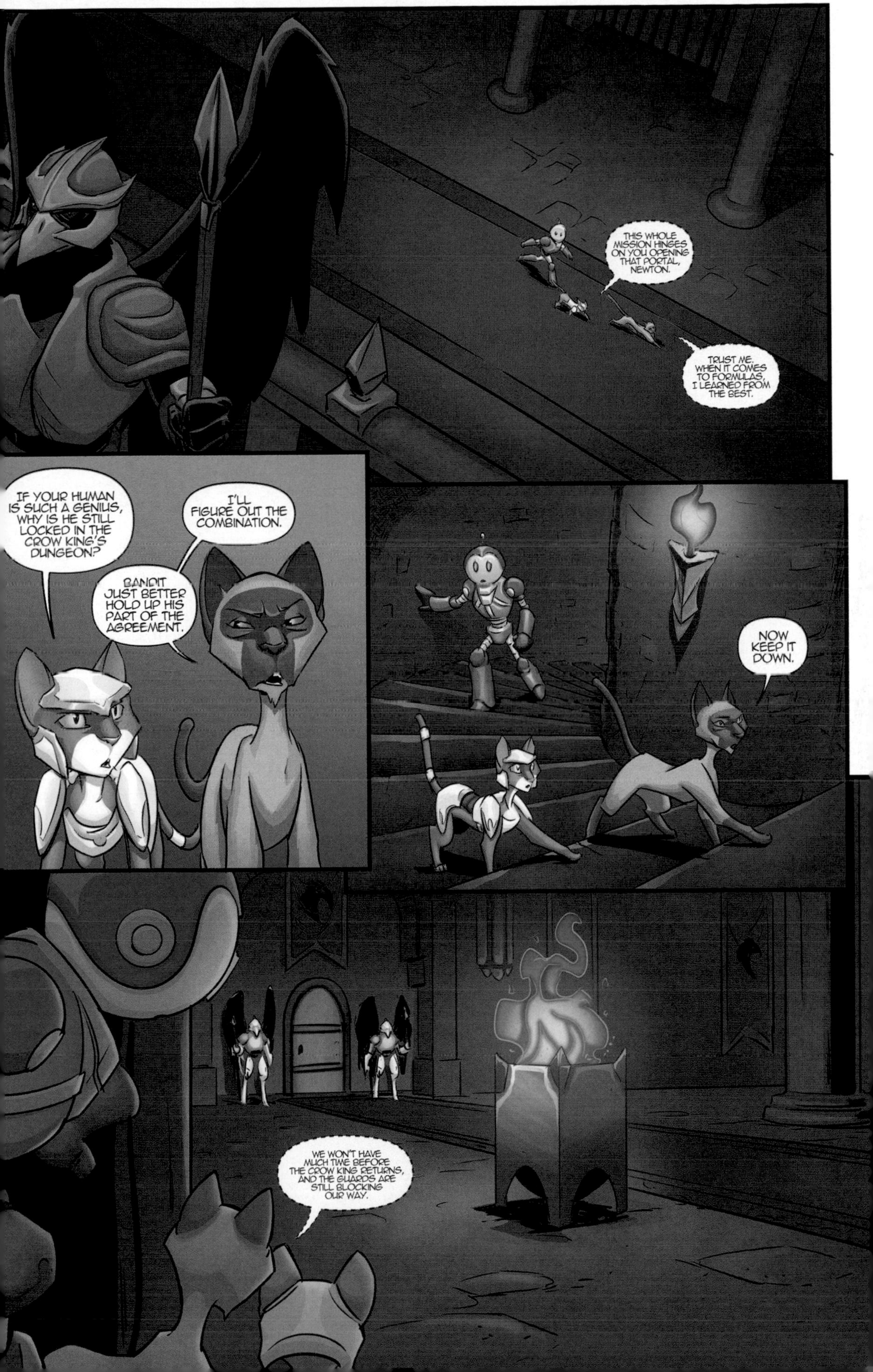
THIS WHOLE MISSION HINGES ON YOU OPENING THAT PORTAL, NEWTON.
TRUST ME. WHEN IT COMES TO FORMULAS, I LEARNED FROM THE BEST.
IF YOUR HUMAN IS SUCH A GENIUS, WHY IS HE STILL LOCKED IN THE CROW KING'S DUNGEON?
I'LL FIGURE OUT THE COMBINATION.
BANDIT JUST BETTER HOLD UP HIS PART OF THE AGREEMENT.
NOW KEEP IT DOWN.
WE WON'T HAVE MUCH TIME BEFORE THE CROW KING RETURNS, AND THE GUARDS ARE STILL BLOCKING OUR WAY.

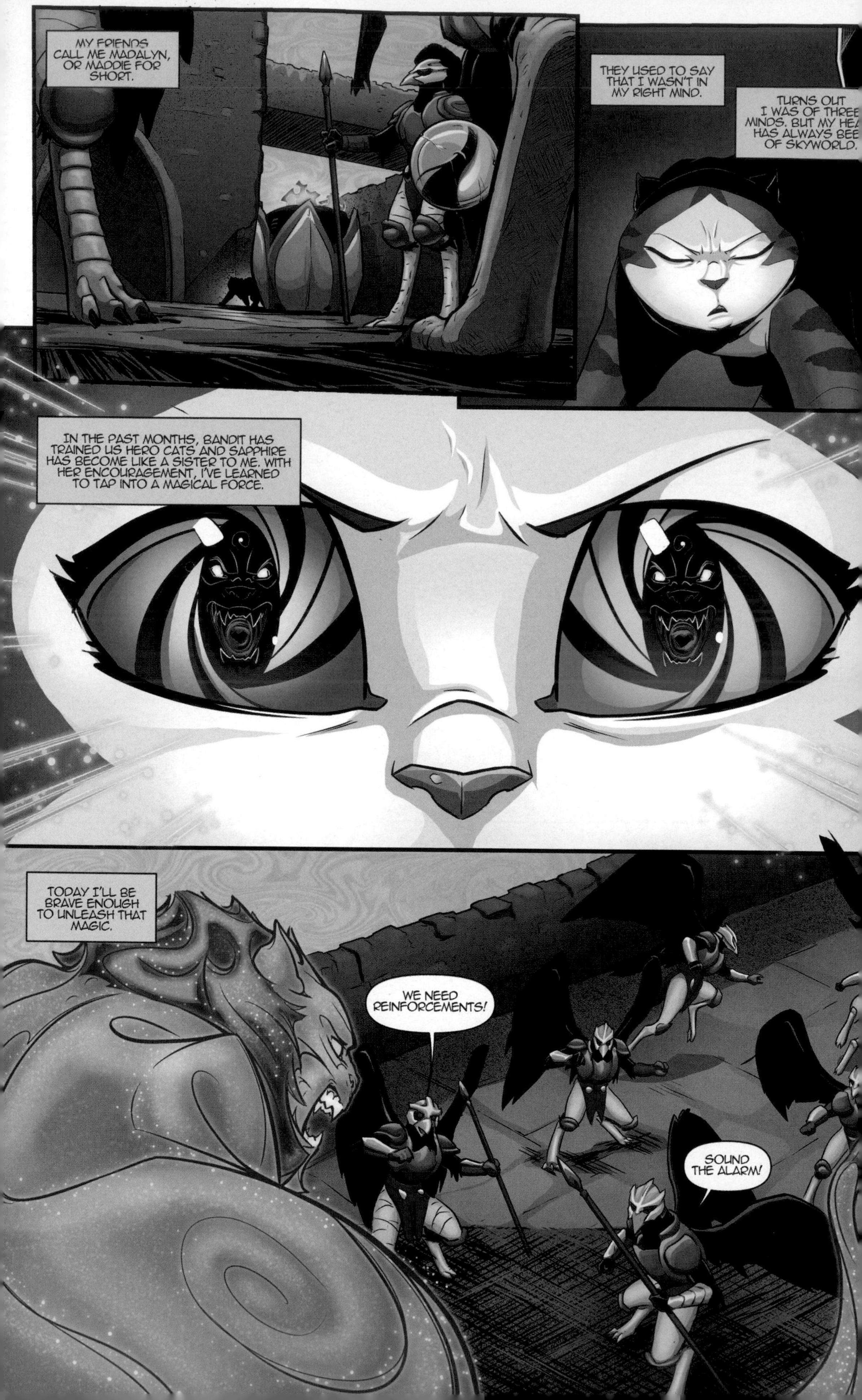
MY FRIENDS CALL ME MADALYN, OR MADDIE FOR SHORT.
THEY USED TO SAY THAT I WASN'T IN MY RIGHT MIND.
IN THE PAST MONTHS, BANDIT HAS TRAINED US HERO CATS AND SAPPHIRE HAS BECOME LIKE A SISTER TO ME. WITH HER ENCOURAGEMENT, I'VE LEARNED TO TAP INTO A MAGICAL FORCE.
TODAY I'LL BE BRAVE ENOUGH TO UNLEASH THAT MAGIC.
WE NEED REINFORCEMENTS!
SOUND THE ALARM!

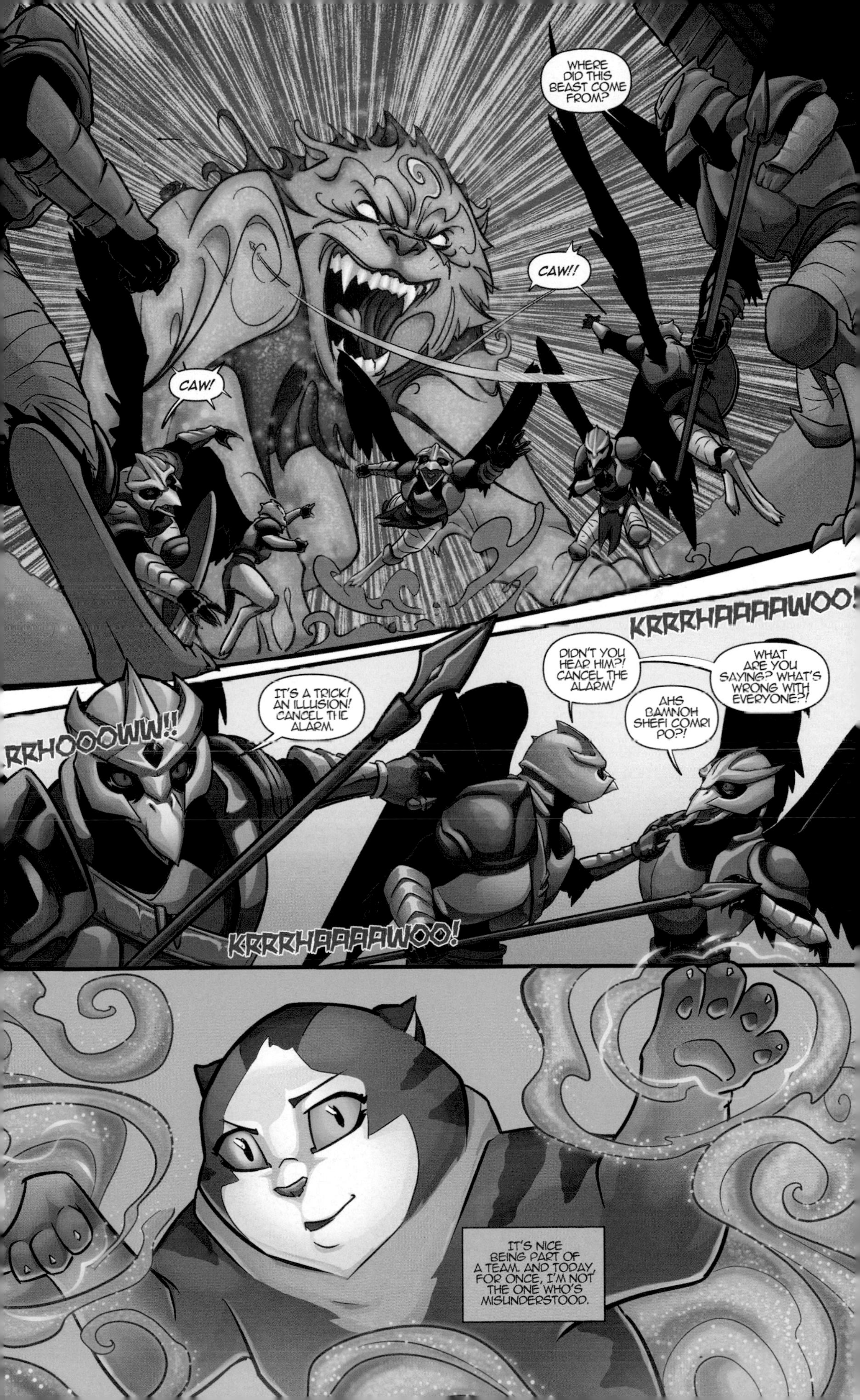
WHERE DID THIS BEAST COME FROM?
CAW!!
CAW!
KRRRHAAAAAWOO!
RRHOOOOWW!!
IT'S A TRICK! AN ILLUSION! CANCEL THE ALARM.
DIDN'T YOU HEAR HIM?! CANCEL THE ALARM!
AHS BAMNOH SHEFI COMRI PO?!
WHAT ARE YOU SAYING? WHAT'S WRONG WITH EVERYONE?!
KRRRHAAAAAWOO!
IT'S NICE BEING PART OF A TEAM. AND TODAY, FOR ONCE, I'M NOT THE ONE WHO'S MISUNDERSTOOD.

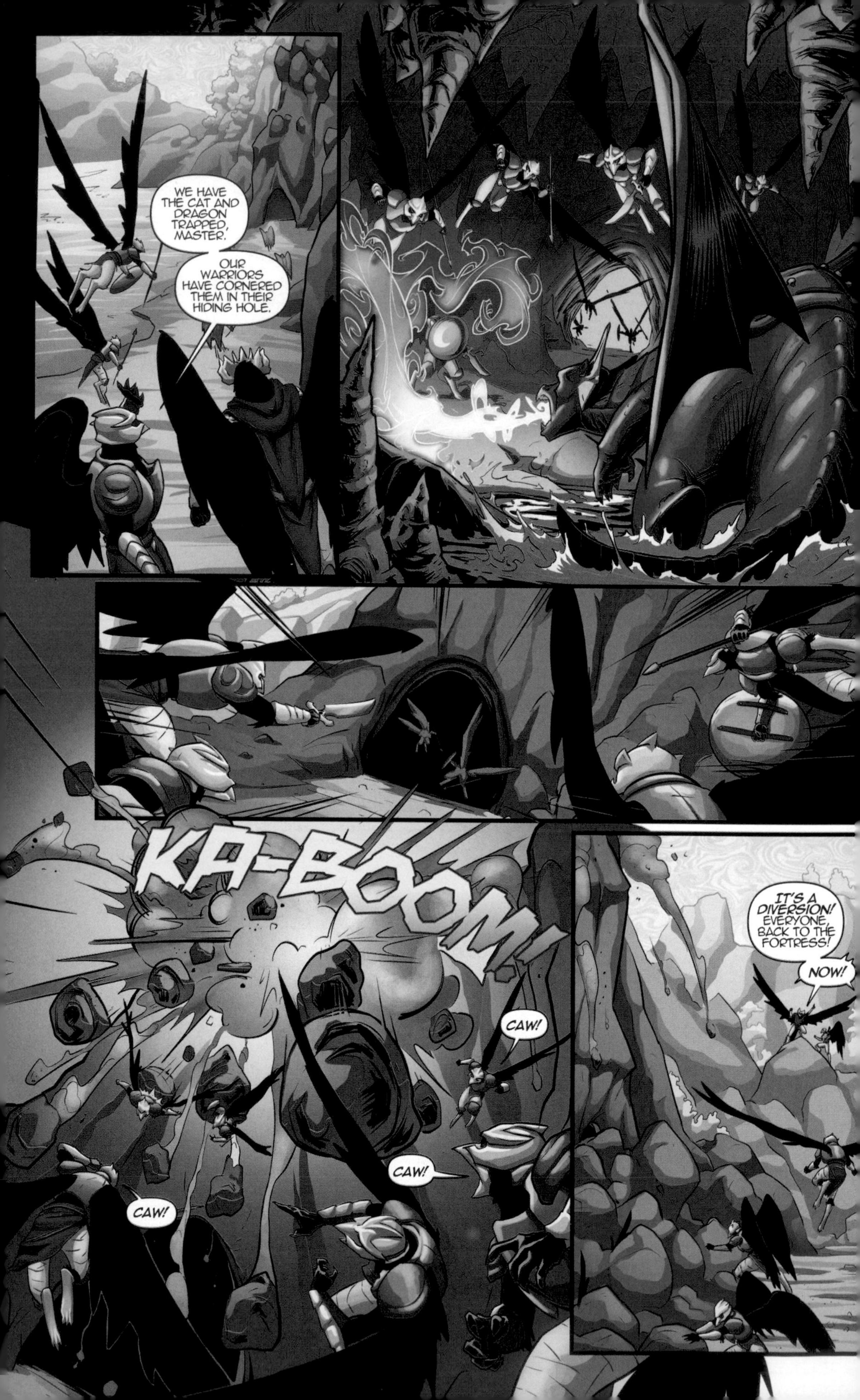
WE HAVE THE CAT AND DRAGON TRAPPED, MASTER.
OUR WARRIORS HAVE CORNERED THEM IN THEIR HIDING HOLE.
KA-BOOM!
CAW!
CAW!
CAW!
IT'S A DIVERSION! EVERYONE, BACK TO THE FORTRESS!
NOW!

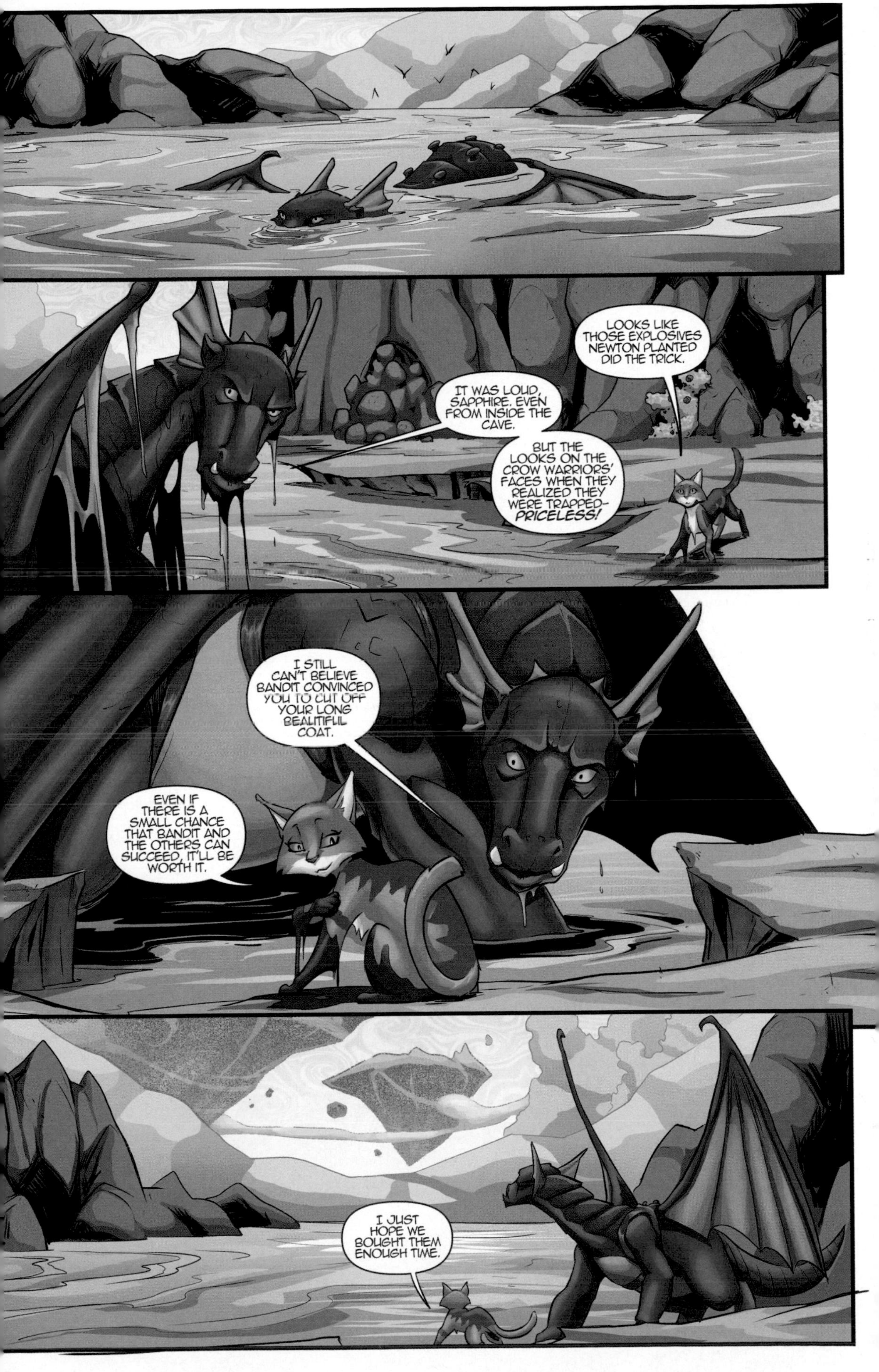
LOOKS LIKE THOSE EXPLOSIVES NEWTON PLANTED DID THE TRICK.
IT WAS LOUD, SAPPHIRE. EVEN FROM INSIDE THE CAVE.
BUT THE LOOKS ON THE CROW WARRIORS' FACES WHEN THEY REALIZED THEY WERE TRAPPED-*PRICELESS!*
I STILL CAN'T BELIEVE BANDIT CONVINCED YOU TO CUT OFF YOUR LONG BEAUTIFUL COAT.
EVEN IF THERE IS A SMALL CHANCE THAT BANDIT AND THE OTHERS CAN SUCCEED, IT'LL BE WORTH IT.
I JUST HOPE WE BOUGHT THEM ENOUGH TIME.

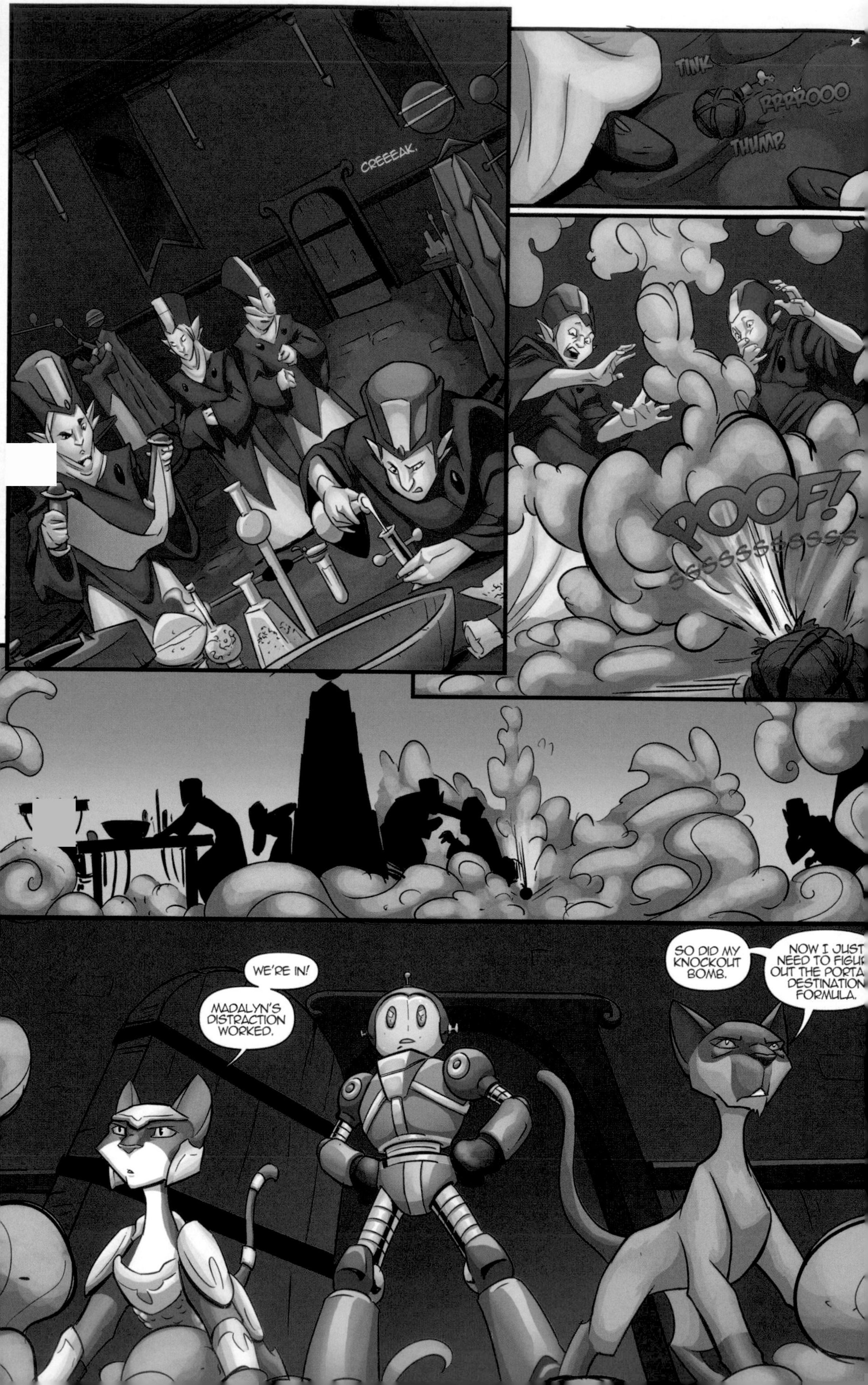
CREEEAK.
TINK
RRRROOO
THUMP.
POOF!
SSSSSSSSSSS
WE'RE IN!
MADALYN'S DISTRACTION WORKED.
SO DID MY KNOCKOUT BOMB.
NOW I JUST NEED TO FIGUR OUT THE PORTA DESTINATION FORMULA.

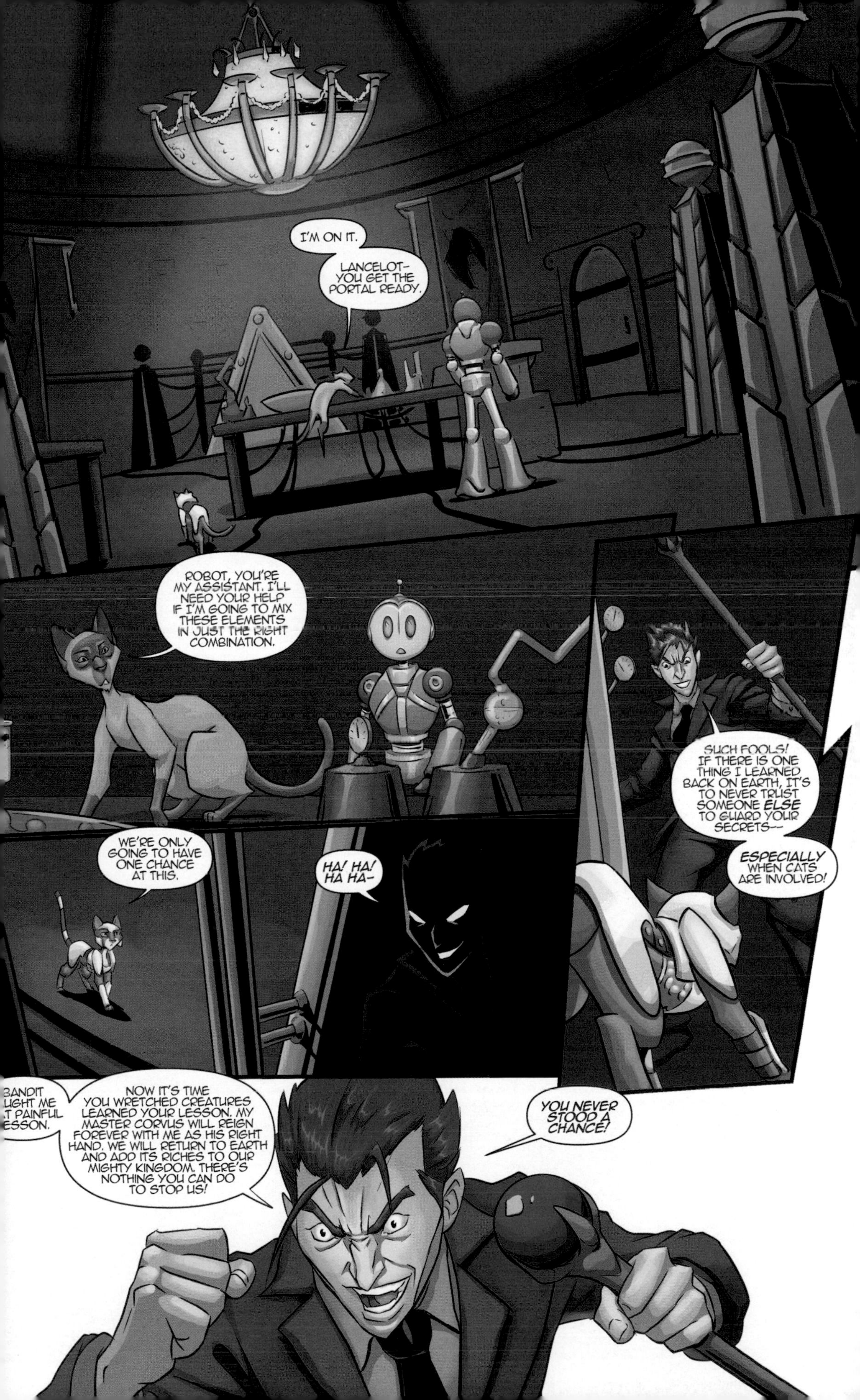
I'M ON IT.
LANCELOT- YOU GET THE PORTAL READY.
ROBOT, YOU'RE MY ASSISTANT. I'LL NEED YOUR HELP IF I'M GOING TO MIX THESE ELEMENTS IN JUST THE RIGHT COMBINATION.
WE'RE ONLY GOING TO HAVE ONE CHANCE AT THIS.
HA! HA! HA HA-
SUCH FOOLS! IF THERE IS ONE THING I LEARNED BACK ON EARTH, IT'S TO NEVER TRUST SOMEONE ELSE TO GUARD YOUR SECRETS--
ESPECIALLY WHEN CATS ARE INVOLVED!
BANDIT UGHT ME T PAINFUL ESSON.
NOW IT'S TIME YOU WRETCHED CREATURES LEARNED YOUR LESSON. MY MASTER CORVUS WILL REIGN FOREVER WITH ME AS HIS RIGHT HAND. WE WILL RETURN TO EARTH AND ADD ITS RICHES TO OUR MIGHTY KINGDOM. THERE'S NOTHING YOU CAN DO TO STOP US!
YOU NEVER STOOD A CHANCE!

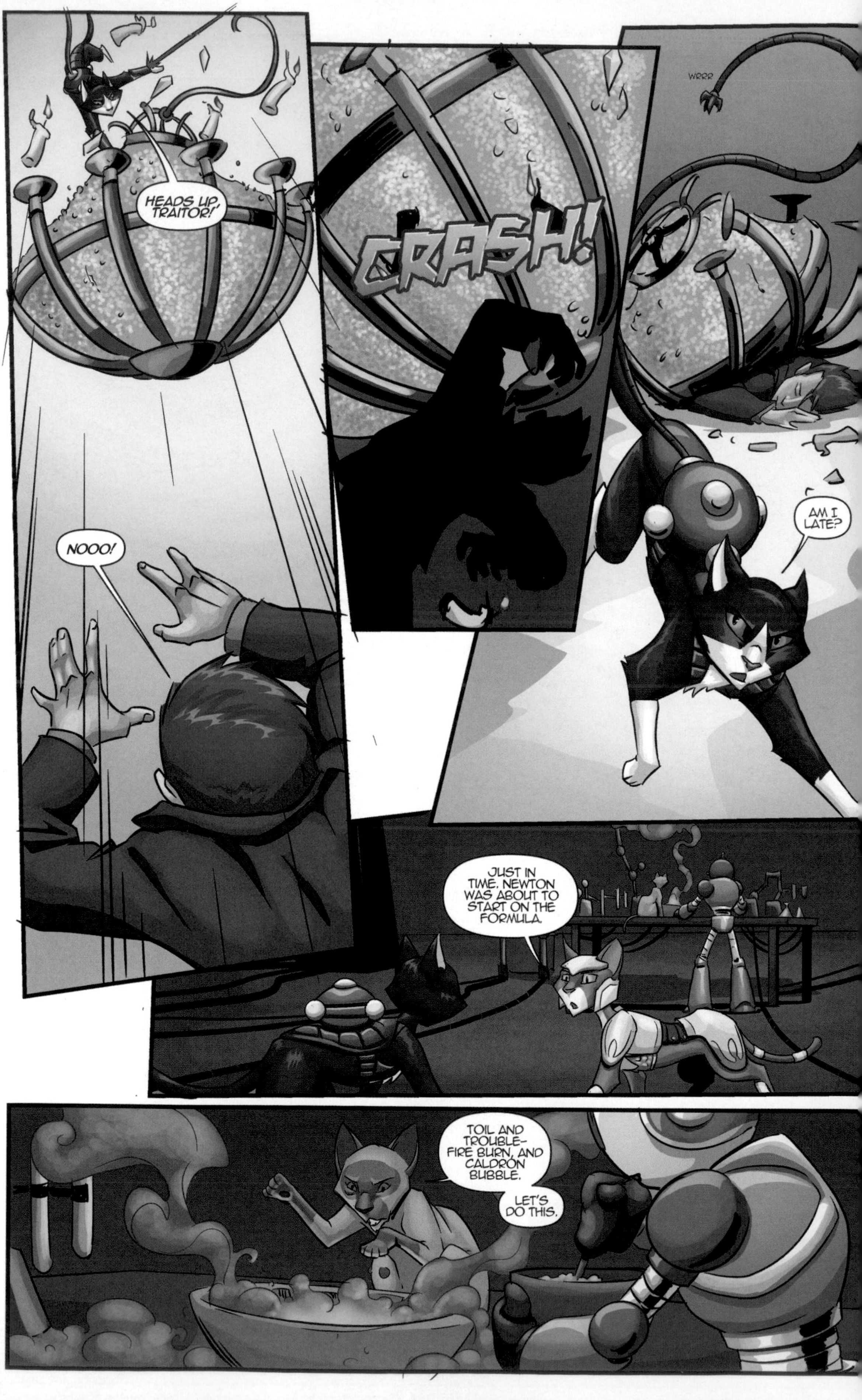
HEADS UP TRAITOR!
NOOO!
CRASH!
WRRR
AM I LATE?
JUST IN TIME. NEWTON WAS ABOUT TO START ON THE FORMULA.
TOIL AND TROUBLE-FIRE BURN, AND CALDRON BUBBLE.
LET'S DO THIS.

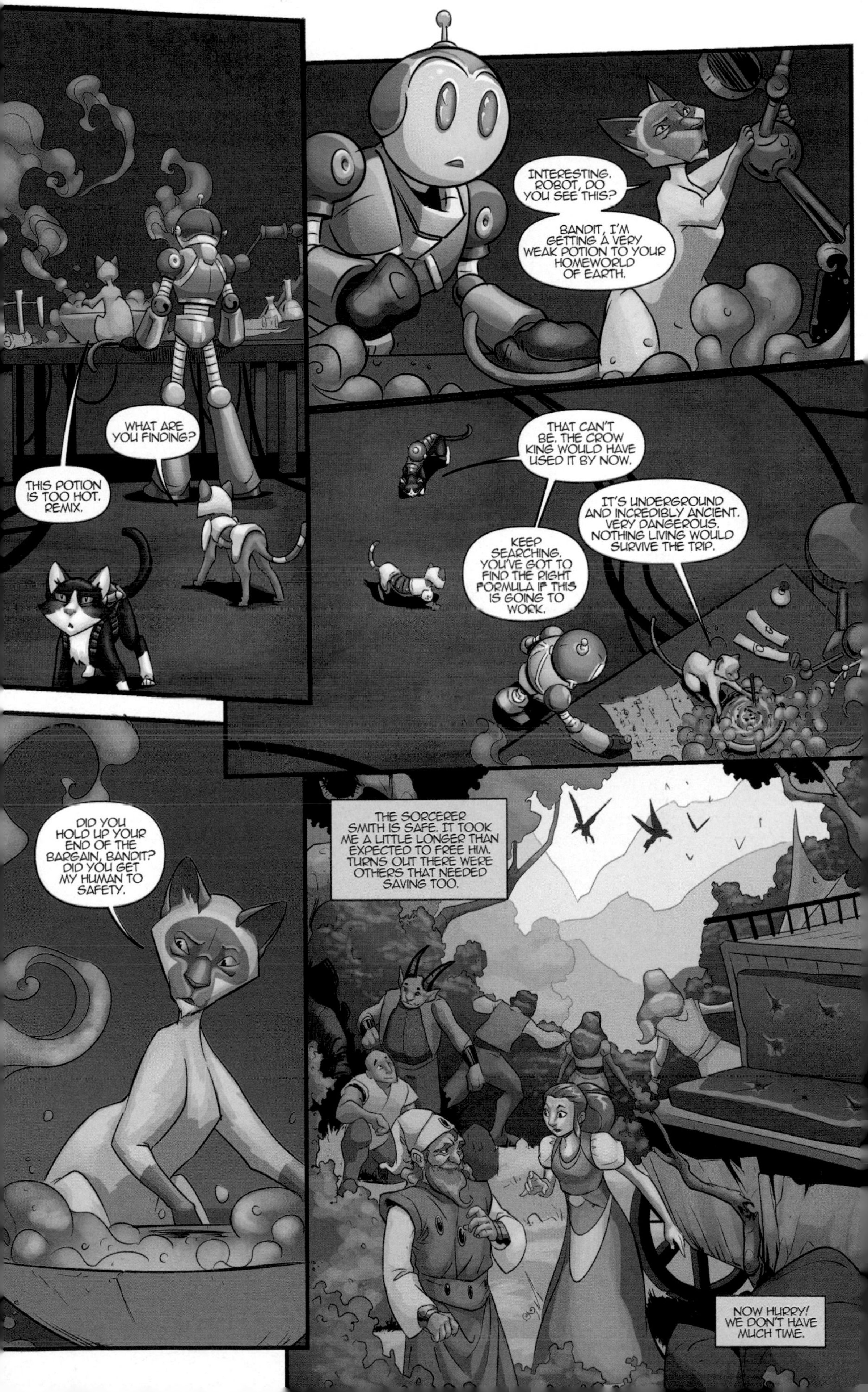
WHAT ARE YOU FINDING?
THIS POTION IS TOO HOT. REMIX.
INTERESTING. ROBOT, DO YOU SEE THIS?
BANDIT, I'M GETTING A VERY WEAK POTION TO YOUR HOMEWORLD OF EARTH.
THAT CAN'T BE. THE CROW KING WOULD HAVE USED IT BY NOW.
IT'S UNDERGROUND AND INCREDIBLY ANCIENT. VERY DANGEROUS. NOTHING LIVING WOULD SURVIVE THE TRIP.
KEEP SEARCHING. YOU'VE GOT TO FIND THE RIGHT FORMULA IF THIS IS GOING TO WORK.
DID YOU HOLD UP YOUR END OF THE BARGAIN, BANDIT? DID YOU GET MY HUMAN TO SAFETY.
THE SORCERER SMITH IS SAFE. IT TOOK ME A LITTLE LONGER THAN EXPECTED TO FREE HIM. TURNS OUT THERE WERE OTHERS THAT NEEDED SAVING TOO.
NOW HURRY! WE DON'T HAVE MUCH TIME.

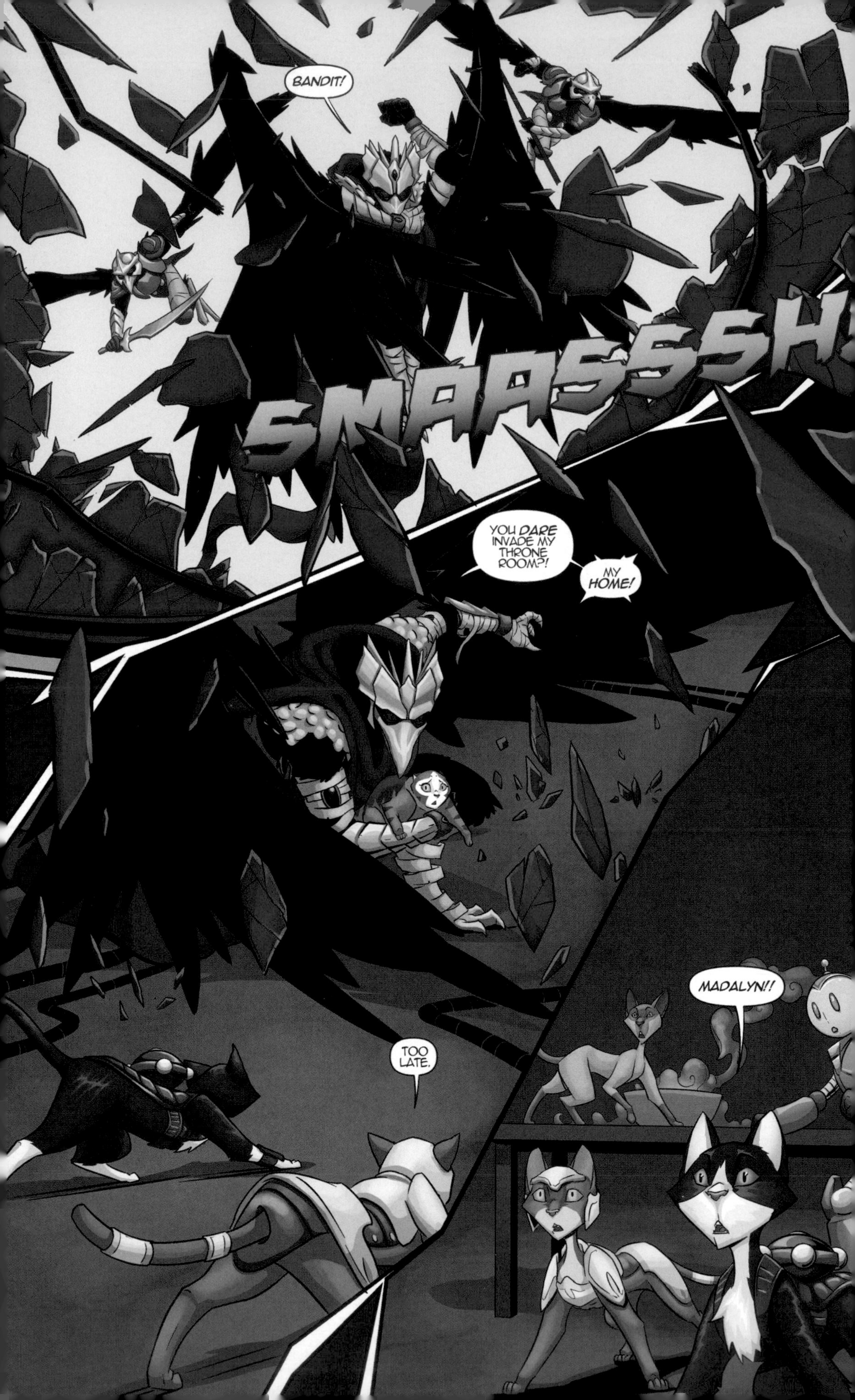
BANDIT!
SMAASSSH!
YOU DARE INVADE MY THRONE ROOM?!
MY HOME!
TOO LATE.
MADALYN!!

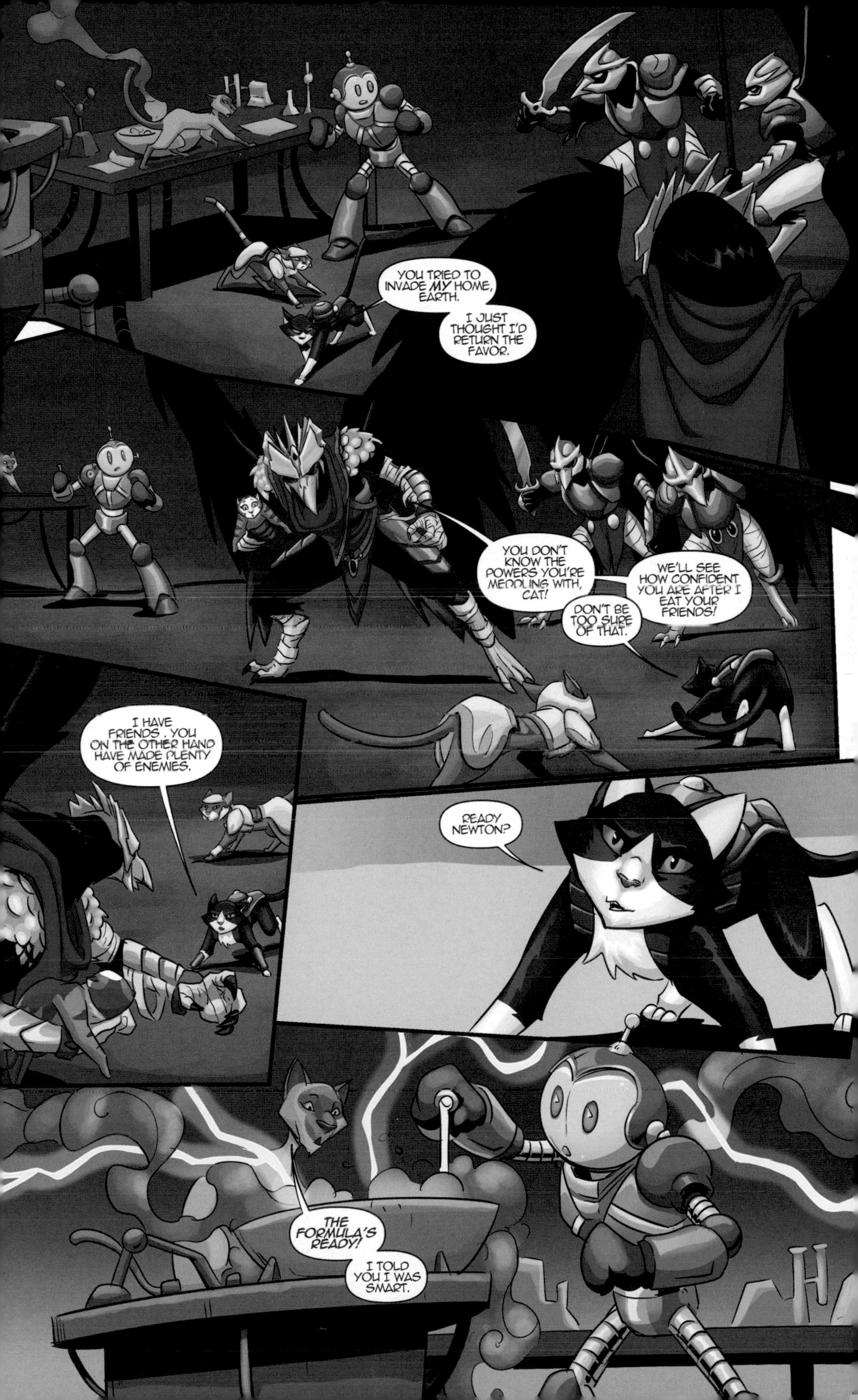
YOU TRIED TO INVADE *MY* HOME, EARTH.
I JUST THOUGHT I'D RETURN THE FAVOR.
YOU DON'T KNOW THE POWERS YOU'RE MEDDLING WITH, CAT!
WE'LL SEE HOW CONFIDENT YOU ARE AFTER I EAT YOUR FRIENDS!
DON'T BE TOO SURE OF THAT.
I HAVE FRIENDS. YOU ON THE OTHER HAND HAVE MADE PLENTY OF ENEMIES.
READY NEWTON?
THE FORMULA'S READY!
I TOLD YOU I WAS SMART.

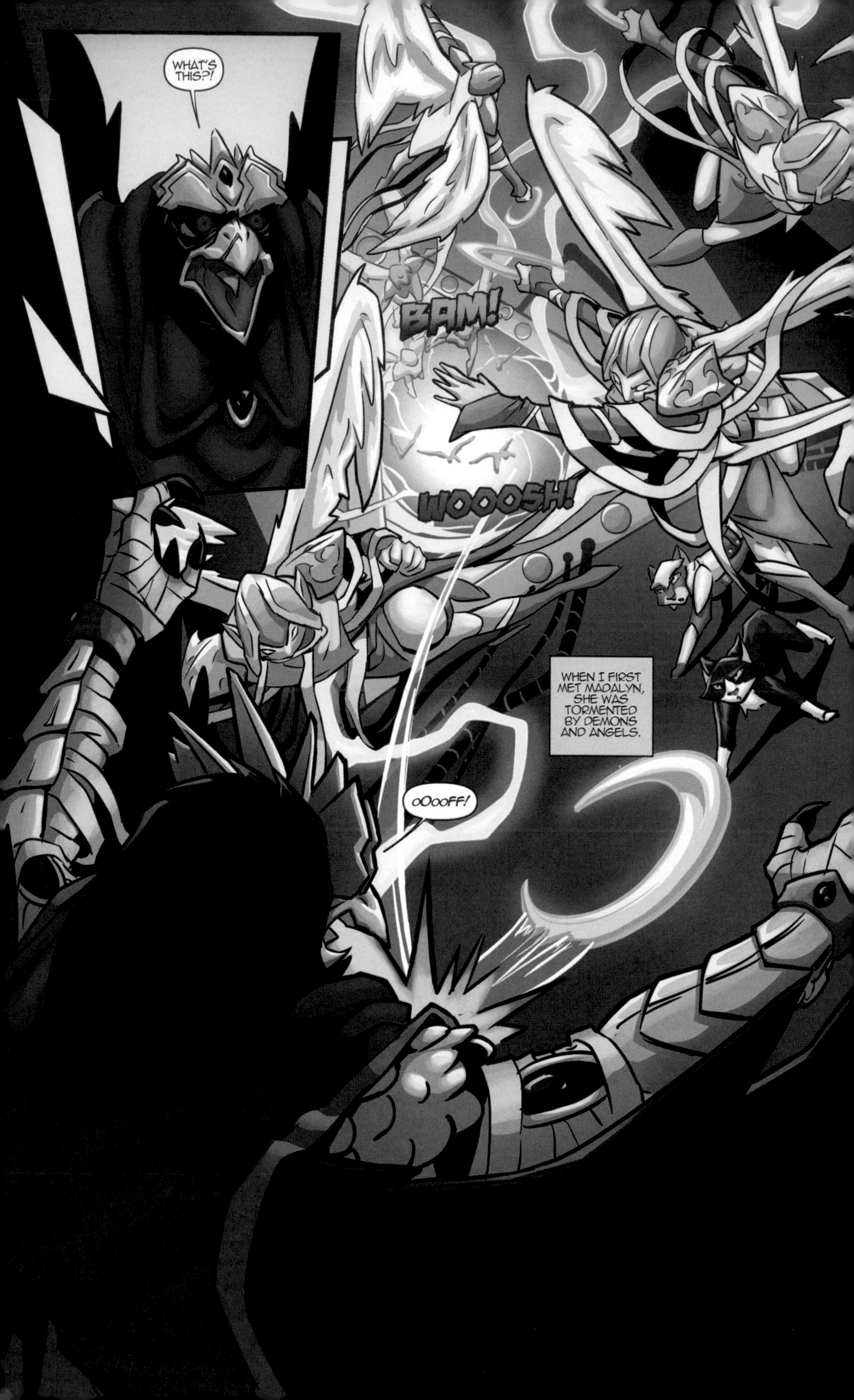
WHAT'S THIS?!
BAM!
WOOOSH!
WHEN I FIRST MET MADALYN, SHE WAS TORMENTED BY DEMONS AND ANGELS.
OOooFF!

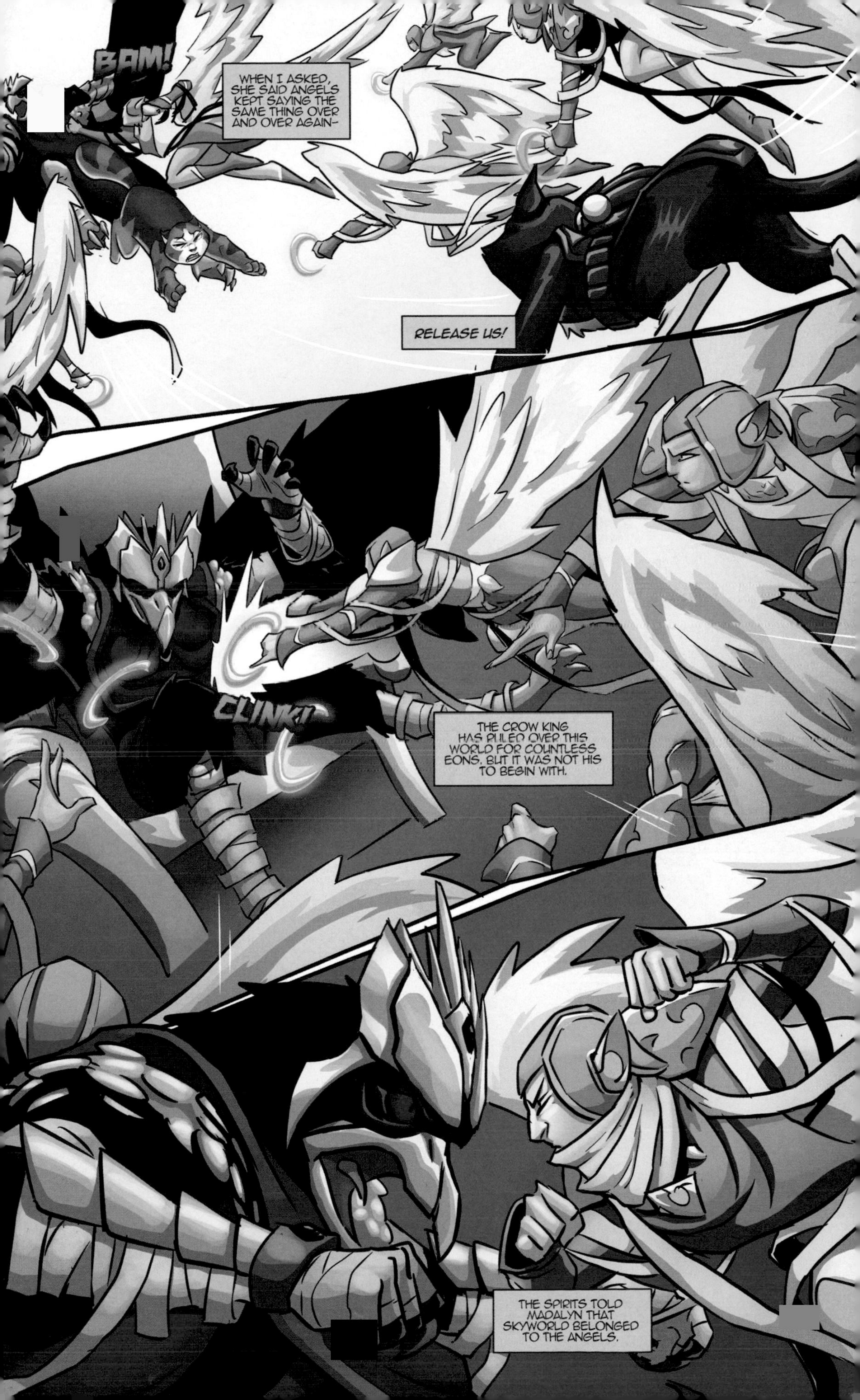
BAM!
WHEN I ASKED, SHE SAID ANGELS KEPT SAYING THE SAME THING OVER AND OVER AGAIN-
RELEASE US!
CLINK!
THE CROW KING HAS RULED OVER THIS WORLD FOR COUNTLESS EONS, BUT IT WAS NOT HIS TO BEGIN WITH.
THE SPIRITS TOLD MADALYN THAT SKYWORLD BELONGED TO THE ANGELS.

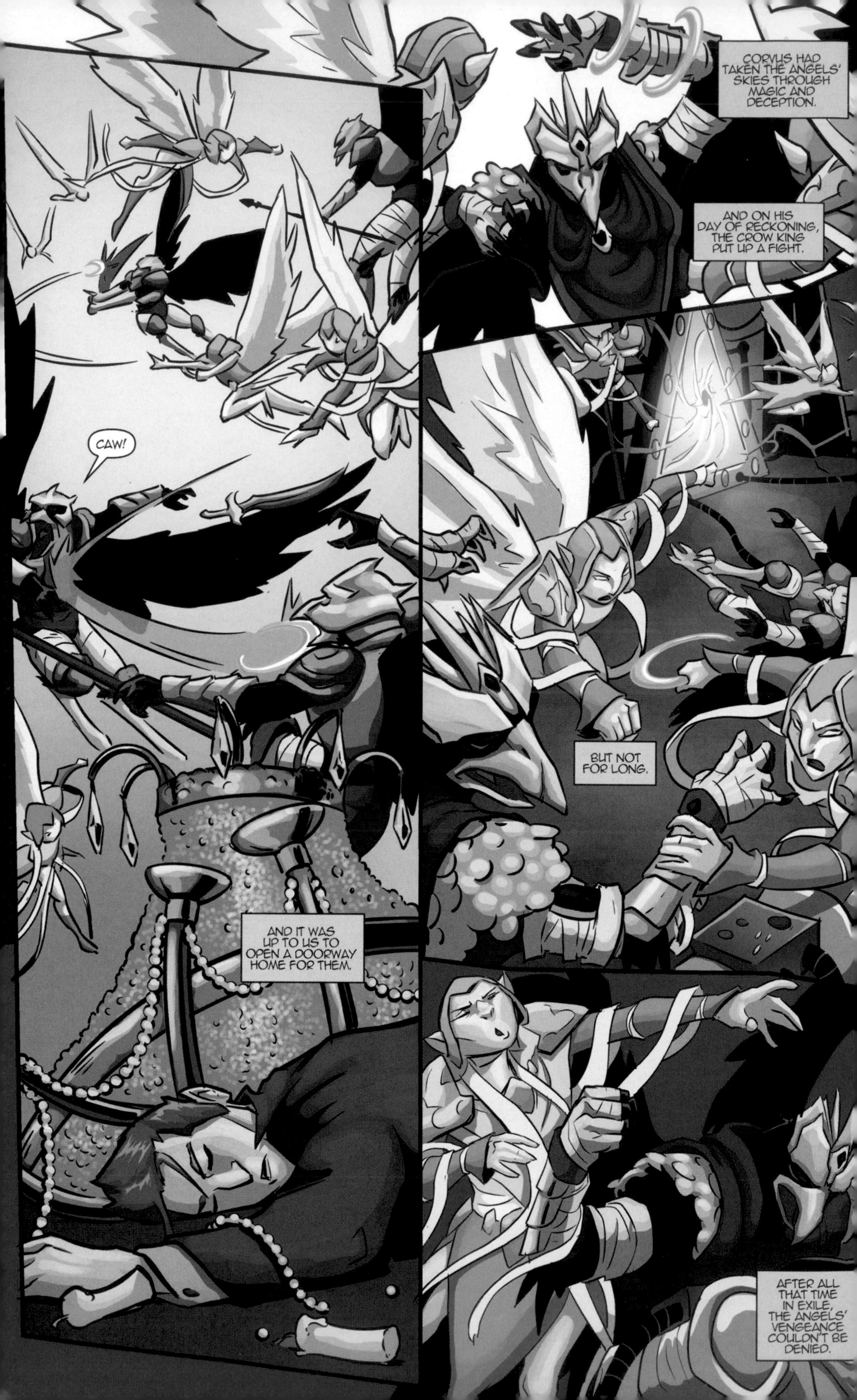
CAW!
AND IT WAS UP TO US TO OPEN A DOORWAY HOME FOR THEM.
CORVUS HAD TAKEN THE ANGELS' SKIES THROUGH MAGIC AND DECEPTION.
AND ON HIS DAY OF RECKONING, THE CROW KING PUT UP A FIGHT.
BUT NOT FOR LONG.
AFTER ALL THAT TIME IN EXILE, THE ANGELS' VENGEANCE COULDN'T BE DENIED.

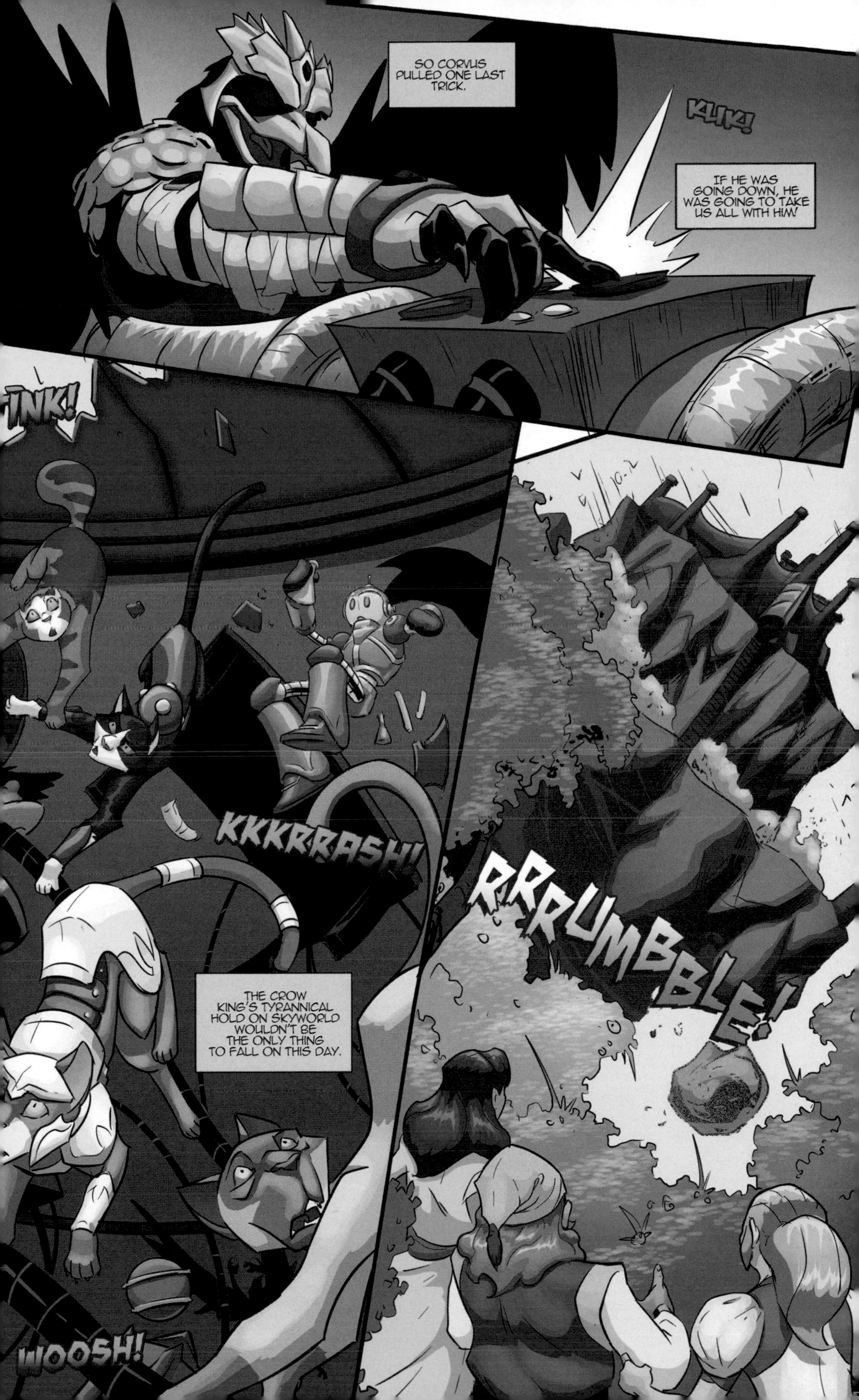
SO CORVUS PULLED ONE LAST TRICK.
KLIK!
IF HE WAS GOING DOWN, HE WAS GOING TO TAKE US ALL WITH HIM!
INK!
KKKRRASH!
RRRUMBBLE!
THE CROW KING'S TYRANNICAL HOLD ON SKYWORLD WOULDN'T BE THE ONLY THING TO FALL ON THIS DAY.
WOOSH!

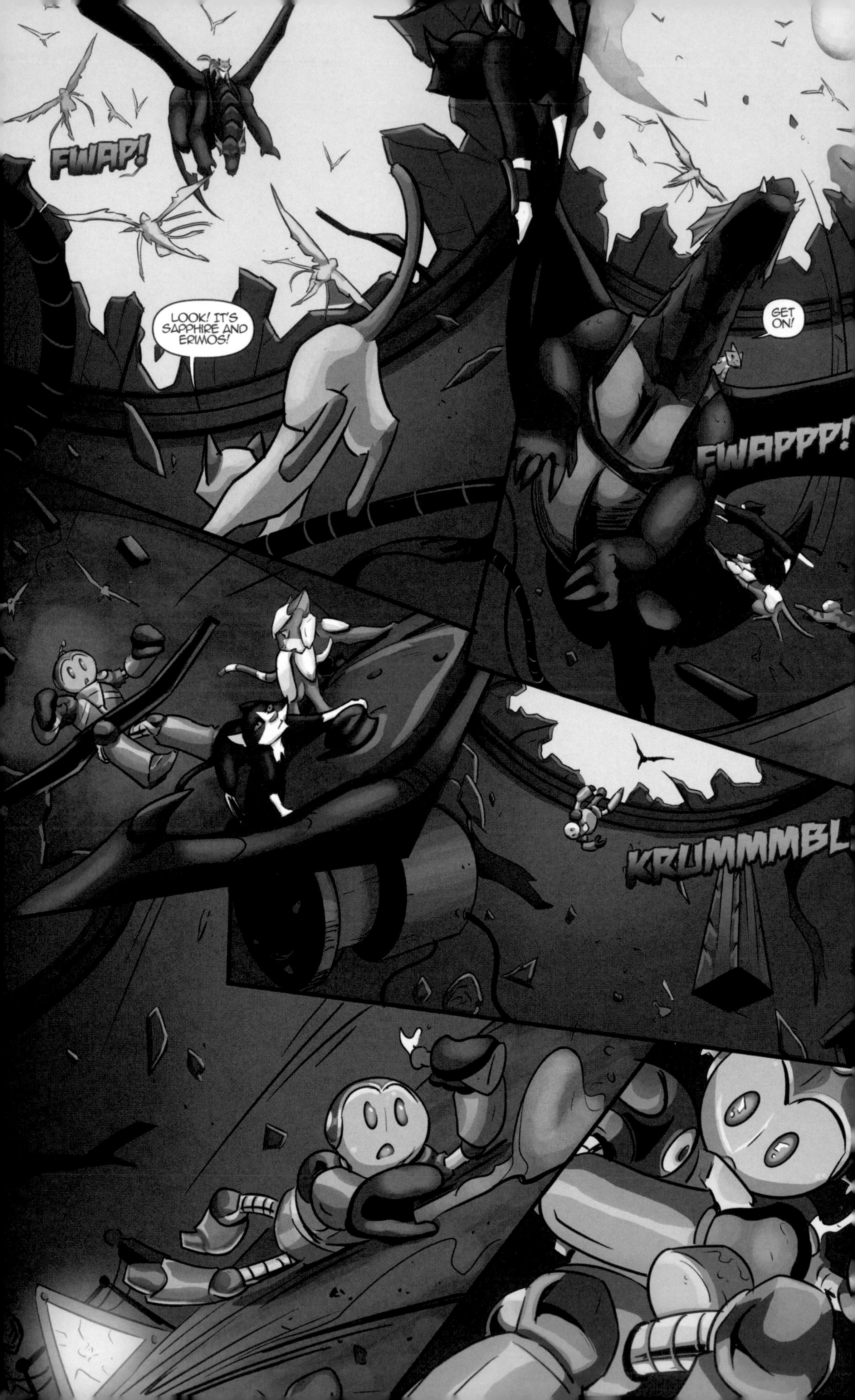
FWAP!
LOOK! IT'S SAPPHIRE AND ERIMOS!
GET ON!
FWAPPP!
KRUMMMBL

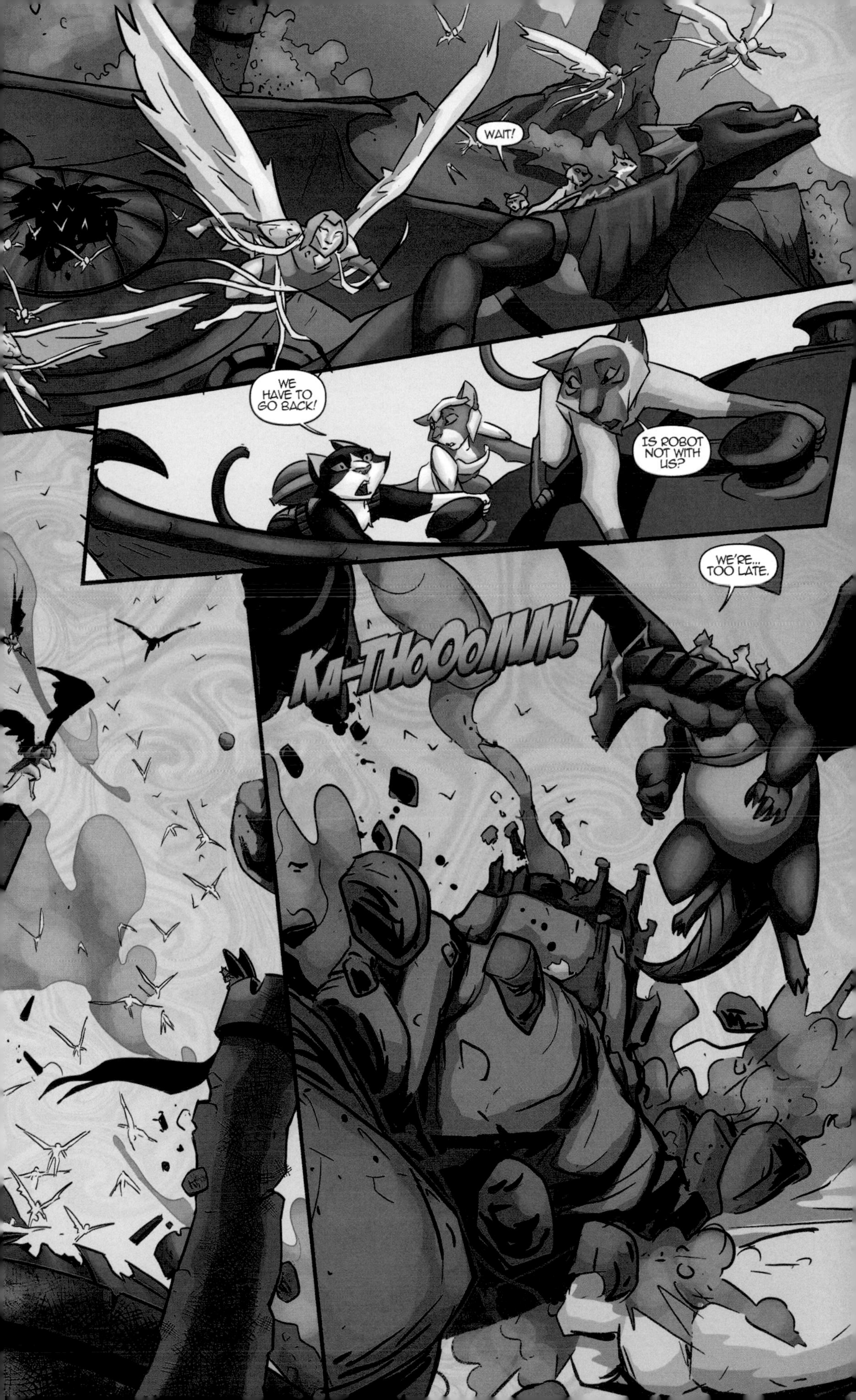
WAIT!
WE HAVE TO GO BACK!
IS ROBOT NOT WITH US?
WE'RE... TOO LATE.
KA-THOOOMM!

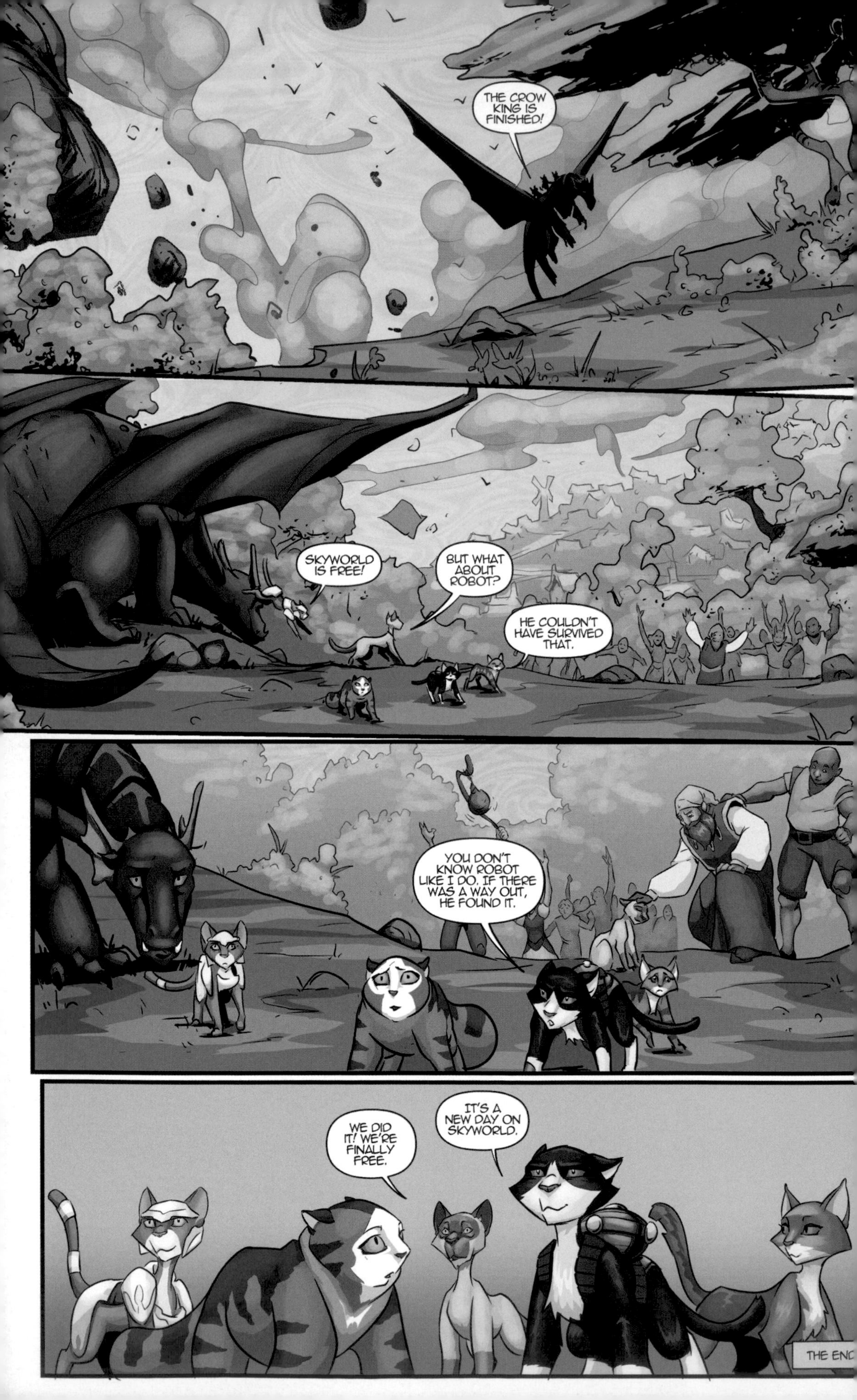
THE CROW KING IS FINISHED!
SKYWORLD IS FREE!
BUT WHAT ABOUT ROBOT?
HE COULDN'T HAVE SURVIVED THAT.
YOU DON'T KNOW ROBOT LIKE I DO. IF THERE WAS A WAY OUT, HE FOUND IT.
WE DID IT! WE'RE FINALLY FREE.
IT'S A NEW DAY ON SKYWORLD.
THE END

HERO CHAT

RETURN TO STELLAR CITY!

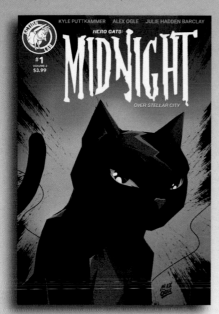

ON SALE NOW,
MIDNIGHT VOLUME 2.

AND IN OCTOBER,
HERO CATS #19.

HEY KIDS & CATS!

BANDIT AND HIS NEW FRIENDS HAVE TRIUMPHED!

IT'S A BRIGHT NEW DAY ON SKYWORLD. ANGELS HAVE RETURNED! DOES THIS MEAN THE CITIZENS OF RIDGEWALK VILLAGE WILL FINALLY LIVE IN PEACE? WILL WE EVER SEE THESE HERO CATS AGAIN? AND WHAT ABOUT ROBOT?
- STAY TUNED!

MEANWHILE, WE CAN FINALLY REVEAL WHERE SKYWORLD IS ACTUALLY LOCATED! JUST TURN THE PAGE AND YOU'LL SEE. ALL THE HERO CAT'S ADVENTURES ARE CONNECTED IN A VERY SPECIAL WAY.

KYLE@GALACTICQUEST.COM
WWW.HEROCATSONLINE.COM

HERO CATS #18, August 2017
Copyright Kyle Puttkammer, 2017 Published by Action Lab Entertainment. All rights reserved. All characters are fictional. Except for Bandit. He's my cat. Any likeness to anyone living or dead is purely coincidental. No part of this publication may be reproduced or transmitted without permission, except for small excerpts for review purposes. We like it when you give us positive reviews.
Printed in Canada.

First Printing.

Bryan Seaton - Publisher
Dave Dwonch - President of Marketing
Shawn Gabborin - Editor in Chief
Jason Martin - Publisher - Danger Zone
Nicole D'Andria - Marketing Director
Jim Dietz - Social Media Manager
Scott Bradley - CFO
Chad Cicconi -Head in the Clouds

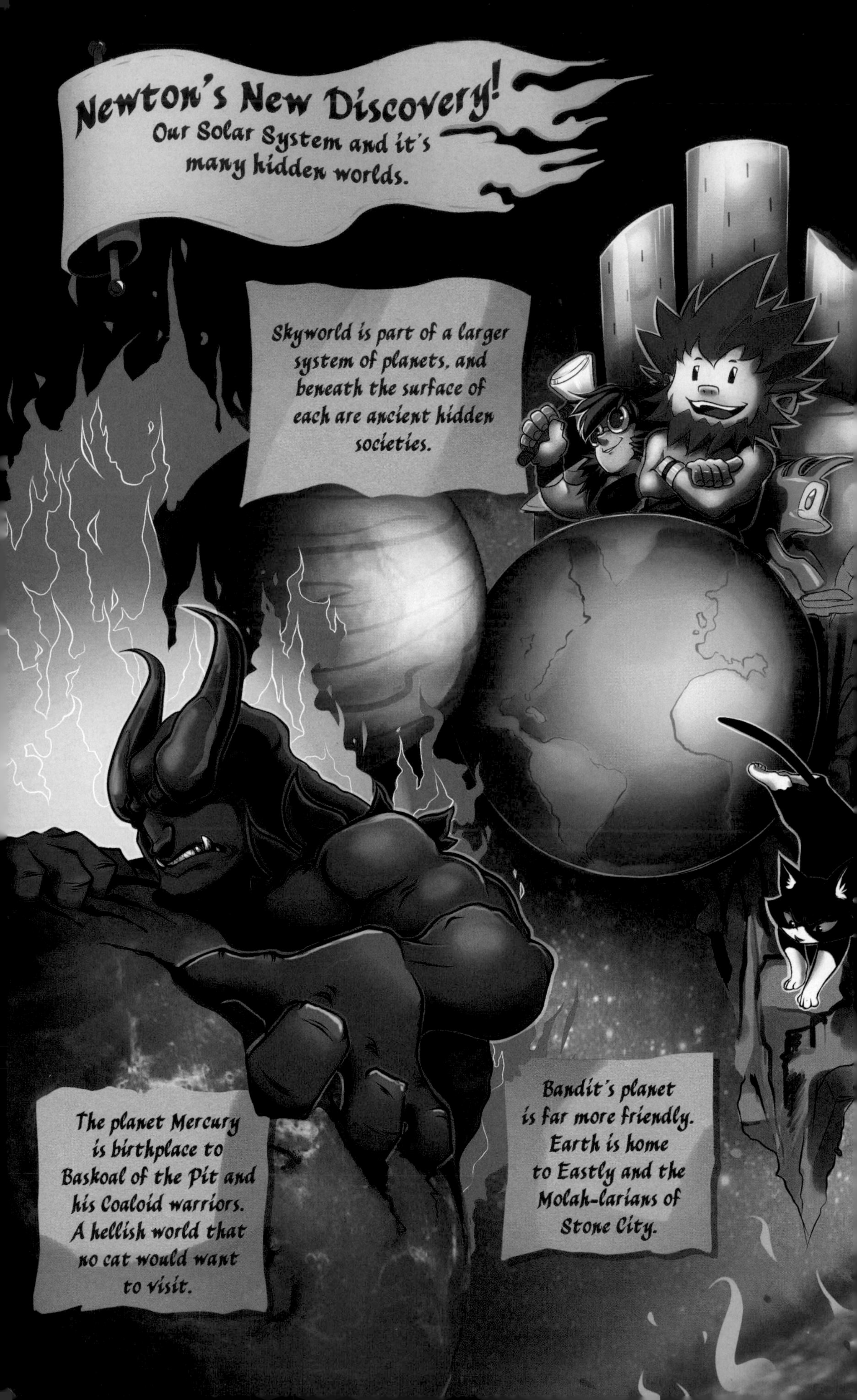
Newton's New Discovery!
Our Solar System and it's many hidden worlds.
Skyworld is part of a larger system of planets, and beneath the surface of each are ancient hidden societies.
The planet Mercury is birthplace to Baskoal of the Pit and his Coaloid warriors. A hellish world that no cat would want to visit.
Bandit's planet is far more friendly. Earth is home to Eastly and the Molah-larians of Stone City.

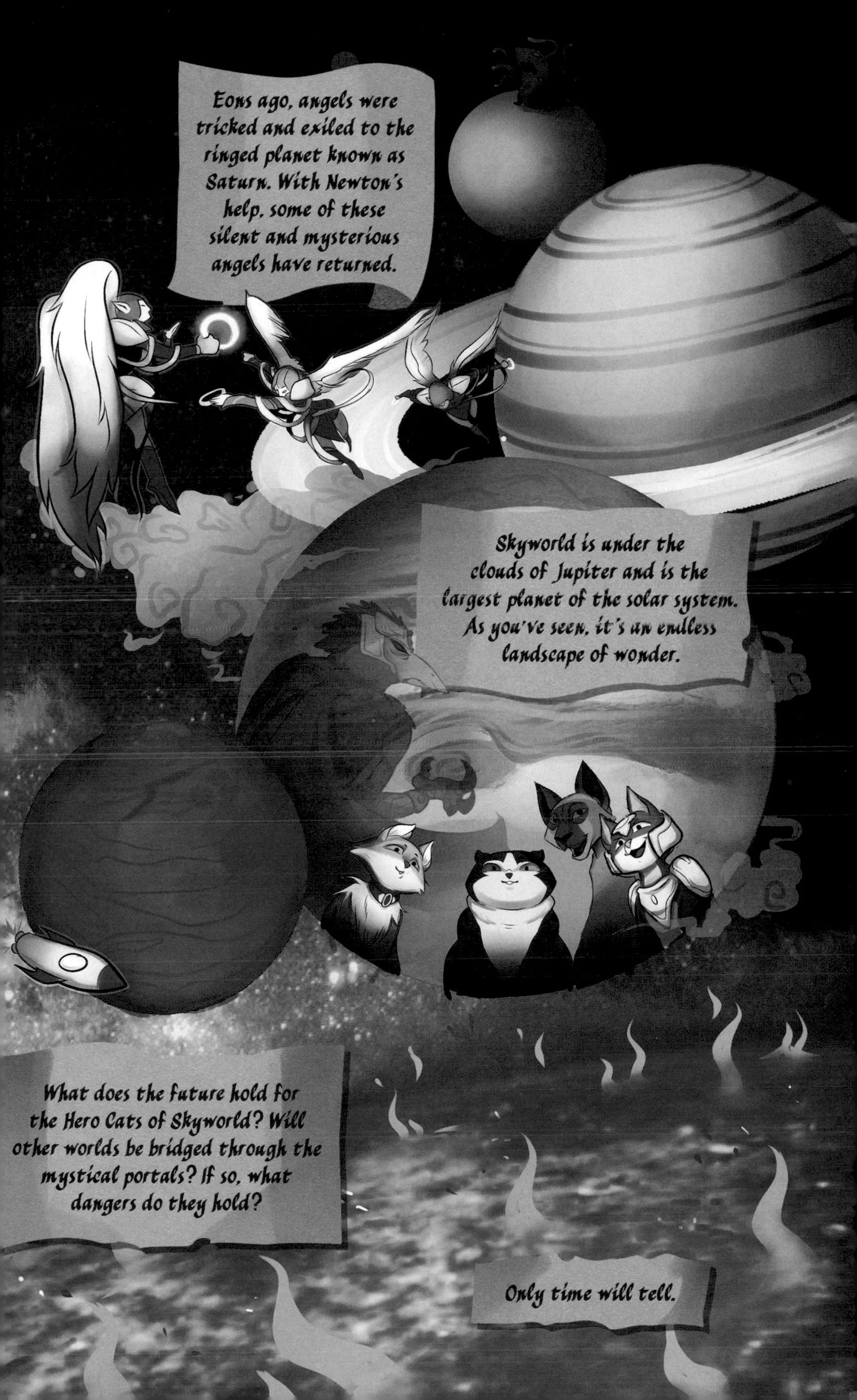
Eons ago, angels were tricked and exiled to the ringed planet known as Saturn. With Newton's help, some of these silent and mysterious angels have returned.
Skyworld is under the clouds of Jupiter and is the largest planet of the solar system. As you've seen, it's an endless landscape of wonder.
What does the future hold for the Hero Cats of Skyworld? Will other worlds be bridged through the mystical portals? If so, what dangers do they hold?
Only time will tell.

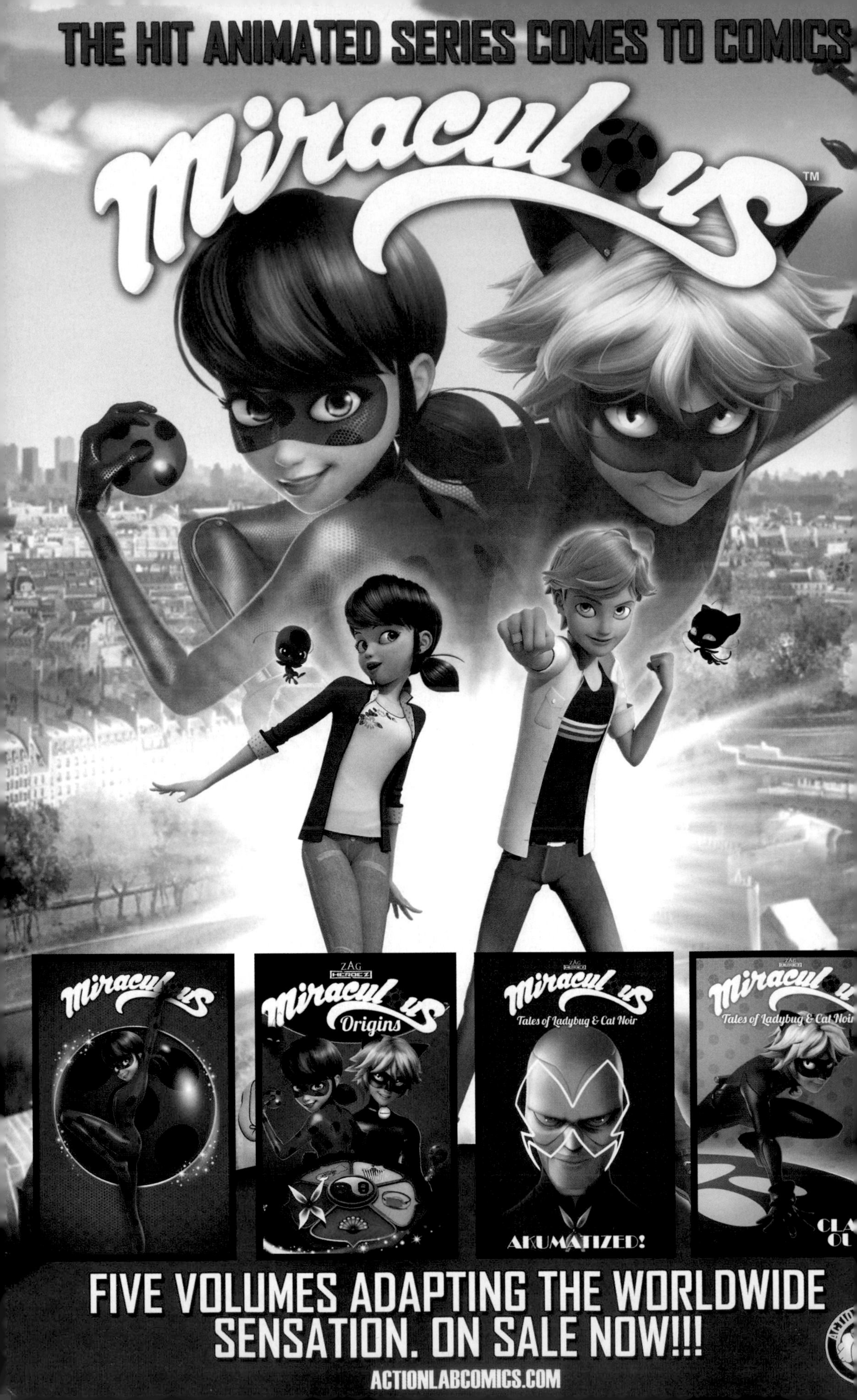
THE HIT ANIMATED SERIES COMES TO COMICS
Miraculous™
Miraculous
ZAG HEROEZ
Miraculous
Origins
ZAG HEROEZ
Miraculous
Tales of Ladybug & Cat Noir
AKUMATIZED!
ZAG HEROEZ
Miraculous
Tales of Ladybug & Cat Noir
FIVE VOLUMES ADAPTING THE WORLDWIDE
SENSATION. ON SALE NOW!!!
ACTIONLABCOMICS.COM

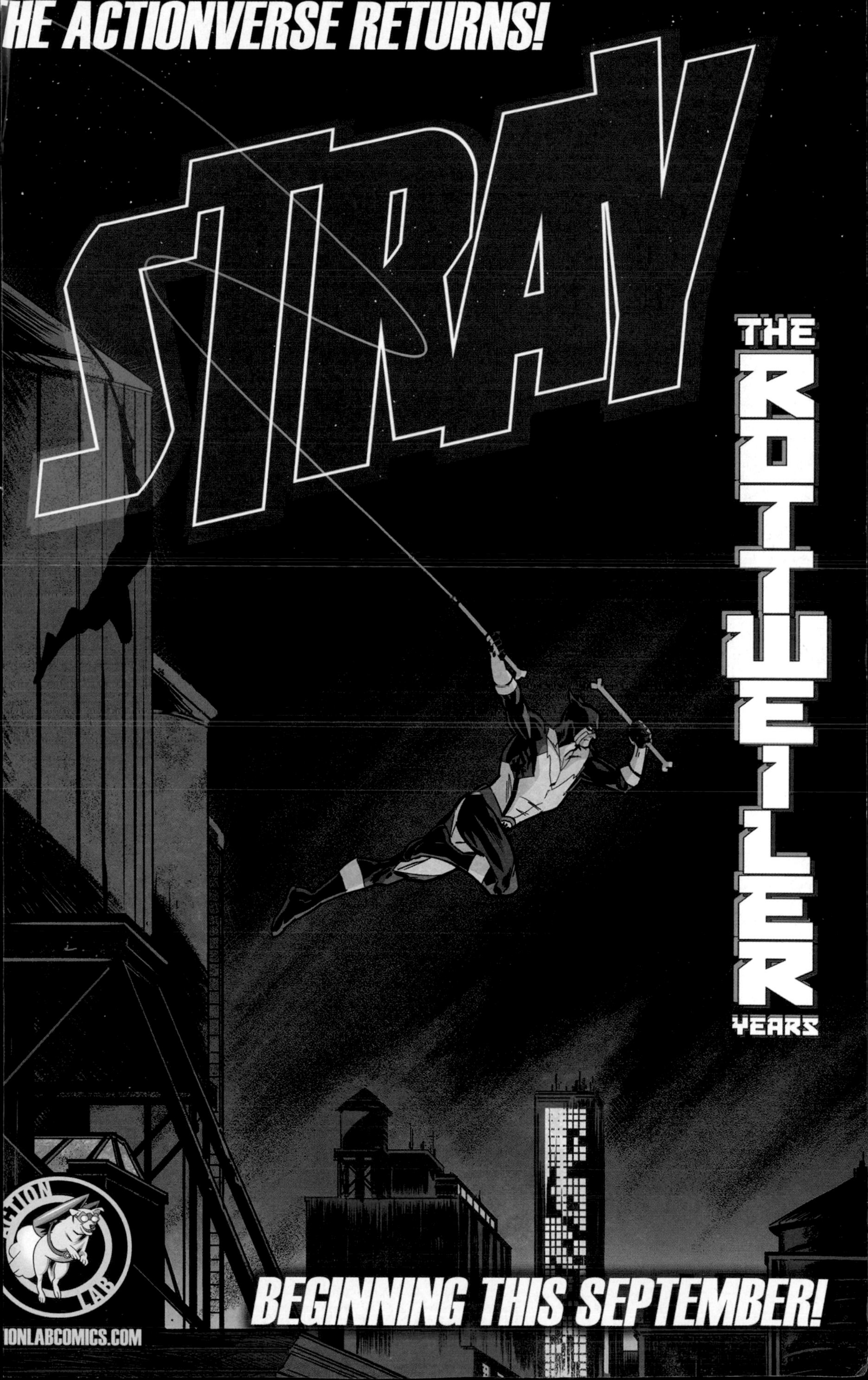
HE ACTIONVERSE RETURNS!
STRAY
THE ROTTWEILER YEARS
ACTION LAB
BEGINNING THIS SEPTEMBER!
IONLABCOMICS.COM

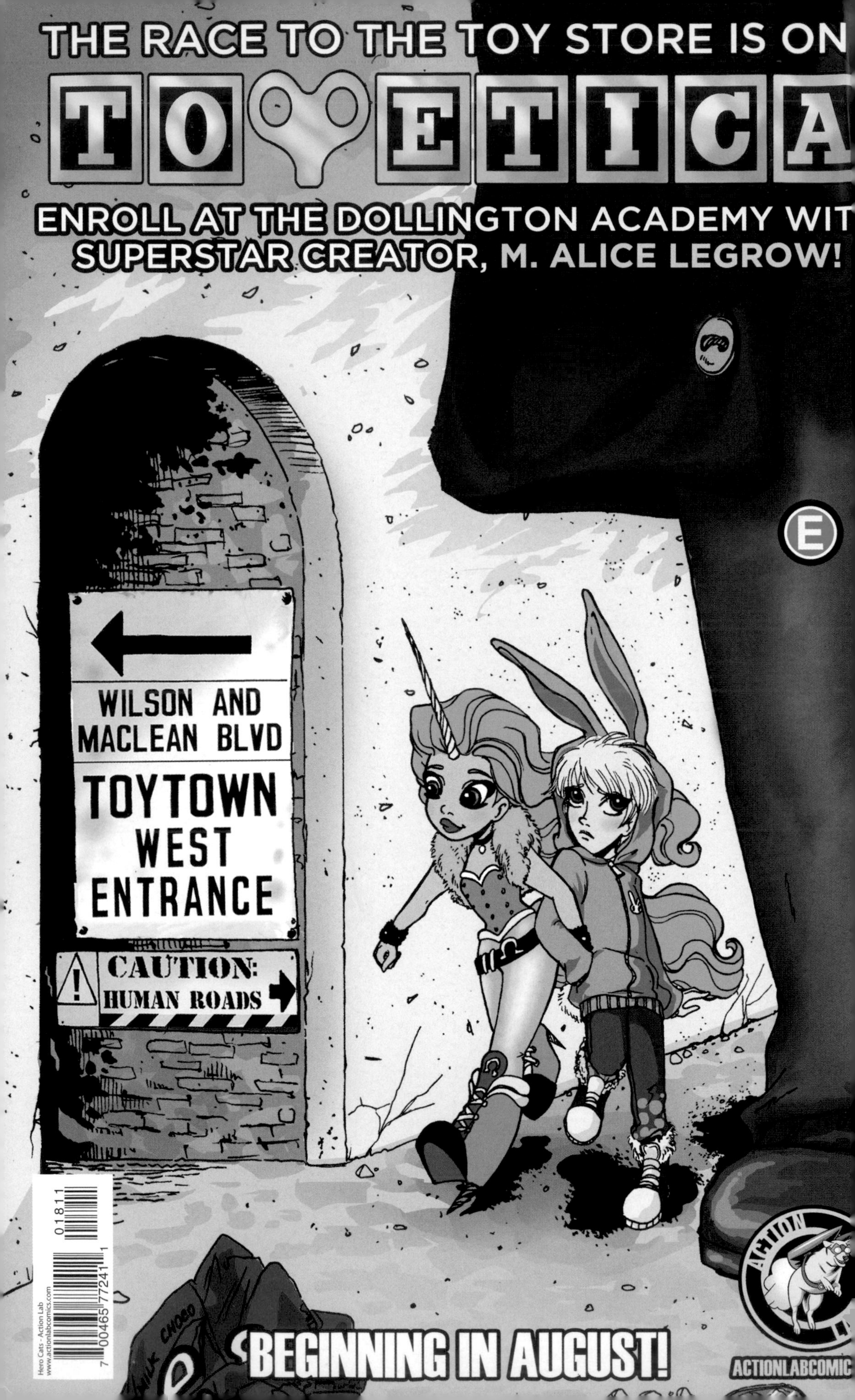

THE RACE TO THE TOY STORE IS ON
TOYETICA
ENROLL AT THE DOLLINGTON ACADEMY WIT
SUPERSTAR CREATOR, M. ALICE LEGROW!
E
WILSON AND MACLEAN BLVD
TOYTOWN WEST ENTRANCE
CAUTION: HUMAN ROADS
BEGINNING IN AUGUST!
ACTIONLABCOMIC